KT-418-030

# JAMIE BUXTON

**TEMPLE BOYS**

**EGMONT**

# EGMONT

*We bring stories to life*

First published in Great Britain in 2014 by Egmont UK Limited
The Yellow Building, 1 Nicholas Road, London W11 4AN

Text copyright © 2014 Jamie Buxton

The moral rights of the author have been asserted

ISBN 978 1 4052 6800 4

1 3 5 7 9 10 8 6 4 2

www.egmont.co.uk

A CIP catalogue record for this title is available from the British Library

Typeset by Avon DataSet Ltd, Bidford on Avon, Warwickshire
Printed and bound in Great Britain by the CPI Group

55466/1

All rights reserved. No part of this publication may be reproduced, stored in a
retrieval system, or transmitted, in any form or by any means, electronic, mechanical,
photocopying, recording or otherwise, without the prior permission of the publisher
and copyright owner.

Stay safe online. Any website addresses listed in this book are correct at the time of going to print.
However, Egmont cannot take responsibility for any third party content or advertising. Please be aware
that online content can be subject to change and websites can contain content that is unsuitable for
children. We advise that all children are supervised when using the internet.

| Northamptonshire Libraries & Information Services NC | | |
| --- | --- | --- |
| Askews & Holts | | |
| | | |
| | | |

*For my dear friend Leon Arden,*
*who gave me the idea.*

*For the king has come to seek a flea, as one
who hunts a partridge in the mountains*
The Book of Shama-el


*Stone disobedient children*
The Book of Spoken Words

*Flea smelled the dump before he saw it. A bad place, deeply unclean. The thick air bounced with fat black flies and once Flea had seen a body there. Swollen, revolting, compelling, it had lain for three days until the Temple persuaded someone to move it with promises of spiritual purification. But that was nothing compared to what he had just seen today. Nothing at all, really.*

*Big white moon, gusting wind and the sky pulsing silver and black, black and silver. The rolling clouds sent the walls into a slow endless topple towards the valley floor. Flea dragged his right hand against the stone blocks. Their rough mass told him the walls still stood so the Temple still stood, and the dead were not walking so the world had not ended. Not ended yet.*

*Maybe he still had time to put things right. Maybe he could find out how a man he had just seen die was going to change everything.*

*He heard the dogs start up again in the distance and forced his feet to shuffle into a broken run. The quicker he moved, the sooner he'd find Jude, and the sooner he found Jude the quicker he'd be sorted. Jude would know. Jude would help him.*

*And all would be well.*

*Wouldn't it?*

three days to go

# 1

The cold woke Flea and drove him out of the shelter.

It was a grey dawn. Misty dawn. Damp, dewy dawn with dark drips on tawny stone walls. Flea flapped arms, stamped feet, blew hard and waved a dirty hand through the thin cloud of his breath. He looked at the gang's shelter and wondered if it was worth burrowing between the sleeping bodies in the hope of getting a bit more sleep. He decided against it. He hated violence, especially when it was directed at him.

The shelter filled the end of an alleyway, its sagging roof slung between the Temple walls and the back of a baker's oven. The gang had nicked its timbers from a half-built house in the new town. The roof was scraps of leather taken from the tanneries and painfully sewn together. Rain dripped through the thread-holes and sometimes the leather got so heavy the whole thing collapsed, but most of the time it worked.

Flea could put up with a drip or two, and the roof falling in. For him, quite apart from practical issues, the shelter was a battleground for status, a battle that he lost every night. In cold weather the older members of the gang – Big, Little Big, Smash and Grab – would hog the oven wall and when it was hot they moved away from it. Flea was constantly pushed around, ended up being too hot or too cold and, either way, was always the first to wake.

The sky was a low grey roof above the walls of the alley. For days now clouds had pressed down over the City, trapping the smoke from the Temple's fire altar so it drifted through the alleyways in a greasy haze. Everyone's eyes stung and every surface was sticky with fat. And out-of-towners were flooding into the City for Passover, the Feast of the Death Angel. More people meant more sacrifices, and more sacrifices meant yet more smoke . . . The mood wasn't good.

A lump of shadow detached itself from the wall and began to waddle along the gutter towards him. Flea blinked, rubbed his eyes and blinked again.

'RAT!' he yelled. He scrabbled for a rock, found a pebble and flung it as hard as he could. It clicked harmlessly off the stone gutter and the rat continued towards him with hardly a pause.

'RAT! RAT! RATS!' Flea backed up against the shelter, feeling behind for a weapon, anything to fend the brute off. Another was coming – they must have smelled the crumbs in the shelter. His hand closed on a stick, which he grabbed. Unfortunately it was holding up the front of the shelter, which collapsed.

Furious shouts as the heavy leather roof collapsed on unsuspecting sleepers.

'RATS!' Flea yelled again.

'What the . . .?' Big, the gang leader, stuck his head out of the shelter. 'FLEA!'

'BUT THEY'RE COMING! LOOK!'

Big's blunt features were blurred by sleep. He rubbed his face, grabbed the stick from Flea and sent the rats scurrying away down the hole at the end of the alley.

'What bloody use are you, Flea?'

Flea was panting. 'I had a bad experience with rats,' he said. 'When I was a grave robber.'

'When you were a grave robber's slave . . .'

'It doesn't matter! He sent me down a hole. I got attacked. Look. LOOK!'

Flea pulled out his lower lip to show the small pale scars on the inside. The hole in question had been a cliff tomb outside the City walls. The way in had been too narrow for both Flea and a lamp, so he had been forced to rummage through the old bones for jewellery by touch. In the utter black, scraped by the rocks, aching with the effort and choking on the dust of dead people, he had felt the darkness bunch, writhe and squeal. The grave robber had pulled him out, screaming, with one rat hanging off his mouth and the other dangling from his ear.

Flea had been sacked, of course. Grave robbing was meant to take place in silence – rats or no rats.

'Leave it or we'll shove you down the rat hole to be eaten alive,' growled Big. 'I mean it. Now fix the shelter.'

'I can't. You've got the stick.'

'And you've got trouble.' Big raised the stick above his head.

'Don't!' Flea pleaded.

'Then get water. Get bread. Get milk.'

Flea grabbed the water skin. The skinny girl Flea had spotted hanging about near the shelter for the past week was just around the corner. She was smiling like she'd seen the whole thing. So he yelled at her to stay away from him if she knew what was good for her and set off for the fountain.

# 2

The City was built on two hills. The Temple sat on one and the rich lived in the elegant palaces of the Upper City on the other. Squeezed in between the hills and spreading out at either end was the Lower City, a dense maze of streets and alleyways zigzagging up and down the slopes. Houses of two and three storeys were crammed together in jagged blocks or stacked in precarious cliffs. The streets were so narrow that if you leant out of your window, you could practically reach into the house on the other side. Flea knew the City like a hunter knows the forest, as a place of danger and opportunity. But he wasn't after game; food and money were what he wanted.

The City was crowded at the best of times, but in the

run-up to the Feast it was stuffed so full you'd think the high old walls would burst. The Law stated that for the night of the Feast, everyone in the country had to come and stay within the City walls. Most people made a few days' holiday of it. Every house was crammed. Every rooftop groaned. Every alleyway was blocked with milling out-of-towners.

Flea pushed his way up the winding alleyway to the fountain, the district's only source of water. As he drew closer, the crowd grew thicker and angrier. People were grumbling that lodgings were more expensive, wine was more expensive, food was more expensive and, most of all, that the Temple was robbing them blind. To pay your Temple tax you had to convert your money into Temple silver. To make a sacrifice you had to a buy a holy lamb or holy dove and, again, you had to convert your money to Temple silver. Every which way, you lost and they won. And what about the disgraceful water shortages that never got any better? The new aqueduct was meant to bring more water to the City, but who got it first? The priests, who were hoarding it in giant reservoirs under the Temple and leaving the City high and dry.

The Temple Boys despised the visitors, but relied on them like everyone else in the City. They were like a great flood that left behind a vast deposit of money: for the Temple, for the market traders, for the innkeepers, for the butchers, bakers, candlestick-makers, for anyone

9

who owned four walls and a roof, but most of all for the beggars, thieves and pickpockets.

As Flea worked his way through the crowd, he kept an eye out for easy pickings – coins on the ground, open purses and the like. But he decided on balance it would be better to stay honest. In a dense and angry crowd like this getting away would be hard and if you were caught you'd be beaten, kicked, even killed.

*Not worth it*, Flea thought, but then, neither was hanging around. He pushed his way through, shouting, 'Water for the leper! Water for the leper boy,' ignored the furious stares, filled the water skin, slung it across his shoulders and staggered off.

Halfway down the hill where two streets met, the Grinderman, a travelling knife-sharpener, was setting up his wheel.

Flea called to him. 'Hey! Why are you lazing around when there's work to do?'

'Why chase after work when work'll find you out all too soon? Lambs' throats are waiting to be cut and knives are waiting to be sharpened,' the Grinderman said. 'Anyway, what are you doing here? I'd thought you'd be off to the Black Valley Bridge this morning.'

'Why would I go there? Did a priest drop his purse?'

'Pay me and I'll tell you,' the Grinderman said.

Flea pretended to throw a coin that the Grinderman pretended to catch and then bite.

'Usual fake rubbish,' he said. 'Now I'm not going to tell you about the magician who's coming to town.'

'What magician?'

'I said I'm not telling.' The Grinderman grinned gappily and tapped the side of his long nose. 'He's not from Gilgad and I wasn't told about him by a guy who saw him make pigs dance. He's not got a legion of demons behind him all bound to do his wishes. He can't turn water to wine, or make cripples jump over the moon, nor conjure banquets out of thin air, neither. And you didn't hear it here first.'

Flea cupped a hand to his ear. 'Hear what?' he shouted and set off for the shelter, his mind racing. He knew all about street conjurors: there was one on every corner at the time of the Feast, but all they really cared about was making your money disappear. Real magicians were something different, though. He'd heard that they could send a child up a rope and make them disappear, call up red-eyed demons in clouds of black smoke and persuade people to do things they didn't want to. That really was some magic he should try and learn. Maybe then he'd have the power to persuade the gang to go to the Black Valley Bridge with him.

# 3

When Flea got back to the shelter, Big was sorting out jobs for the day.

Big was the tallest and strongest member of the Temple Boys and their only real fighter. He'd been abandoned as a baby because he wasn't born perfect – a few toes had been missing. Unlike most abandoned babies he'd lived because an elderly couple took pity on him, but when they died he'd taken to the streets. Spots pocked his face and his nose was flat. Flea thought he looked as if he'd run into a wall.

Little Big was his deputy and banker. He had a slight twitch that made his head jerk every few seconds or so, especially when he was talking, but he had a grip like a dog's jaws, which was useful when he was shaking you down for your takings at the end of the day.

All money was shared. Basically, the rest of the gang paid Big to protect them – mostly from Big himself.

'Listen up!' Big said. He was standing on the edge of a cracked stone water trough with Little Big sitting at his feet. 'We'll pair up today and work Temple Square. Crouch and Hole-in-the-Head, you two together. Crouch needs a stick, someone.'

Crouch was bent double and it hurt him to lift his head. Hole-in-the-Head had lost an eye and he shaved his head in patches so it looked like he had a skin condition.

They always did well because Crouch's usual expression was heartbreakingly brave and hopeful.

'I've got an idea,' Flea said, but Big just carried on talking.

'Halo and Crutches – you two hang out by the washing pools. Halo, you've got to cry. Crutches, you've got to comfort him, but it's hard because you're in such pain yourself. What's your story?'

'Can we be from out of town and we're on our own because our parents haven't got the money to pay the Temple tax?' Halo said. He was the pretty one and smaller even than Flea. But, unlike Flea, the rest of the gang were always nice to him.

'We'll get nice and dusty and say we walked all the way,' Crutches said in his odd, deep voice. He was a surprisingly good pickpocket even though he could hardly use his legs.

'Good,' Big said. 'Who's left? Gaga, Snot, Red, Clump, Smash and Grab.'

'And me!' Flea said. 'But listen. If we head for the Black Valley Bridge and . . .'

Big did not even glance at him. 'Tell you what. Snot, it should be you teamed up with Crutches and crying. Halo, you and Gaga go to the top of the steps and beg as people are going in. Gaga, make that funny noise, and Halo, just look sad.'

Gaga nodded his head and said, '*Gagagaga.*' It was

the only noise he ever made, hence his name, and he let people know what he thought by nodding, shaking his head or punching them. Snot sniffed marshily and spat out a huge gob of mucus. Gaga punched him.

Big said, 'Quite right. No gobbing, especially near the Temple. You'll get the Temple Police after you. Now then. Clump, Red, Smash and Grab: you know those shelters that've gone up the other side of the west wall? Can you handle them?'

'People stare at my scars, so I'll be the diversion,' Red said. He was burned down the left side of his body and found it hard to close his left eye.

'We could have a fight,' Clump said. 'I'll attack you then Smash and Grab can sneak in round the back.'

'Why can't *we* fight?' Smash and Grab asked, both saying the same thing at the same time.

'Because I can't run, can I?' Clump said. His twisted right foot slowed him up. 'You two can get in and out faster than us. As soon as we see you leave, we'll kiss and make up.'

'Yeah, kiss my scars,' Red said, and got a laugh.

'But I . . .' Flea said.

'Right, that's it,' Big said. 'Get moving.'

'It's not going to work!' Flea shouted at their backs. 'All the other gangs will be at the Temple, especially today. But if we head for the Black Valley Bridge we might have a chance!'

No one turned. No one listened. Muttering angrily, he set off behind them.

# 4

Flea hadn't been a member of the Temple Boys for that long. The autumn before, he had seen them at work and thought he would try to join them.

He was at a loose end. He'd been a runner for a small-time gangster called Mosh the Dosh, but quit when he overheard Mosh was planning to sell him to a grain merchant from the coast. He'd tried to get in with an Upper City gang, but a dozen other street children with exactly the same idea had chased him off. He couldn't return to grave robbing and had already run away from the stink of a gluc factory, where his job had been to tend the fires under the massive cauldrons of bone, skin and slaughterhouse offcuts. But going solo was too dangerous. Only that morning he'd seen a beggar lying in the gutter with his throat cut, stripped of his all clothes. Passers-by stepped over him, round him, ignored him as if he didn't exist.

So he'd been watching the world go by in the Upper City when he'd spotted two red-headed boys, twins, loitering by the entrance to a yard not far from him. It looked as if they were trying to hide at the same as watching the street, but they stood out like a pair of sore thumbs. It was obvious they were waiting for someone to rob.

A merchant came out of the inn with a swirl of flowing robes. He stroked his oiled beard and put a scented handkerchief to his bulbous nose, as if the smell of the street was just too, too much for him. The twins stiffened like dogs spotting a rat. Flea thought they made pretty rubbish thieves.

Then a boy on crutches, who had been leaning against the wall, swung himself across the road and tapped the merchant on his arm.

The merchant looked down impatiently, listened, then glanced across at the scowling twins. Understanding dawned on his face. He patted the boy on the head, reached into a pocket and handed him a coin. But as he made off down the street his hand strayed to his hip, where he patted a small bulge.

Flea smiled and waited. *Two purses*, he thought. One for loose change, one rather more promising – and the merchant had just given away where it was. The twins made a great show of scowling at the merchant as he set off down the street. What he did not spot was another boy walking towards him, who seemed to trip and cannon into him before running off.

The merchant shouted at the boy's retreating back, walked on and then patted the place where his fat little purse had been. It was gone. He fumbled his robes, looked at the ground and stared accusingly towards the twins. They hadn't moved. He looked down the street, but even if he had been able to spot the small boy, it wouldn't have made any difference: Flea's expert gaze had seen him pass the purse to a one-eyed boy, who in turn had handed it on to a boy with a twitch. It was the perfect set-up.

The merchant yelled, 'Stop thief!' But who to stop? The stream of people in the street flowed on, sweeping away the twins and all the other gang members.

'Misdirection' was the longest word Flea knew. It was the art of making someone look so hard at one thing that they missed what was going on under their nose. He had just seen it in action.

Flea had a few tricks of his own. He followed the twins all the way back to the den and had been hanging around with the Temple Boys ever since.

But that was then. Now Flea and the gang were close to the Temple, picking their way through the dark alley over the rubbish that had accumulated in the past few days.

At the end of the alley they could see Temple Square bathed in sunlight: a big, clean space, watched over by the Temple Police who in turn were watched over by Imperial Roman soldiers. That was the system – if the Temple Police ever lost their grip and a riot started, for example, then the Romans would step in and start killing.

The soldiers didn't care. They were as hard as stone and as obedient as well-trained dogs.

But before the gang could split up and get to their tasks, the alleyway was blocked by a hulking figure with a broken nose and greasy hair plastered forwards on to a bulging forehead.

'What's this?' he said. 'A bunch of rejects heading for the Temple?'

The thick leather straps around each wrist marked him out as one of the Butcher Boys, a gang from the Lower City who hung out near the slaughterhouses. Normally they didn't come this close to the Temple, but the rich holiday pickings had lured them up the hill.

'We've got a right.' Big tried to square up to him. 'We belong up here. We're the Temple Boys. We work the Temple.'

'You're pathetic losers,' the Butcher Boy spat back. 'You've got no rights unless I say so. Now get lost.'

'Who's going to make us?'

Flea admired Big for trying. On the other hand, he knew things would only end badly if they carried on like this. Big would fight, then the others would join in, then the rest of the Butcher Boys would get involved and the Temple Boys would be badly beaten. He felt an all too familiar hot swirl of fear in his guts. Someone had to do something.

'Wait!' he shouted as loudly as he could. He wished

his voice did not sound quite so thin, but it had done the trick. The thug looked down at him.

'You talking to me?'

'Yeah, you. Wait,' Flea repeated. 'We don't even want to hang out at the steps. We're going somewhere better.'

'Piss off.'

'But that's just what we want to do,' Flea said. 'We don't want trouble. We just want to get on.'

The Butcher Boy looked at Flea, then away, then at Flea again. Then he smiled.

'All right,' he said. 'Where?'

'The Black Valley Bridge,' Flea told him. 'There's a magician coming to town. He can make pigs fly and dead men dance. He'll snap his fingers and the Temple'll turn to mud, then he'll snap them again and it'll turn back to stone.'

'Believe that, do you?' The Butcher Boy looked over his shoulder and called out to a minion who was watching his back, 'De lickle Temple Boys believe in magic!' He turned to Big. 'Suckers. Get on out of it. But if I see you anywhere near the Temple, you're dead.'

Flushed and furious, Big pushed Flea out of the way and led the Temple Boys across the square.

# 5

As soon as they were out of sight of the other gang, Big grabbed Flea and pinned him against the wall.

'What was that about?' he demanded. His breath coated Flea's face like a sour mask.

'I got you out of trouble, didn't I?'

'You made me look like a prat. I'm not scared of the Butcher Boys.'

'Maybe not you, but the rest of us wouldn't stand a chance. And anyway, if the Butcher Boys are in the Square, the rest of the gangs will be there as well: the Water Gang, the Mad Dogs, the Holy Rollers . . . They'll squeeze us out wherever we go. There won't be a decent pitch left.'

Flea knew he was talking sense, but also knew that might not save him. He should have kept his mouth shut.

Silence, then: 'I had it sorted,' Big said. 'Don't you forget it.'

'I'm sorry,' Flea said. 'Really sorry.'

He felt Big's grip on his tunic loosen.

'And what was that crap you were on about? About a magician?' Big looked suspicious.

Flea opened his eyes and tried to look honest and sincere. 'It's true. I swear it. The best magician in the world is coming to town by the Black Valley Bridge.'

'How come we haven't heard?'

'He's coming from up north, from Gilgad or somewhere. A merchant told the Grinderman and the Grinderman told me. I just thought, what with the crowds and them all being tourists, there'll be rich pickings.'

Big dropped Flea. 'Rich pickings, you reckon? Robbing tourists?'

Flea nodded. 'That's what I thought. They'll all be gawping at the magician.'

Big almost cracked a smile. 'And that's why you're an insect and will always be an insect. We're not going to waste our time stealing pennies off out-of-towners. This magician's from Gilgad, right, the other side of the back end of beyond. He'll be clueless. What does he do after he performs all his tricks? Well?'

Crouch was the quickest to catch on.

'He'll take a collection.'

'Exactly. He'll empty everyone's pockets, and then what do we do? I'll tell you. We'll empty his. We're the Temple Boys. We know how to handle a conjuror. We'll give him a welcome to the City he'll never forget.'

Big went through the plan. Red was lookout again. Crouch and Halo were to get the magician's attention by asking a lot of stupid questions; he and Little Big would work out who was carrying the purse. Clump, Snot, Hole-in-the-Head, Gaga and Crutches would surround them, then Grab would cut the purse free and Smash would leg it. They'd all rendezvous back at the shelter at noon.

'What about me?' Flea asked.

'What about you?' Big answered. 'You can just . . . hop off.'

He looked around the rest of the gang until he got a couple of sniggers. Then they set off for the Black Valley Bridge.

# 6

The Black Valley ran below the eastern City walls. To reach the bridge from Temple Square the gang hurried alongside the western temple walls, turned right into the blaring chaos of the sheep market with its pens and purification baths and headed for the eastern gate.

The crowd was surging and chaotic. Clearly they weren't the first people to hear about the coming of the magician.

In the choke point of the narrow city gate, Flea found himself wedged between a porter carrying a sack of grain and a fat man's belly. 'Is he here? Do you really think he's the Chosen One?' a voice called out.

'That's what I heard,' the porter close to Flea answered. 'Miracle worker. There was this leper up at Bethany: one touch and he was better. He made a man with a withered leg go dancing up and down the street – completely cured – and he does eyesight too!'

'Miracle worker?' the fat man jeered. 'He's got to be

a lot more than that if he's the Chosen One. King David – he was the Chosen One, and he was a proper warrior and a king as well. You think this conjuror can match up to King David? Next you'll be saying he walks on water!'

That drew a big laugh from the crowd; then all other words were lost in the rising din.

Flea freed himself from the crush and pushed on. Ahead, he saw Red climbing a tree near the bridge. Flea shinned up after him until he was far above head height and could see all the way across the Black River Valley.

An old stone bridge crossed the steep valley in a single span. Both the bridge and the road on either side were blocked solid. Gawkers ambling out of the City to see the action met out-of-towners streaming into the City for the Feast. All the passing places on the bridge were occupied by black-robed Wild People selling souvenirs to the tourists. Imperial soldiers had set up a roadblock to try and take matters in hand, but were just making things worse. To complete the chaos, a donkey pulling a cart into the City had met a camel carrying a mountainous bundle of hay out of it. Neither was prepared to pass the other – or reverse.

From high in his tree, Flea surveyed the scene cheerfully. His plan had worked. By a mixture of luck and guile he had persuaded the Temple Boys to do what he wanted. If the day went well, surely he'd be properly accepted by them. He felt happy.

'Bloody tourists,' he said to Red. 'Don't see how anyone's going to get through this.'

Red ignored him.

'You know Big's plan to rob the magician? I thought –'

Red said, 'Leave it.' He snapped off a long, thin twig and started poking a man's turban with it. The man turned on his neighbour; angry words were exchanged. Red gave a stiff lopsided grin, wiped a tear away from the corner of his ruined eye and handed the stick to Flea to have a go.

Flea tried to get the conversation going again. 'So, how long do you give this magician before the Temple Police throw him out of town? A day?' He dropped the twig on the angry man's head.

Red snorted. 'Half a day if he's lucky, but it won't be down to the Temple Police. This is the Feast. The City's going mad. If he's a troublemaker the Imps won't even let him cross the bridge. You watch.'

They stopped for a moment to watch the Imps, Roman Imperial soldiers, failing to organise the chaos on the bridge.

'There seems to be a lot of people to meet him.'

'Maybe he's that good,' Red answered.

Flea shook his head. 'If he's that good, why haven't we heard of him before? I heard someone asking if he was the Chosen One. What was all that about?'

'Shut up, insect,' snapped Red. 'Can't you stop talking? Can't you stop . . . thinking?'

Flea did shut up, but quickly began to feel bored. The sun was weak, but the sky was bright white and made his eyes water. He narrowed them to slits and scanned the landscape on the other side of the bridge, the rocky slopes of the Black River Valley and then the pale scar of the road winding down from a notch in the soft shoulders of Olive Tree Hill.

He couldn't stop thinking of what he'd just heard in the crowd. *Is he the Chosen One?* What if this magician really was someone special? Suppose he was a great king in disguise, a cross between King David the Giant-Killer and King Solomon the Magician? That really would be something, and in years to come he'd be able to say, *Ah, yes, I remember when the Chosen One first came to the City. Of course, no one had any idea who he really was and I had a bit of a job persuading my friends to come and see him, but I had a feeling, you see. And you know what we were planning to do? Rob him.*

As Flea drifted off on his own train of thought, the clouds broke up and the sun pierced through. Suddenly, there were clear blue skies to the east, but for a single small cloud. If he squinted and forgot the cloud looked like a dog, he could almost imagine it as a chariot drawn by a winged horse, and he could almost definitely see the magician in the back with a golden bow and a quiver of burning arrows.

And now the winged horse was pulling back its lips to show long red teeth, jagged as saws. The feathers on its wings were as sharp as swords – one sweep of them and Roman heads would tumble. But the archers on the battlements had seen the threat. Now they were pulling their bows back into quivering arcs.

'Watch out!' Flea cried. And as the arrows leapt upwards in a black swarm the magician raised his right arm. Fire shot from an outstretched finger and he drew it across the blue dome of the sky to create a blazing barrier so the archers' arrows flamed and fell in charred twists. Now he started shooting his own arrows. They smashed into the battlements, turning soldiers into flaming, screaming, dancing monsters before they tumbled to their deaths.

The magician reined in his snorting steed and circled Flea's tree in his chariot, wreathed in smoke, shining with strength, and at the sight of him, the crowd fell to the ground, wailing and moaning in terror.

Only Flea – Flea the Brave, Flea the Magnificent – dared to meet his calm and level gaze.

'Well done, courageous Flea. You have saved me, you have saved your friends and you have saved your City. As your reward, Flea . . . Flea . . . FLEA, you idiot! Wake up! What are you doing up there?'

Flea blinked and looked down. Big and most of the rest of the gang were at the bottom of the tree.

'What's going on, insect?'

'Nothing,' Flea said. 'Nothing.'

'Well, since you're up there, keep watching! Don't go all *la la* like you usually do.'

Big opened his mouth into a stupid gape and rolled his eyes up into his head. Flea scowled across the crowded bridge.

And really did see something.

# 7

On the other side of the valley, a dense little group was moving down the road from Olive Tree Hill with purpose. People seemed to be clearing the road ahead of it. Above the background noise Flea thought he could hear faint cheers.

'Something's happening!' he called down to Big, who grabbed Snot. Together, they wormed their way through the crowd towards the bridge. Halo scrabbled up into the tree with Flea and Red. Flea helped him on to the branch and held him tight. Halo was inclined to get excited and fall off things.

In the middle of the bridge, the stuck donkey had managed to back the cart hard against the parapet, the camel was attempting to turn sideways and a man carrying a pitcher of water was stuck between them, trying desperately not to let it fall. At the same time, the heaving press of people was stopping any man or beast from going backwards or forwards and more people were trying to squeeze on to the bridge all the time. To cap matters off, Flea saw Big and Snot jump on to the cart and start stamping and yelling in imitation of the driver.

Problem. They were making so much noise they'd attracted the attention of the Imps. The two Temple Boys on the cart showed clearly above the heads of the crowd and made easy targets for the soldiers, who started to shoulder their way towards them, all leather plates and polished buckles.

And now something strange was happening on the far side of the bridge, behind the soldier's backs.

The little group Flea had seen had arrived and the crowd started moving to either side of the road. Some of the people bowed their heads. Others put their hands across their chests as a mark of respect. Some even knelt, so at last Flea could see them from his vantage point . . . Not a wizard in his flaming chariot with an army of demons, but a dozen or so of the shabbiest travellers that Flea had ever seen.

This was the *Chosen One* and his followers? This bunch of dusty tramps? But Flea couldn't be disappointed for too long, because things on the bridge were looking horrible for Big and Snot. They were still jumping up and down on the cart, but with their backs to the approaching Imps. They had no idea of the danger they were in.

Flea saw the Imps look at each other, saw the metal flash as they drew swords. The man with the pitcher dropped it and it shattered. He yelled a warning at the boys on the cart, but could not make himself heard. Then a small man in a dusty grey robe was suddenly standing between the soldiers and the boys, hands outstretched, palms out.

He was one of the travellers and Flea couldn't work out how he had moved so fast.

The Imps stopped and stared, swords still raised. Flea held his breath. The Imps would smack him with their shields, batter him with their sword hilts, and when they'd finished with him they'd turn on Big and Snot.

But the small man just stood there and smiled. And smiled. And smiled.

# 8

The soldiers looked at each other. Sunlight glinted on their swords.

'What do you want?' one of them asked the small man in his harsh, foreign accent. His voice carried over the hushed crowd.

'I'm sorry, friends,' the small man said. 'I just thought I might be able to help with this traffic jam.'

He had narrow shoulders and a dramatic head, with long hair swept back from a widow's peak and dark, dark eyes set between a heavy brow and a boxer's cheekbones. His tunic might have been brown once and was now fading to grey, or perhaps it had been grey and was so stained it seemed brown.

At this moment the donkey gave a short, despairing honk and sat down. The cart tipped over, throwing Snot and Big down so they sprawled in the dust between the small man and the Imps.

The crowd had fallen silent and the mood had changed. All eyes were on the Imps. People were watchful, but ready. Flea saw the Imps' eyes darting to the right and the left as they were forced to reconsider. No help anywhere near. Massively outnumbered.

They slid their swords back into scabbards. 'Get on with it, then.'

The small man helped Big to his feet, then Snot, who sniffed marshily and gobbed.

'Nice,' the small man said. Then, 'Tell you what, why don't you unhitch that unfortunate beast and walk it over here to me? Think you could do that?' A showman's smile lit up every part of his face. Big pointed to himself, then at the donkey. 'Me?' he asked.

'Only if you're not too busy,' the small man said.

Another of the travellers – skinny with cropped, rust-coloured hair and dressed in a striped robe – joined them. He showed Big how to free the donkey from the shafts and Snot how to calm it. Then Big and Snot led the donkey out of the chaos and over to the far side of the bridge. The small man climbed on to its back and, suddenly, the world went mad.

People began cheering, shouted, surged forwards, surged back. On the other side of the road a man shinned up a dusty date palm. He started pulling the leaves and branches from it and throwing them down. People caught them. Some waved them; others threw them under the hooves of the donkey. The man's fellow travellers pushed ahead of him, somehow forcing a clear way down the middle of the bridge.

'Did you see that? Did you see what the magician did?' Red shouted.

'Is that him? Are you sure? He just looks like a tramp to me,' said Flea.

'He only went and saved Big and Snot. He only stopped the Imps arresting them. He only rubbed their Roman noses in the dirt.' Red slapped Flea on the back, held up Halo so he could have a look, slapped Flea again.

Flea could not get excited. Disappointment didn't do justice to his feelings; betrayal was more like it. This small man with the showman's smile could not be a famous magician, let alone the Chosen One. It was the biggest let-down of his life.

'That can't really be him, can it?'

'You're the expert,' Red said. 'You brought us here.'

Which was true and just added to the sense of deflation.

'But we can't rob him now,' Flea said. 'He's seen us. He's ruined our plan.'

Red looked at him, appalled. 'Of course we can't rob him,' he said. 'He just saved Big and Snot from the Imps.'

'But –'

'Forget about the plan. This is better.' Red dropped Halo to the ground as the donkey passed underneath them, then followed behind, punching the air and shouting.

The cheers rose louder and louder as the magician, still riding the donkey, approached the City, the crowd trailing behind him like a long cloak. Still sitting in his tree, Flea saw Red say something to one of the magician's followers – a tall, broad-shouldered man with a face like a twisted root. To his amazement he saw the man turn back, stoop, pick up Crouch and Halo, and carry them off under his arms.

He felt a jab of jealousy and resentment, but not wanting to be left alone, he dropped from the tree and caught up with the crowd as it streamed towards the Temple.

# 9

Flea was a vulture hanging on broad, ragged wings high above the City.

He was drawn by the stench of blood. His broad wing tips feathered the column of warm, meaty air that roared skywards from the Temple's fire altar. His keen eyes scanned the courts below and nothing escaped his piercing gaze: the livestock pens to the north where the newly washed lambs glowed white; the high towers and dazzling gold rooftops of the Temple; the crowds that milled in the huge outer court; the gathering press of people in the inner courts; and, right in the middle, the inner sanctuary where the fire blazed and the slaughter floor was wet and red. A dozen lambs slaughtered at a time, a hundred doves; thousands killed in a day. Mountains of flesh, fields of gore, rivers of blood.

But for what? People never said, but Flea sometimes wondered if the Temple's invisible god had a vulture's tastes and greed. Or maybe not quite a vulture, which preferred raw flesh to cooked and was always hungry. Apparently the god of the Temple only visited the Sanctuary once a year. Maybe he didn't have to eat. Maybe he just liked to smell the meat.

The rumbling in his stomach brought Flea back to earth when he reached Temple Square. Well, he did have to eat, and one of the reasons he usually kept away from the Temple was that the smells from the fire altar always reminded him of how hungry he was.

He took stock of the situation from his level, which was approximately halfway up everyone else's. The magician, his followers and the enormous crowd had disappeared into the Temple, forcing their way through the tunnels that carried them up, up, up to the level of the first huge courtyard.

Flea had missed them, which meant none of them could have stopped to ritually cleanse themselves. Usually that was enough to get you barred from the Temple, but the guards must have looked at the crowd and decided it was too dangerous to try and stop it. What was going on?

He washed his hands and feet at the communal pool and splashed the worst of the dirt off his face. He forced his way into the middle of a group of gawking tourists – out of sight of the guards – and let them sweep him up through the vaulted hall and on into the Temple itself.

The outer court covered the entire top of the Holy Mountain and was like another world, a flat bright land of white flagstones, bounded by painted pillars, hemmed by golden rooftops. It had its own noise: a buzz of holiness and a hum of chants, pierced by cries and shouts.

Right in front of Flea, a fanatic from the northern desert – one of the Ranting Dunkers – was screaming about *the end of the Temple, the end of the City and the end of everything!* The farmers surrounding him seemed more interested in the insect life in his hair than his words and Flea wondered how long he'd last before the Police threw him out.

Flea climbed on to a wicker chest crammed with black-market doves and looked around. To his right a class of trainee priests were humming like bees and swaying like wheat in the breeze as they recited words from the Holy Book. To his left parents rested, while their children played tag round the pillars of the colonnade and kicked the priests' shadows up the arse. Behind him, official money changers were yelling out their rates, and dealers were trying to entice the crowds to buy their doves and lambs (*All blessed! All perfect! All pure!*) for sacrifice.

But straight ahead and close to the entrance of the inner courts was a surging knot of people. Flea jumped down, ran across the marble flagstones and wriggled through the crush to the front. The crowd was pressed around a clear space where the magician was being confronted by two priests from the Temple. They were plump and sleek, white robes shining, oiled hair gleaming. 'So, what are you calling yourself these days?' one of the priests asked in a loud, carrying voice. 'Yeshua, the Great Conjuror of Gilgad, or Master? Don't tell me you want people to call you Lord!' he laughed.

Flea was taken aback. First he was the Chosen One.

Now he was Master or Lord. Right then, in contrast to the priests, the magician looked even smaller and dirtier than he had on the bridge.

'Oh, and don't be surprised that we know who you are,' the priest continued sarcastically. 'I remember when you were considered a bit of a star: the wonder child who toddled up those steps into the Council Chamber twenty-five years ago and kept the old men riveted with your wisdom. But you couldn't cut it, could you? Couldn't stick the course. Or do you really expect us to believe that you prefer to tramp around with a band of tarts, thieves and collaborators?'

*Interesting*, Flea thought and he peered at the magician to see if any traces of Wonder Child remained. Not as far as he could see, but Flea had to admit that he was quite a cool customer. The man had lowered his eyes and was idly tracing shapes on the flagstones with his toe.

The priest blustered on. 'We're waiting, Yeshua. Did you hear my question? Or do we have to pay you to talk these days?'

Everyone was watching now and Flea began to find the whole thing very interesting indeed. In fact, the hair on the back of his neck was prickling because he had suddenly realised that it wasn't just pickpockets that played with misdirection. It was magicians too. Even though the magician was saying nothing, he had the eyes of the crowd, and the less he spoke the more they stared at him.

Flea let his eyes drift around, trying to work out what was really happening.

There!

The rusty-haired man with the striped robes who had helped Big and Snot with the donkey was the only person in the crowd *not* looking at the magician. Instead, he was rummaging gently in his shoulder bag.

The priest was growing annoyed. 'I'm disappointed,' he said. 'Perhaps your life as a tramp and a beggar has addled your brain because I thought you came here to talk. I know, let's see if you can answer a direct question. How about this: have you got any money on you, or do you think you're so special that you don't have to pay Temple tax like all these good people around us?'

While the priest babbled on, Flea worked his way through the crowd until he was close to the rusty-haired assistant. He watched like a mouse might watch a cat.

'I repeat,' the priest said. 'Have you got any money on you?'

Success! As the priest mentioned money, the assistant's right hand strayed to his belt and patted the place where he had hidden his money bag.

Flea smiled. The rest of the gang might have blown their chances of robbing the magician, but he'd show them how it was done.

And now, better still, the magician reacted. A simple, sweet smile softened his rough features and he turned to the red-haired man: 'Brother Jude, you're in charge of our savings. Anything left in the purse?'

With a wry expression, Jude reached into the shoulder bag and pulled out a limp leather pouch fastened with a drawstring. He tossed it to the magician, who caught it, held a hand up for silence and shook it. Laughter erupted – the crowd knew all about running out of money. When the magician reached in and pulled out a pebble they cheered and stamped their feet.

'Broke again,' the magician said, dropping the pebble at his feet. Then he added, 'Unless my young friends can help?'

He pointed to Crouch and Halo, who had managed to worm their way through to the front of the crowd. The two could not have made a bigger contrast: Crouch bent double like an old crow and Halo with his fair skin, big dark eyes and curly hair. Crouch frowned, then put a hand on Halo's shoulder and pushed him gently forwards.

The magician shook the purse upside down, then held it out to Halo. The boy approached it cautiously, snatched it like a starving dog and shook it, then handed it back. While the crowd laughed and pointed good-naturedly, Flea saw the magician slip the purse to Jude, who had moved smoothly up behind him. When he saw the purse again in the magician's hands, it looked different. The switch had been made.

'Good,' the magician said. 'Now then, what do you think is in the purse?'

'Nothing,' the crowd shouted.

'Nothing? Are you sure?'

'YES!'

'Child, what do you think?'

Halo looked up at him. 'Nothing,' he said in his high voice. 'Otherwise I'd have nicked it.'

More laughter.

'Would you like to look inside?' The magician handed it back.

Crouch held the purse open while Halo put his small hand inside and his face lit up. To gasps and cheers he pulled out a beautiful, smooth, ivory egg.

'Hand it back to me, friend.'

The magician closed his hands around the egg, blew on them, muttered a few words and then opened his arms wide. A spotlessly white dove exploded from his hands and flapped its way into the blue sky. The crowd cheered again, before falling silent as the magician stooped low by Crouch's side and whispered in his ear.

Grinning, Crouch reached into the purse that he was still holding. With a great show he pulled out a gold coin and he held it up. More laughter and cheering all around, then the magician raised his hands for silence.

Flea nodded in appreciation. A decent trick, good enough to con a easy-going crowd in a holiday mood.

But not good enough to con him.

The priest hadn't finished, though.

'Not so clever,' he sneered. 'Not so clever at all. That dove was dedicated to God and you let it free. And as if defiling the Temple with your filth wasn't enough, that coin tells us all we need to know about people like you. A Roman coin. The currency of our conquerors. You come to the Temple, the beating heart of our religion, and the only coin you can produce has the hated Imperial stamp on it! What were people shouting at you? That you were the Master? Well, whose man are you, Yeshua? The people's or the emperor's?'

Rusty-haired Jude was watching the magician closely. Flea had made his way right next to him. He pressed up close and located exactly where the money bag was tied to Jude's waistband. His light fingers began to work at the knot that held it.

The magician answered the priest for the first time. 'You know the answer to that, my friend,' he said in a rich, level voice.

'But your coin's got the emperor's head on it!' The priest sounded triumphant.

The magician took the coin back from Crouch and looked at it closely. 'So it has,' he said. 'There's the big man himself. Now, what do you think I should do with it?'

'Shove it where the sun don't shine!' a heckler called out, and the magician laughed, a proper, warm laugh.

'I'd love to, but let's see what the priest has to say, because we all know how much the Temple loves its money!'

A huge roar of appreciation – excellent for Flea. The knot was loosening. The money bag was almost free.

The magician waited for quiet, then took a step towards the priest, and another, until he was right in front of him and had to look up, like a child.

'You asked what had changed about me since I was last here, but I don't think I really have changed that much. I think it's this place that's changed. You think that I'm somehow a lesser man for carrying an Imperial coin, but you deal with Roman money every day. Even worse, you try and make me insult the emperor while you live under his shadow all the time.'

He pointed to the parapet of the Roman Fortress that loomed over the northern walls of the Temple. It was bristling with Imperial soldiers. He pointed to the roof of the portico from which more soldiers looked down, as they did every Feast day, ready to pounce at the first sign of trouble.

'Even the high priest has to beg the Roman commander for his ceremonial robes, and at the end of every festival he has to give them back so the commander can lock them in his storeroom!'

The crowd began to mutter. No one liked to be reminded of the power the Romans held over them.

'And you have the nerve to criticise me for using an Imperial coin?' he continued. 'The emperor can have his coin back, but what about the people? What about the coins in the Temple treasury? Coins poor farmers have sweated blood to earn and have starved themselves to bring here as taxes. Isn't it enough that we pay taxes to feed the Imperial army? Do we have to pay for the Temple too? The Temple used to protect the people, but now it only protects itself. The Temple grows richer while the country grows poorer. The Temple clings on to Rome like a weak child hangs around a bully. This isn't a temple. This is a market stall! Friends, if you want freedom, free yourselves from the Temple!'

With a practised countryman's flick the magician threw the coin high in the air in the direction of the Fortress and started to walk to the southern colonnade, taking the crowd with him.

As he did so, Flea gave the string holding the money bag one last tug. But before he could grab it, Jude's hand clamped down hard on his.

# 10

There was nothing he could do. Flea's hand was round the purse; Jude's hand was round his. He was stuck.

Caught.

Doomed.

'Not bad, little thief, not bad. But not good enough,' Jude whispered, looking down.

Flea looked at the crowd and saw how he was being left behind. He struggled, went limp, struggled again.

'And stop worming around or I'll turn you in. What do you think the punishment will be? Will they cut off an ear, or will they just stone you? Ever been to a stoning? They bury you up to your neck in the ground and –'

'All right, all right!' Flea said between gritted teeth.

'Good. Now, we're going to talk.'

'Why? What do you want from me?'

A hard squeeze made him squeal.

'Not your place to ask,' Jude said, and Flea allowed himself to be dragged across to the low railing that separated the outer court from the inner. Only when they were there did Jude loosen his grip a little.

'I'm curious,' he said. 'What on earth did you think you were doing?'

'What do you care?' Flea said.

He looked at the man with rust-coloured hair properly. He had a thin, horsey face with long teeth. There was a star-shaped scar in the middle of one cheek and he appeared to have lost most of his teeth on that side of his face.

'About you? Nothing. But to be honest, I'd stick my head in boiling oil before I handed anyone over to the Temple Police, even my worst enemy.'

'If you don't let me go, *I'll* be your worst enemy!' Flea tried to kick him, but could not reach.

The grip tightened again.

'All right, all right. I'm one of the Temple Boys,' Flea said. 'We're a gang. The boys on the bridge you helped – they were Big and Snot. The one who's all hunched over, that's Crouch. The pretty one is Halo. I'm –'

'You're Flea.'

'How did you know my name?'

'Magic – what else? Actually, on the way here your friend Big was telling me about his gang: all your names and where you live. Apparently, all he has to do is snap his fingers and you'll do anything he asks.' Long-toothed smile. 'Now, can I let you go so we can talk? All right? Good.'

Flea flexed his hand while Jude put the money bag safely inside his satchel.

Jude rubbed his face and it sounded like a rock scraping on gravel. 'Bottom of the heap, are you?'

'Yes,' Flea said reluctantly.

'Finding it hard?'

'Suppose.'

'I know all about that,' Jude said. 'Although my case is slightly different.'

Flea looked at him with interest.

'You see, even though I'm the dogsbody, I'm actually the original member of Yesh's gang,' Jude continued. 'Except because we're grown-ups we don't call it a gang, we call it a *movement*. And I'm not the fixer, I'm a *facilitator*. And we don't go around doing tricks and talking to people, either. We're *reaching out*, we're *engaging*, we're *communicating*. And worst of all, we have a plan to follow and a mission to fulfil. We're showing people the way.'

'So leave,' Flea said.

'Quit? That would be like giving up. Anyway, who'd look after Yesh?'

'You don't trust the others?'

'I don't trust him,' Jude said.

'So why should I care?' Flea tried to growl. 'Anyway, what do you want?'

Jude blinked, then laughed. 'You're a horrid little so-and-so. I was going to hire you for a day's work – good wages too – but if you're –'

'How much?' Flea said quickly. The thought of money snapped him out of his bad mood.

'That got you interested. How much do you make in a typical day?'

'A shekel,' Flea lied.

'Nice try. I know how these things work. I bet you have to pool it anyway, or pay off Big.'

'Half a shekel.'

'I'll pay you half that,' Jude said. 'And feed you. And I promise not to tell anyone that I caught you red-handed trying to rob me –'

Jude broke off and looked over Flea's head to the far distant southern end of the Temple. It was where the money changers took the visitors' coins and exchanged them for Temple gold. You often got arguments there – the exchange rate was crippling and the actual cost of buying a dove or a lamb for sacrifice was high – but this was different.

'Sounds like trouble,' Flea said.

'That's what I'm worried about. They said they were planning something.'

'Who? What?'

'Yeshua. The others. I said it would make enough trouble just coming to the City, but no, he said he had to make a big statement and really show people what he was about.'

'And what is he about? At first I thought he was a magician, but then . . .' Flea protested.

'That's just what people call him when they want to put him down. Don't you understand? He hasn't come here to turn water into wine or pull eggs out of children's ears, he's come to . . . What's going on now?'

Because the sound was growing even louder. Howls. Screams. And now fighting.

The magician's words had obviously hit home with the crowd. The money changers and traders had never been popular. Now the crowd was taking out years of frustration on them. As Flea watched, a man clutching a moneybag broke free from the crush, but he was chased down and disappeared under a billowing sea of robes. Flea saw a trader trying to sneak towards the western gate with a wicker basket of white doves. He was spotted and started to sprint, holding his tunic up with one hand and the basket with the other. A small mob gave chase and surrounded him. A dove fluttered upwards, blood-stained and panicked, and just as it looked as if it might fly free a hand reached out and dragged it back.

The trumpet blast was harsh and shocking. Jude grabbed Flea. 'The Temple Police! Will your gang have the sense to get out?'

'The ones that can run will. But the others will be in big trouble – Clump and Crutches especially. They're breaking the Laws of Perfection.'

'And things will be even worse if the Imps wade in,' Jude said. 'He's gone and done it this time. Look, get out now! I'll find your friends and if I don't see you later, see you tomorrow. Outside your shelter!'

And he was gone.

# 11

Flea huddled in the entrance to the shelter along with Big, Little Big, Crouch, Halo and Crutches. The woman who lived in the hovel opposite was shaking out a rug and her stuck-up daughter was airing the mattresses and giving them a good beating – they crammed their house full of out-of-towners for the Feast and lived off the rent for the rest of the year.

Dust flew. The daughter stared at them. Flea made faces at her, but it was pretty clear why she was interested. Big had a split lip, Little Big had a black eye and seemed groggy. Crutches had been knocked over and kicked. Crouch was curled up on his side, his hair still wet from spit and his tunic torn. There was no sign of Snot, the twins, Gaga, Clump, Hole-in-the-Head or Red.

Halo was sobbing loudly and when Big cuffed him, Flea exploded. 'What are you doing? You should never have gone into the Temple. You were meant to rob the magician, not join up with him and his washed-up followers.'

'Flea,' Big said. 'Shut up before I hang you upside down.'

Flea ignored the threat. 'I thought we were meant never to trust anyone bigger than ourselves. We could have cleaned up. At least I had a go.'

'Flea!' Big's tone became more urgent.

'This is what happens when you suck up to adults . . . tramps! . . . . northerners! . . . con artists! show-offs . . .'

'FLEA!'

'WHAT?' Flea screamed back. Everyone was laughing him, then looking past him, then at him and laughing some more. 'WHAT, YOU BLOODY BASTARDS?'

'Behind you, prat.'

He turned.

The missing gang members, the magician and his followers were filling the alleyway. Yeshua had his hands on Clump and Gaga's shoulders, eyebrows raised. The others, with the rest of the Temple Boys, stood behind him.

Everyone seemed amused. To cover his confusion, Flea decided to carry on where he left off. 'So? So they're not dead? Big deal. We meet a magician and he doesn't kill us. Great trick. It was a riot! Halo and Crouch could have got stoned to death for taking part in that stupid conjuring trick. People were saying they were witches. The rest of us could have got killed or trampled to death. We didn't know where you were!'

'You should have stuck with us,' Red said. 'It was fine.'

'And what happens tomorrow if there's a curfew? Or a lockdown? How do we beg? How do we eat? Does the magician know how to fix that?'

A short silence was followed by sniggers. Flea realised that he'd missed something.

'Keep up, moron,' Big said. 'They've invited us to eat with them tomorrow night. It's a big deal, a feast with wine and everything. And there's no curfew, either. The Temple wouldn't dare.'

'No one told me!'

'Do us a favour,' Big said. 'Don't say another word.'

'And do me a favour,' Yeshua said. 'Spend some time with us and get to know us a bit better. Will you, Flea? Please?'

Flea felt the force of the magician's clever, intense eyes and looked away.

Yeshua said, 'We've got a tough one here, friends. Going to have to do more than my usual tricks to get him interested.'

Flea looked for Jude, but he wasn't there. 'One day you'll meet a real magician who'll blast you off the face the earth with lightning bolts,' he muttered.

'Until then, you've just got me.'

'We should have robbed you.'

'You wouldn't have got much.'

'I mean after you'd collected from the crowd.'

'We don't do that.' He smiled a steady, warm smile that somehow spread beyond Flea to take in the rest of the gang. 'Now, can we join you? That looks like a fine shelter. Did you make it yourselves?'

And in no time at all, Yeshua and his followers were sitting down by the shelter as if it were the most natural thing in the world.

Flea shook his head. All he felt was a profound

suspicion. He had to admit that the magician had a sort of power – he couldn't think of any other word – that could pull smiles out of a person like a butcher dragged the guts from an animal, but did it *really* make them happier? Did it change a thing?

When Clump asked Yeshua how he did the trick with the egg and the dove, Yeshua opened his eyes wide and said, 'Trick? How dare you. Have none of you heard of magic?'

'But can you . . .' Clump's voice tailed off.

The gang exchanged glances. They knew exactly what he wanted to ask. A month ago Clump had stolen the gang's takings and bought a cure for his twisted foot from a travelling doctor. The foul-smelling ointment had done no good at all except earn him a black eye for nicking the money and a foot that reeked of camel dung and rancid lard, which was probably what the ointment was made of.

'I know what you want,' Yeshua said. 'You want to know if I can cure people. The answer is *yes*, I can sometimes.'

Yeshua looked around the gang, meeting and holding their eyes. Once, twice he did it and then, without anyone uttering a word, Gaga stood and approached him as if he were on a string. Yeshua put his hands on Gaga's head, looked upwards, muttered something, then bent down and whispered in Gaga's ear. Gaga smiled uncertainly, cleared his throat, smiled shyly and said, 'Thank you,' in a little hoarse voice.

They were the first words any of the Temple Boys had ever heard Gaga speak. Everyone got up and made a fuss of him – slapping him on his back, asking him to say something else. Everyone apart from Flea, who felt sick in a way he could not understand.

He slouched to the end of the alleyway where the woman and her daughter were standing by their mattresses and staring at the gathering with undisguised curiosity.

The followers pooled their money and two of them went off with Big and Red to get some food. When they came back with bread, cheese and fresh vegetables, one of the followers produced a cloth and they spread the food out, then sat around it.

'Flea, come and join us,' Yeshua called.

Flea felt as if he were being torn apart, with half of him wanting to accept Yeshua's invitation, but the other too proud. He went round the corner and sat down, hugging his knees with his back against the alley walls and the laughter of people having fun burning inside him. What was wrong with him? The man had just cured Gaga and even that didn't impress him. There was just something about Yeshua, something that tried to draw you in. That was it! He wanted to draw you in, but to what?

'What are you doing?' a voice said. He looked up in

surprise. The skinny girl who was always hanging around was standing in front of him. She was about Flea's height, with gangly, skinny limbs. Her tunic was even shabbier than Flea's. She had half a loaf of flatbread in one hand and an orange in the other.

'What does it look like?' Flea snapped.

'It looks like you're sulking,' the girl replied. 'Here, want some bread?'

Flea tried to wave her away.

'What's going on?' she persisted. She pointed at the magician and said, 'Who's that man?'

'Don't you know? He's only meant to be the Chosen One,' Flea said.

'Who chose him?' the girl asked. Flea opened his mouth to answer, then realised he didn't know. 'If you ask me, he's trouble,' she went on. 'I heard people talking about him. They said he's come to the City to mess things up.'

'How?'

A shrug.

'Well, if you don't know, there's no reason to hang around, is there?' Flea snarled.

'No reason for you to, either,' the skinny girl said calmly. 'Why don't you come with me? You could have some bread. I'll even give you bit of orange.'

Flea's mouth watered, but he said, 'You think I need your food? Anyway, I've got to stay here. Someone has to look out for the gang.'

The girl gave him a level look that made him hate her. Then it was her turn to shrug.

'See you, then,' she said and walked slowly off. But she had given Flea an idea. If he found out more about Yeshua, maybe something that showed he was using them, then he would have something real to tell the gang.

When Yeshua and his followers finally got up to leave, Flea hid. When Big and Little Big came looking for him, his heart lifted – for a moment.

'That's it,' Big said. 'You've just proved you're a total loser.'

'Yeah,' Little Big said. 'Loser.'

'What do you mean, *loser*?' Flea protested. 'You're the loser. Who's hanging out with –'

'Just shut it, Flea,' Big said. 'No one cares what you say. In fact, we've decided to kick you out.'

'You what?'

'We're kicking you out of the Temple Boys. Not that you were ever in the gang. You just bored us into letting you stay.'

'But I do stuff. I get the water. I –'

'Yeah, you were useful, but now you're not. You're just annoying. We're moving on and you've made it clear what you think.'

'But I'm allowed to say –'

'Shut up.'

'. . . to say . . .'

Big picked up a stone and tossed it from hand to hand.

'. . . what I think.'

The stone thumped hard into the middle of Flea's chest and suddenly he was sitting down, feeling as if the air had been sucked from the world around him.

'But –' he managed to gasp.

'Just get out.'

Big picked another stone and Flea staggered to his feet and out of the alley, folding his arms against the pain.

# 12

It was the worst night of Flea's life. Worse than the night he left the glue maker (even though it had been snowing then), worse than the night he escaped from Mosh the Dosh's house (he had picked a hole in the roof and scraped his back on a nail), worse than the night after the rats in the tomb had bitten his mouth and his lips had swollen up and he'd had feverish nightmares of giant rats, wearing grave-shrouds and dancing.

Why was it worse? Because everything was his fault. *He* had suggested they go and see and the magician. *He* had argued against them taking their chances in Temple Square. And *he* had refused to join the others when Yeshua had invited him to.

Twilight turned to night and the dark was cold. He

walked up and down the street outside the alleyway, flapping his arms, then headed for the water fountain: sometimes a street seller would set up a charcoal brazier that you could huddle around. But the weather was too foul and no one was out. Once he thought he saw the skinny girl disappear around a corner in front of him and he ran to try and find her, but there was no one there. He was chasing shadows.

Wherever he went the cold wind found him. He settled down in the street close to the gang's shelter, his back against the wall, hugging his knees.

two days to go

# 13

It wasn't the cold that woke Flea but the pressure of a finger under his ear. In the end, he'd curled up on the woman-across-the-alleyway's rubbish dump. The faint warmth of decomposition made it less frigid than hard earth and paving stones.

He opened his eyes. A very black sky, very bright stars and a man-shape blocking them.

'Here. Too cold to be lying around.'

Flea recognised Jude's voice. He started as something warm landed in his lap.

'Don't unwrap it! It's a hot stone. You don't do that in the City?'

'D-do w-what?' Flea had to clamp his teeth to stop them chattering.

'Heat stones during the day and put them in your bed at night. Maybe it's a northern thing. You have to be careful, though. Some stones explode when they get too hot. How does that feel?'

'All r-right.'

In fact it felt wonderful. Wrapped in his hands, cradled against his belly, the stone felt like a small, personal sun.

'How did you find me?' he asked.

'My keen sense of smell. That was a joke. I was going to roust you out of your shelter, but Shim, one of Yesh's followers, said you didn't join them, so I kept my eyes peeled. Anyway, if you're warm enough, stand up. We've got a busy day.'

'We?' Flea rubbed his eyes.

'I'm paying you for a day's work. Part of the deal?'

'The whole deal, as far as I can remember.' Now Flea felt both light-headed and sharp. He saw a flash of teeth in the starlight.

'Well that's good.' Jude sounded amused. 'I don't imagine you have a better offer.'

Flea bridled. 'If you think I'm desperate . . .'

'You? Desperate? Never. It's me that needs the help.'

'Say something that surprises me,' Flea replied. But when he looked up, the moonlight had caught Jude's face and he was not smiling.

Quite the opposite. His face was twisted into an odd shape, almost as if he was trying to stop himself from crying. Flea opened his mouth to jeer, then thought better of it.

He heard himself ask, 'So what . . . do you want?'

'Fewer questions from you.'

Jude set off quickly down the twisting alleyways of the dark City, heading north in the direction of the sheep market. He was wrapped in a blanket and, hot rock or not, Flea wouldn't have minded a corner of it. He blew clouds of vapour from his mouth and tried to keep up.

By the time they reached the sheep pens, the sky was

getting lighter and the market was waking up. Sellers haggled with buyers. Priests were on hand to bless the new sacrifices, slaves throwing down straw in front of them to stop their holy robes from being despoiled by unholy dung. Trembling lambs glared white in the grey light. The air was thick with sheep fug and bleats.

'What are we doing here?' Flea asked. He hated the sheep market; the lambs seemed to know what was about to happen to them.

'My official duties for the day are to go and buy a sheep for our feast.'

'Shouldn't take long.'

'And a couple of other pieces of business. That's where you come in.'

'What do I do?'

Jude looked at Flea. 'Keep your eyes open and your mouth shut. If it works out, I'll be back in favour and that might help you.'

'How?'

'If your gang wants to hang out with mine and I say you're part of my gang, then your gang will start sucking up to you as sure as this little lamb's going to be grilled.' Jude turned swiftly to business. 'Here! What do you want for this one?'

He was calling to a Wild Man, a nomad from the eastern desert dressed from head to toe in black. The man's daughter, with hair the colour of desert sand and eyes lined heavily with black pencil, was kicking her heels against a wall. She stuck out her tongue at Flea. Her feet were bare, her clothes were rags and the chain that looped from her nose to her ear was gold.

'What are you staring at?' Flea asked.

'Your face,' she said. 'What are you doing with Jude?'

Flea glanced across at Jude, who was haggling in a relaxed, practised way. 'Helping him.'

'Hah! He must be desperate,' the girl jeered.

'He's paying me.'

'What? A mite? Two?'

'Half a shekel,' Flea lied.

The girl's eyes widened and she jumped down off the wall. 'Father! Double the price! The rumours are true. It's the end of the world and Jude's throwing his money away!'

The two men looked at her and laughed. Then they touched hands and Jude walked off with this head up, not looking to left or right.

Flea had to jog to keep up with him. 'How do you know *them*?' he asked. It wasn't often he felt superior.

'Unlike you, I have a lot of friends.'

'But they're not . . . our people. They're unclean.'

Jude laughed. 'You're not so clean yourself and anyway, do you really think you know who you are?'

'Huh?'

'Who are your parents, Flea?'

'I don't know. Dead, I think.'

'Remember them?' Jude asked coldly.

'No, but . . .'

'So for all you know, you're a Wild Boy yourself.'

'I'm not!' Flea said, suddenly hot. 'I can't be.'

A lump blocked his throat. He had a memory that he guarded like a dog guards a bone: a courtyard, a storehouse, towering earthenware jars, a woman who looked at him from a doorway. He knew that once this had been his home and she was his mother, but he didn't like to think about it too often because the feeling choked him.

Jude pulled Flea round and saw the look on his face. 'I'm sorry,' he said. 'That was wrong of me. I just meant that it doesn't matter whether you're high priest or Wild Boy or child of the streets. What's in here: that's what counts.' He thumped his chest.

Flea said nothing.

'What?' Jude asked. 'You want me to say sorry? Beg forgiveness? Crawl on my knees? Why are you staring at me like that?'

'Just imagining what you'd look like hacked to bits.'

'How many?'

'Fifty.'

'Ouch. I'm hurt.'

'Good.'

'Cut to the quick.'

'That's such a lame joke.'

'I'm all in pieces.'

'It was funny at first, now it's not.'

They walked on.

'Anyway,' Flea said. 'What did the Wild Girl mean about the end of the world?'

'Hold your idiot tongue,' Jude said urgently. 'Talk like that could get you into trouble. Haven't you felt the mood in the City?'

'No different from usual.'

'Good god. How are you still alive? Use your eyes,' Jude said. 'Look!' He pointed to a corner where a group of men were huddled together, talking. One of them put his head up, whispered something urgently and the group dispersed. Then Flea saw three other men approaching, moving smoothly as if they knew no one could touch them: Temple spies. You could always tell them by the way they walked as if they owned the City but never stopped looking around.

'And there,' Jude said. More spies were closing in from the other direction. 'And in the middle of all that, Yesh starts a riot in the Temple.'

'You thought that was stupid?'

'Stop asking questions, Flea.'

'Or wrong? Why does it matter?'

'It matters. That's all you have to know.'

'Oh, I get it,' Flea said. 'You want to protect him

from danger. Nothing bad about that.'

Jude looked Flea straight in the eye. 'Stop. Asking. Questions. And. Do. What. I. Say. This is where you start to earn your keep.'

# 14

Flea's job was to stick behind Jude, look unimportant and check to see if anyone was following him. He was good at not being noticed and was pleased that Jude didn't spot him when he looked back.

Jude turned off the street of the spice sellers and into a small yard where half a dozen donkeys and two camels with patchy coats were tethered to wall rings. He spoke to the groom, who shrugged and shook his head. Round the corner was another yard, and close to that a couple more. In each one, Jude asked questions, but always got the same shrug or shake of the head. Flea noted how Jude's shoulders slumped each time he was sent on his way.

But what was he doing? There was no sign of haggling, so he wasn't looking to hire a beast. Rather he seemed to ask a couple of questions, often repeating them, before moving on. So he was trying to find something out.

To the west of the sheep pens Jude followed a series of twisting alleyways so narrow the houses almost met above their heads and the air was as still and thick as a stagnant pond.

Even Flea did not know this part of the City and he became even more cautious. He watched as Jude squeezed down an alleyway beside a half-ruined warehouse. In front of the sagging doors, traders were selling stale vegetables, laid out on the ground. From inside came the sound of hammering. Smoke was belching from a chimney, which probably meant it was some kind of factory.

Cautiously he followed Jude down the alley and peered round the corner into a dank, sunless court that stank of animal dung. At the back of it was a shelter where a stringy brown donkey nosed at an empty manger and a camel stared haughtily at a wall.

Jude was talking to an old man.

Suddenly the scene on the bridge from the day before flashed into Flea's mind. That old man was the donkey driver and here, surely, were the two useless beasts that had caused the traffic jam. What were they both doing here, sharing the same stall? Jude was arguing and the old man was shrugging and looking blank, but there was something sly about him. Now Jude was reaching into his purse and pressing coins into the old man's hand, who shrugged, then said something. Jude seemed to ask for confirmation, nodded and walked away, a very different expression on his face. Thoughtful, worried, but more determined.

As Flea followed Jude out of the alley, he noticed a

tall man stooping in front of one of the vegetable sellers. The man was pretending to smell the herbs, but his eyes were darting to left and right. When Jude turned in his direction, he looked away quickly.

*No reason to do that*, Flea thought and hung back.

Jude set off. The man standing at the vegetable stall put down a large green bunch of parsley, straightened up and ambled off in the same direction. In spite of his height, he managed to look apologetic and insignificant as he bobbed and weaved through the crowd.

Flea followed them south into the heart of the City, wondering how he could warn Jude without being spotted. When Jude paused at the entrance to the covered market – a warren of narrow streets, roofed over to keep the sun out in summer and the rain out in winter – Flea moved near to a large woman whose shopping was being carried by an equally large slave.

He pushed closer, then waited while the tall man fiddled with his sandal strap. As soon as Jude plunged into the gloom of the market, the tall man followed and so did Flea.

This was better, Flea thought. He knew the covered market. He'd spent days in here the winter before, sheltering from the cold, and the gloom made it easier to steal from the stalls. He liked the smells that enveloped him: the head-rush of spices; the nose-tickle of soap and oil; the stink of blood and butchery. A shard of light speared through a hole in the roof and lit up the tall man and Flea could see him more clearly. Thin lips in a bony, clean-shaven face, curled into an empty, tortoise smile. Questioning, arched eyebrows cloaked quick, darting eyes.

Flea squatted by a bucket of skinned sheep's heads, trying to ignore the naked eyeballs. *Maybe he can't see you, but* we *can*, they seemed to say.

But the man had lost Jude. He swore under his breath and backtracked, stopping right in front of Flea, so close that the hem of his tunic brushed up against Flea's upturned face. Flea smelled old smoke, but more importantly he saw a little pocket sewn into a fold of the garment right in front of his nose.

*Destiny!* Flea thought. *It would be criminal to let an opportunity like this pass.*

Flea's hand dipped into the pocket and felt something small and smooth. He caught it between two fingers and when the man moved away, he just seemed to be left holding it. Palming it, he was about to set off again when two hands clamped down heavily on his shoulders.

'Where do you think you're going?' Jude hissed in his ear. Flea had no idea where he'd come from.

'That man was following you,' he hissed back.

'The tall one? Where did he pick me up?'

'Just outside the alleyway where you found the old man, the camel and the donkey.'

Jude's eyes momentarily widened. 'That far away? I only just noticed him. How close did you get to him?'

'Close enough to get this.'

Flea opened his hand to show the thing he had stolen: a small, carved ivory tube, about the size of a man's middle finger and still pocket-warm.

'Not so clever. He's going to miss it. Wait a minute: describe him.'

'Wearing grey. Long neck. Looked like a tortoise. Black eyebrows. Smelled of smoke.'

'Did he smile a lot?'

'All the time.'

'Can you get us out of here?' Jude's voice was suddenly urgent.

'Yes, I know this area.'

'Then do it – and lose that thing you stole, whatever it is.'

Flea nodded and was off. He knew many escape routes out of the market. The one he chose took them between a soap seller and a spice warehouse into a gap so narrow even he had to squeeze sideways. Then there was a wall to climb and a view down into a tiny roofless room where dull-eyed children picked through sacks of dried lentils and didn't look up.

Flea led Jude across the rooftops, crossing streets where the houses came close enough together to jump the gap and on until the streets widened and the houses were built out from the hillside. They stepped from a roof straight on to a small strip of carefully terraced garden.

Jude checked the sun. 'All right,' he said. 'This is far enough. Now then, Flea. You and I need to talk.'

# 15

In the narrow garden was a pomegranate tree, pruned so that thin twigs spread like fingers from the thicker arms. Dark rows of earth, freckled with ash, were turned and ready for seeding. But it was cold on the rooftops. Flea hugged himself and wondered where spring was.

'Did you get rid of that thing you stole?' Jude asked.

'Chucked it down a chimney,' Flea lied.

'Good. Here's the money I owe you.'

Flea didn't look at it. 'Don't you think I deserve a bonus?'

Now that his time with Jude was coming to an end, he was ambushed by sadness. It had been good to feel useful. It had been better to feel needed. What did the rest of the day hold in store for him? Nothing. He had been thrown out of the Temple Boys. He was alone again.

Jude snorted. 'For doing what we agreed? In your dreams.'

'For keeping my mouth shut. That's what you really want, isn't it?'

'About what, in heaven's name?'

'About the man who was following you. About the way you looked at every donkey and camel in the City until you found the ones that blocked the bridge yesterday. About paying their owner to tell you something.'

'You . . .' Jude grabbed Flea by the wrist and pushed him back against the tree, thrusting his face in close. Flea could see every hair of his beard, the spit threaded between his lips, the red starburst of the scar on his cheek. 'Do you honestly think that if I strangled you here and now anyone would care? Perhaps that's why I hired you, because I could use you and then throw you away when I was done.'

Fear stuck Flea with a splinter of cold.

'I'm sorry,' he said. 'I take it back. I'll leave you alone.'

Jude gave a cold laugh and dropped him. 'On the other hand, I chose you because I thought you were clever . . . and I was right.'

He looked away over the flat rooftops, eyes narrowed and a muscle pulsing in at the back of his jaw. Flea massaged his wrist and waited for as long as he could manage. 'So?' he asked.

'All right. I won't pay you a bonus, but I will pay you for more work. Lucky that you're working for me – Yesh would just say there are riches waiting for you in heaven. Ground rules first. One: Fleas should learn not to bite the hand that feeds them. Two: Fleas shouldn't bite off more than they can chew. Three: clever fleas jump away from trouble, not into it. Got that?'

Flea protested. 'I can't help seeing what I saw. It's far better you explain so I don't get it all wrong. Please.'

'Please. He actually said "please". That's more like it.' Jude chewed his inside cheek. 'Well, if I tell you just enough to keep out of danger it might help. I think the man following us was Roman. He's not . . . he's not a man you want to be interested in you.'

'Who is he then?'

'If he's the man I think, his name crawled away and died of shame a long time ago. He's got the governor's ear, the Roman prefect himself; and he's ambitious. It doesn't help that the governor's more or less given up governing so he'll listen to anyone with a strong opinion. And this man has a simple idea . . . If people don't do what you want, hurt them until they do.'

'So he's powerful?'

'He's effective. Like a knife. Some people say he was once one of us. Some people say he was Idumaean, like Herod the Great. Or a Samaritan. Or a . . . well, it doesn't matter because he's a Roman now, and that my friend is the power of Rome. Anyone who thinks like a Roman, *is* a Roman. But I don't understand why he was following *me*. And that's a worry.'

'Maybe he made a mistake,' said Flea.

'He doesn't make mistakes.'

72

'So maybe it was something to do with the donkey and the camel blocking the bridge.'

'I told you to forget that.' Jude looked away.

But Flea knew he was on to something. 'I can't. You can twist my arm all you like, but you can't make it go away. It doesn't make sense. I'll just think and think about it and probably think wrong. There was a traffic jam on the bridge. It was caused by a camel and a donkey owned by the same man. The magician sorted it out then rode the donkey into the City and everyone went mad. Then you found the owner and gave him money . . .'

'Flea! Back off!'

'Saying *back off* doesn't work with me. You told me to follow you, so I followed you. If you'd said, *Watch out for anyone who's interested in me, but keep away from them*, I'd have been more careful.'

Jude rolled his eyes upwards. 'I didn't know he was following me,' he said between gritted teeth.

'Exactly. You can't possibly know everything's that going to happen so you might as well tell me everything.'

Jude raised his arms and looked at the sky. 'What sort of creature have I hired? All right. All right. But if I'm going to hire you again, it will be for your low cunning and sneakiness, not for your endless questions. Is that clear?'

'So you are hiring me?' Flea felt a smile creep across his face.

'One more day.'

Flea had to stop himself from punching the air. He folded his arms and leant back against the terrace wall like this sort of thing happened all the time, like he was taking it all in his stride. 'So, you were about to tell me about the old man, the camel and the donkey.'

'It was part of a plan,' Jude said, after thinking for a moment. 'It was part of a plan cooked up by Yesh and all the other followers. The trouble is, they didn't tell me. That's why I needed to find out about it.'

'Let me get this right,' Flea said slowly. 'The others, Yeshua and the others, wanted there to be a big snarl-up on the bridge.'

'Correct.'

'And they wanted Yesh to sort it out?'

'They wanted to be certain there would be a crowd and, above all, they wanted a donkey.'

'But there are donkeys everywhere.'

'There had to be a donkey on the bridge and obviously it had to be the right donkey, so the donkey owner didn't make a fuss. It was all set up. Remember the guy with the water pitcher? I think he was probably the signal that it was all arranged. It meant everything was in place: the camel, the donkey – everything.'

Flea felt dizzy. It was like peering into a pool of water. You saw the surface, but then, suddenly, you could see *below* the surface, further and further down.

'But why?' he said.

74

'That's a very short question with a very long answer. Do you really want to know? Good, so sit down and listen because I'm going to tell you a story.'

Jude settled down with his back against the pomegranate tree and Flea sat next him. After a quick look around the little garden to make sure they were alone, Jude began.

'A long time ago when the world was young, me and Yesh used to travel around the villages of Gilgad doing tricks. Doesn't sound like much, but it was a living and the best time of my life. Sometimes he did the patter and I did the magic, and sometimes it was the other way round, but people paid us wherever we went – maybe with coins if we were in a town, maybe with a meal and a place to bed down if we were in a village. Sometimes we'd fetch up in a huddle of huts in the middle of nowhere – howling desert all around and wild dogs and lions. You couldn't imagine how anyone scratched a living from the rock and sand, but there'd always be a bite or two to eat and a pile of hay to sleep on and the stars up above in the desert sky if you wanted something to look at. We were . . . *I* was . . . happy. I knew it wouldn't last. Yesh's father was a carpenter, but Yesh was never going to settle down to that. I just thought if I could keep him moving, keep him living on his wits, he might forget . . .'

'What?'

'His *difference*. Yes, that's the word. I thought he might

be busy enough to forget his difference. And then things changed. It all happened so slowly I didn't even notice and by the time I did, it was too late.'

Jude looked at Flea.

'Something you need to know about Yesh. He could have been anything he wanted, except he didn't want to be anything you or me could dream of. That's part of his difference. He's a one-off. An original. When he started doing a new sort of trick and people began to think it was real magic, he didn't exactly argue with them – and that made things dangerous. Every village has a priest, and while they might turn a blind eye to conjuring, real magic is witchcraft and you can be stoned for that. I tried to warn him, get him back to what we were doing before, but he said he was on the verge of something really important. He thought a change was coming to the world and people, his people, should be ready for it.

'Soon he was pulling in the big crowds, really big crowds, and he picked up more people, which turned into an inner circle of followers until we were thirteen, including Yesh. You saw them with him yesterday. We all got on at first, but then one evening, when we were sitting round the fire, I suddenly realised that instead of everyone talking and sticking it to each other they were all just *listening* to him.

'Next thing, when we came back to places we'd already been, there were people waiting for us, and I found out all kinds of stuff I somehow hadn't noticed before. He'd turned the water into wine, breathed on a dead sparrow and brought it back to life, cured people of leprosy and blindness. For a while we were followed around by an old pigman who swore Yesh had pulled little demons out of his throat and given them to his pigs to eat. Another person swore he'd fed a whole crowd with a handful of fish and a couple of loaves of bread – that's the sort of audience he was pulling in . . .

'Truth was, he always thought his talk was more important than the magic. He found a way of getting through to people better than the priests ever could. He talked about a world where everything was turned upside down – good for the poor, hard for rich, where you could make yourself pure just by doing good things.'

Jude paused, and when he started talking again he wore the expression of someone taking bad medicine.

'Then last year he ran into this Ranting Dunker called Yohan, blast his miserable guts. Yohan lived on the edge of the desert and had a following himself, but he said he was nothing compared to Yesh. He said Yesh wasn't just the best conjuror in the world, nor even the best healer. No, he said he was the Chosen One himself, and Yesh's other followers – the ones he'd picked up along the way – didn't laugh it off, they believed him. They started calling my old friend *Master*, which was annoying enough, then *Lord*. And now, to cap it all, suddenly I realise they're planning something big, here, in the City, on the busiest day of the whole year, *and I don't know what it is.* You with me, Flea?'

'I think so – and it all had to start with Yesh sitting on a donkey?'

'That's it. The man with the pitcher of water was a sign to Yesh; when he got on to that donkey it was a sign to the people.'

'But what's the problem? Why not just go along with it?'

Jude gave a wry smile. 'Coming from you, young Flea, that's a bit rich. When have you *just gone along* with anything? I'm frightened. I'm frightened of how it all might end. Yesh is walking into danger and your gang will go down with him if they're not careful. We need to find out what it is they're up to, and then we stop it. You and me.'

'One small problem. I was just chucked out of the gang, and they never listened to me when I was in it. No way can I stop anything.'

'But you want to get back in?'

'Of course I want to get back in. They're my gang.'

Jude narrowed his eyes. 'Maybe we can use the situation. Maybe you could save them.'

'But I can't save them unless I'm part of them, can I?'

'True. But there is a way.'

'What?'

'Whatever else I say about Yesh, he is a good man. The

best. Let him talk to you. He can't bear it when people reject him. He can't understand why and it gets to him like an itch he's got to scratch. You can use that.'

'What? Join his movement?'

'Nothing like that. Just be yourself, but give him a chance.'

'And then what?"

'Yesh will like you. If your gang sees that he's on your side, chances are they'll take you back.'

Flea nodded. 'Just so long as I only have to pretend to like him.'

'Just think of it as your mission. Now from what I can gather, Yesh is down by the Healing Pool today, so that's where we're going now. All right?'

Flea was on the point of agreeing when something struck him. 'You told me that when the crowd saw Yeshua riding on a donkey it was a signal,' he said. 'What signal?'

Jude's face took on an odd twist. 'Perhaps "signal" isn't quite the right word. It's a prophecy.' And Jude began to chant. '*Be full of joy, oh people of Zion. Call out in a loud voice, oh people of Jerusalem. Look: the king is coming. He is just and he is good and he has power, but he is not proud, for he is sitting on a donkey.*'

'Yeshua's a king?' Flea could not keep the amazement out of his voice.

'He must be . . . he came into the City on a donkey.'

# 16

The Healing Pool was a few hundred paces to the south of the Temple, not far from the gang's shelter. An underground spring fed a square pool that was surrounded by a deep, roofed portico to give shade in the summer. In the hot season it was dank and humid, in the cold it was damp and clammy, but it was always crowded. In the days before the Feast tourists joined the sick to create a solid heaving mass of humanity, jostling to get through the narrow gateway into the pool's enclosure.

Even so, Flea had never seen the courtyard in front of it so crowded and Jude lifted him up on to his shoulders for a better view.

Ahead of them a small, red-faced woman was jumping up and down to try and get a view. Flea leant down and tapped her on the shoulder.

'Excuse me,' he said. 'Can you tell me why so many people are here?'

The woman looked up. 'Because the healer's come! The Chosen One! The new king! Haven't you heard? Just one touch and the heavens open and you see angels and live forever. A miracle, child, a miracle. He's in there now. They're letting people through, but only one at a time. I'm staying here for as long as it takes.'

'The king?'

'That's what they're saying.'

'And he really heals?' Flea thought quickly, then bent down to her and said in a low voice, 'At last! Between you and me, my friend here's got this massive problem. Yesterday his father started coughing and was dead that same day. Then his brother started to cough and died in the night. Now he's not feeling too clever and neither am I. We –' Flea interrupted himself with a racking cough and between fits managed to spit out, 'You don't think it's plague, do you?'

The woman gave him a stricken look and let out a scream. A space around her cleared. She shouted, 'PLAGUE!' and a bigger space opened up. Flea added lolling forwards to his coughing and took the opportunity to whisper into Jude's ear, 'Start coughing like you mean it and move quickly, before they start stoning us.'

The crowd melted away in front of them as they walked to the gate. It was guarded by one of Yesh's followers, a tough, no-nonsense-looking man with eyes like chips of stone, broad cheekbones and a chest like a wrestler. 'Brother Jude. Might have guessed it was you,' he said. 'The idea is to get people to trust us, not scare them away,' he said.

'They'll be back, Tauma, they'll be back,' Jude said, as Flea slipped from his shoulders.

'Don't doubt it, brother,' Tauma said. His eyes took in Flea, then looked away.

'I hear that people are saying he's the king now, come

in all his glory. *Brother*.' Jude sounded contemptuous.

'People will talk,' Tauma answered with a chilly smile.

'If they've been fed stories.'

Tauma stopped smiling and gave Jude a long and level stare. 'Funnily enough, he was asking for you earlier. It was embarrassing when no one knew where you were.'

'Oh, you know me. Always busy with this and that.'

'But on whose business?' Tauma said.

'My Master's, of course.' A look passed between them. Profound suspicion from Tauma, satisfaction from Jude. 'Come on, Tauma, you know I always have Yesh's best interest at heart.'

'No, I don't,' Tauma said, but he stepped aside to let Flea and Jude pass through the gate.

Behind the walls, the atmosphere was hushed. People were crushed under the portico and some were even standing in the shallow water, staring at the far end of the pool. Flea spotted Red and Little Big on the far side of the pool, eyes fixed in the same direction as everyone else, so he pushed through the crowd until he could see what had attracted their attention.

Yesh was standing on a raised stone platform at one end of the pool, to the right of the entrance. The platform was kept clear by his followers, who were holding the whole crowd back, except for a merchant with an expensively curled beard wearing long, heavy robes.

Yesh's voice just carried across the murky water of the pool to Flea.

'All right. What is a sacrifice?' he was saying. 'When we buy a lamb to be slaughtered we're sacrificing a life, but –'

'If you buy a lamb, you own it,' the merchant interrupted. 'You can do what you want with it.'

'But I'm asking who makes the real sacrifice,' Yesh answered. 'You or the lamb? You've spent a few coins, but the lamb's lost everything it has: its life.'

'But the priests say, and the Rules say, that if you do something wrong you make up for it by making a sacrifice at the Temple. Your sins are washed away in its blood. It's simple. It's our custom. It's right,' the merchant replied.

'And by your clothes I see you can afford a lot more sinning than my friend here,' Yesh said. He pointed to a beggar in the front row of the crowd, grey rags wrapped around his skinny body. 'To buy a lamb for sacrifice, he would have to starve himself for a year. You could buy ten lambs and not even notice. By your reckoning, that would mean you are allowed to be ten times worse than him. Is that right?'

'That's dangerous talk,' the merchant said. 'Damn it, it's blasphemous.'

Yesh shrugged. 'You're most welcome to carry on believing you can sin more than your neighbours just because you're richer than they are. You're welcome to carry on stuffing your money into the Temple coffers. You're welcome to make the priests even fatter, if that's what you want. But I'm talking about what goes on inside, my friend. I'm talking about your heart. I'm talking about how you clean your heart, and the only way to do that is to make a real sacrifice and make it willingly.'

The merchant stepped back, shaking his head. A path was cleared for Yesh though the crowd and he made his way down it until he came to a young man on crutches supported on either side by an older man and woman. The woman knelt and kissed the hem of Yesh's clothes. The older man started to explain something, but stopped when Yesh held up a hand. Yesh leant down, prised the woman's fingers from his robe and lifted her to her feet. Then he knelt and touched the leg of the man on crutches. All around, the little sounds of the crowd were sucked up into a single intake of breath.

Yesh walked five paces, then turned. 'Well?' he said. 'Aren't you going to give it a go?'

With trembling hands, the older man and woman took the crutches away. The man lurched slightly, bent down and put both his hands on one knee.

'That's good,' Yesh said. 'One step at a time. It's the only way to do it.'

The young man took a step with his good leg, then threw his bad leg round and forwards. He lurched, straightened and did it again, rowing through the air with his arms. The magician stepped forwards and embraced him. The crowd cheered. Some fell to their knees, while others surged around him. Cries of 'Heal me, Master!' went up. 'Heal *me*!' A man jumped into the water, another went in after him and soon the water was full of men, waving and splashing. 'Heal me! Heal me!'

Flea pushed through the crowd around the pool, away from Yesh, tired from his early start and feeling confused. The sun broke out from behind a cloud and he lifted his face to it.

Spring warmth. Fresh warmth. Through half-closed eyes he watched the water churn as people tried to force their way closer to the magician, the king, the Chosen One or whatever else they were calling out. Had Flea really just seen a miracle? Everyone else seemed to think so, so why wasn't he convinced? He'd seen Gaga talk and a lame man walk. What more did he need?

He leant against the wall and felt something digging into him. He reached inside his tunic, pulled out the carved ivory tube he'd stolen and held it up in the light. Vines spiralled around it, but there was a join in the middle where they didn't quite meet. If you twisted it, a spiralling ridge moved along a spiralling groove, and when one end came off it uncovered a metal spike with thin channels cut into it, clogged with something dark and crusty.

Blood. Flea was revolted and fascinated. He screwed

the thing back together, but his skin was still crawling and he caught the faintest trace of something rotten. A smell that was both thin and strong, like cotton thread, twined itself up his nostrils.

Then Big bustled up, Little Big trailing after him like an ugly shadow.

'What are you doing here? I said you were out of the gang.'

'I'm allowed to come here if I want,' Flea said.

'And I say you're not. We're here with Yeshua. We're security. And I'm telling you to get out.'

'And I'm here with Jude. And he's your man Yesh's first ever follower and best friend and he said it was all right for me to be here.'

Flea planted his feet, folded his arms and waited for the blow to fall.

Just before Big clouted him, one of Yesh's followers, fleshily handsome and better dressed than the others, bustled over.

'Ah, Flea, I assume. Spent the day with brother Jude, I hear?'

'It's all right,' Big said. 'We're getting rid of him.'

'That's the last thing we want,' the man said. 'The shepherd is always pleased when the lost sheep returns, or so the Master says. So, how was Jude, young man?'

'You calling me a sheep?' Flea asked.

'Haha.' The man's smile did not quite reach his eyes.

'Very good. We love laughter and you have a great sense of humour, I can see. Have your friends been telling you about the dinner tonight?'

'No?' Flea looked innocently curious. 'I think they couldn't have quite got round to it.'

'Er, Flea's no longer with us,' Big said uncomfortably.

'Nonsense. The Master wants him to come. Most insistent. He'll never let anyone go, not without with a fight.' The man's very white teeth looked as thick as tombstones and, above his smile, his blue eyes stayed watchful. 'Well?' he urged.

'Tell the Master that . . . I'm all right with that,' Flea said.

'Good. He'll be pleased. Come on, all of you. No time to waste.'

*All going to plan*, Flea thought. *All going to plan.*

# 17

The streets that led to the Upper City were drenched red by the evening sun.

It felt odd to walk with a group of adults and even odder to be noticed without anyone throwing something rotten at you. Old people, young people, middle-aged people came to doorways and windows to watch. Some called out. Some offered water or bread or whatever they had. Others held up babies, pointed the magician out to children or begged him to come inside. When a man called out, 'Show us a trick!' Yesh smiled, clapped his hands and looked up at the heavens as if he were expecting them to open. When nothing happened he shrugged and said, 'Doesn't always work.' He walked on leaving laughter behind him.

Jude fell in step beside Flea.

'It worked.' Flea spoke from the corner of his mouth.

'Watch and learn. I expect that will be a new experience for you,' Jude said.

Flea decided to ignore that. 'So, what's happening?'

'We're on the way to the house of Yesh's uncle, Yusuf of Ramathain, also known as Yusuf the Merchant, also known as one of the richest men in the City. Something's going on.'

'And you said Yesh was planning . . .'

'Exactly, and I'm guessing they're in it together, which makes it all the more important to keep your eyes and ears open. Wine will be flowing like water, but don't touch it – understand? I don't want you reeling around and I want you in a fit state to report anything odd that you see or notice. Now, you need to know the names of the other followers.'

Jude went through the followers' names, with Flea trying to commit them to memory. He'd met two at the Healing Pool: Tauma was the man at the gate, Shim was the creep with the fake smile. Then there were Yak and

Yohan who were always by Yesh's side, wherever he went. Yak had wild hair and an untrimmed beard, but once you knew he was Yesh's brother you could see the resemblance, though he was taller and broader across the shoulders. Yohan was young, with dreamy eyes, smooth skin and a wispy beard. Mat was small and plump as a bee and always busy. If anyone had a problem, they went to him. As for the rest, there was a Bart, an Andros, another Yak, a Shimon, a Thad and a quiet one called Lip.

Trailing behind them, Flea almost managed to convince himself that all was well. Halo was sitting on Shim's shoulders, pretending to beat him like a donkey. Thad and Bart had taken Crutches' hands and were swinging him along like a child. Clump was practically dancing and even Red was walking along with a great big grin on his face.

In the Upper City, the houses hid behind high walls. Flea caught glimpses of pillars, open porches, fountains and clean, empty spaces he had never even imagined, they were so far from his everyday life. The crowd trailing them was quieter now and fell totally silent when they stopped at a high, metal-studded door. Pitchy torches smoked and flared, dropping fire on the pavement.

A small figure was standing on the edge of the crowd, watching. The skinny girl. She waved. Flea tried to look superior, but felt oddly uneasy that she had seen him, as if he had been found out somehow. What had she said to him? That Yesh had come to the City to make trouble. *Well, I'll find out soon enough if I can do anything about it*, thought Flea.

Yesh stood in front of the great doors. He pretended to blow and they opened smoothly. The crowd *oohed* and *aahed*, then clapped.

The doors revealed a great courtyard, and a palace rearing up in stiff cliffs of white marble. They closed on the crowd and shut out the sound of the City. All you could hear was a fountain's silvery splash and very faintly, in the distance, a harp.

'This is the house of a very rich man.' Red's voice was awed. Light spilled like gold from every window and made his scars look livid and shiny.

Across the courtyard, doors led up to an open archway that framed a man dressed in a long blue robe embroidered with gold stars. They shimmered and gleamed as he walked. A long beard spread over his broad chest, which sloped down to an even bigger belly. Very slowly he came down the stairs towards them and bowed to Yesh before kneeling to kiss the marble in front of his feet.

Yesh laid his hand on the man's head briefly. Yohan and Yak helped him to rise just as Mat bustled up to the Temple Boys.

'Stop gawping and listen!' he snapped. 'That is Yusuf of Ramathain. He's just paid the Master the greatest possible honour and I'm not having the evening ruined by you lot. If you're going to eat with us, you've got to clean up. Come. Come!'

They followed him through a side door and down a long, vaulted passageway. At the end of it, heat and noise blasted from an open door. It was a huge kitchen where ovens the size of furnaces roared. A row of cooks chopped, stirred, mixed, while meat sizzled on spits and plucked birds nestled in rows, ready for the oven. The gang was hurried past bowls of fruit and sacks of spices, but Flea hung back. In a dark recess of the kitchen a man was standing alone, watching the activity. His eyes ranged over the Temple Boys, his head nodding as he counted them off. The face snagged on a memory. Flea had caught a glimpse of him before, and recently too, but where?

'Come on, come on, stop staring.' Mat hustled Flea along, ushering him into a side room that smelled of scented oil and mould. The Temple Boys were looking around, apparently confused by the sight of a row of water basins.

'This is where you wash,' Mat said. 'You have heard about washing? Soap, water, oil. Or do I need to get one of the slaves in to show you how it's done?'

'But why?' Big said.

'People wash before they eat,' Mat said.

'Really?'

'Trust me, you'll want to look your best when find out who you'll be eating with.'

Big stepped up to a basin of water and the others followed. Soon Clump was mincing up and down in a parody of a fine lady and Smash and Grab were having a water fight. Slaves brought more water. Another brought clean tunics. Mat fussed and grumbled, sent them back to clean their nails, gave a grudging nod if he thought they could pass or told them that they were late, they were ruining everything, then sent them back to the basins. At last, tingling, oiled and stinking of flowers, the gang stood in front of Mat and he said, 'I suppose that will have to do.'

Flea thought about the lambs being washed before they were sacrificed.

'Baaa,' he said, but no one heard and he followed them down a long corridor that ended in a curtain that moved like water.

And behind the curtain, a monster with a hundred voices was roaring.

# 18

Mat pulled the curtain aside and the gang was suddenly drenched in the din of drunken adults having fun. A thousand candle flames fluttered like a thousand butterflies. The heat was intense, like a blanket that smothered and prickled.

The Temple Boys found themselves in a huge room on a raised platform set with couches where Yesh and his followers were relaxing. Below, on the floor of the great hall, more guests on more couches were staring up open-mouthed. Flea looked for Jude, who met his eye and gestured for him to wait. The rest of the gang stood stock-still, eyes wide.

Yusuf the Merchant noticed them, nodded to Mat and then stood to address the crowd.

'My friends, I know all of you are curious to meet my brother's son and I know many of you would rather I disowned him than welcome him into my house.' He raised a hand to quell a murmur of disagreement. 'And I have to admit it was a bit of shock when he sent young Yohan to me the other day to ask if I could set a few more places at this meal.

'"Who's coming?" I asked. "The high priest and the treasurers?" Yohan shook his head. "The governor and his retinue?" Yohan shook his head. "Surely not the Emperor himself?" And this time Yohan answered, "The twelve poorest, most miserable, most wretched children in the City." And here they are – street kids from the foulest gutter. The lowest of the low. The dirtiest of the dirty before they scrubbed up, and definitely the hungriest of the hungry.

'Now, I don't know about magic, although I've seen Yeshua do things that you wouldn't credit, but I will say this: whether or not you believe that a cripple who's been given the strength to walk again should be allowed into the Temple, whether or not you believe my nephew can make people perfect, whether or not you think he's the Chosen One, bringing a gang of beggar boys to dinner in my palace is real magic. A proper miracle!'

Laughter echoed around the hall. Yusuf waited for it to die down and then held up a hand. 'This wouldn't be the first time I've done something on gut instinct. I can afford this wonderful house because I've followed my instincts. I made it in this great City in spite of being a poor northern boy and I'd like to think my extraordinary nephew can do the same – with a bit of help from his old uncle, of course. He's been called a trickster, a conjuror, a magician, a healer and a lot more besides. But, for the record, he was the cleverest boy I ever saw and he's by far the cleverest man.

'I wanted him to join my business, but his mother wanted him to become a preacher and even though things haven't quite worked out the way she imagined, he is, quite simply, the best person I have ever met. He doesn't just teach, he lives what he teaches.' Yusuf dropped his voice. 'But, friends, there is a message here for us all to think about. When Yesh talks about changing things, he means it, and this is your chance to be involved. Beggars sitting with the great and the good. That's change. I'm sure you can all think of some other changes you'd like to see.'

He paused and looked around the room, then spoke again in a brighter voice. 'Now, I'm told these good lads go by the name of the Temple Boys, so before I sit down, I would ask you to raise your cups and bid them welcome. Gentlemen, the Temple Boys.'

And with that, all the men lying on couches got to their feet. Flea felt hands on his shoulders and allowed himself to be pushed forwards. He looked to left and right and saw the others do the same, saw the happiness shine through all the doubt and confusion, saw Clump lift his hands above his head, and he realised that this should be the high point of his life. The day he was plucked off the street and given supper in the house of the richest merchant in the City.

'The Temple Boys! The first shall be last and the last shall be first!' Yusuf called.

'THE FIRST SHALL BE LAST AND THE LAST SHALL BE FIRST!' every man in the room shouted back and raised their golden goblets.

Mat pushed Flea towards a couch in the middle of the row. He stood by it nervously, then felt someone behind him. He turned and found himself looking up at Yeshua, smiling at him. For the first time Flea noticed the laughter lines around his eyes. He had a gap between his front teeth and his beard had been trimmed and oiled so it gleamed.

'Flea,' he said. 'Flea. There's something I want from you. Something very important.'

# 19

Misgivings flooded Flea's mind and must have shown on his face, because Yeshua laughed again.

'I'm not going to eat you,' he said.

'I didn't –'

'But you're scared. No, not scared. Worried.'

'So?' Flea tried to stand tough, but found it hard.

'Sit with me,' Yesh said.

'Why me? Why not get Halo or Crouch or any of the others?'

'Because you've taken against me from the start and I want to know why. Is it that Jude caught you robbing us and you feel embarrassed? Come to think of it, you definitely *should* feel embarrassed.'

Flea flushed. 'He told you that?'

'You answer my question,' Yesh said firmly.

'We were always going to rob you. That was the plan. I was the only one with the guts to try it.'

'Or the others realised they might get more out of being my friend.'

'Got enough friends,' Flea lied.

Yesh looked at him fondly. 'You know, sometimes we push away what we most need just in case we're not going to get it. When we most need to be loved, we make ourselves unlovable.'

Flea snorted. 'Do you think I'm thick?'

Servants were placing copper bowls of warm water in front of everyone. The water smelled enticingly of lemon. Flea was thirsty and drank, but then saw that all around, people were dipping their elegant fingers into the bowls, washing them, then waiting for servants to hand them spotlessly white linen cloths. He felt his face flush again, and then heard from behind him the sound of loud slurping.

Yesh, drinking deeply, met Flea's eyes from the bowl's rim and winked.

Flea turned away again. What was he supposed to feel? Grateful? Did Yesh really think he was such a pushover?

Food began to arrive, weird stuff that was both sweet and salty and unlike anything Flea had tasted before. While Yesh talked to his uncle, Flea took a sip of wine, found he liked it and took another.

On the couch next to his, Yak was feeding Halo. Big

was showing Tauma a few of his favourite wrestling moves, which involved throwing himself around on the floor, but no one seemed to mind. Jude was at the end of the row of couches. When Flea waved, his hand seemed far away and he became fascinated by the way he could wiggle his fingers. It all seemed quite funny.

More wine.

More astonishing pastries.

More wine.

More meat: bird of some kind.

Flea grew hot and lay on the cool floor for a while. People laughed at him and he didn't care, except the noise got trapped in his head and suddenly it didn't matter that Jude had told him to keep his eyes and ears open. Instead it became very important to leave the room because if he didn't he was going to be sick.

He staggered to his feet, blundered into a slave, found a passageway that seemed cooler than the great hall and followed the coolness until he saw the outside.

Bliss.

He heard a fountain. Even more bliss. He tripped, but didn't care. The fountain was in the middle of a beautiful courtyard and fell into a raised pool. Flea weaved his way to it and dipped his head into the water. The shock was like being reborn. He came up gasping, then plunged his head down again, opened his eyes, blew silver bubbles and watched them rise. Then he crawled round the side of the fountain and propped himself up against it so he could see the moon, which seemed to be drifting at some speed from left to right, but somehow never disappeared. When it stopped zooming around he'd be ready to rejoin the party, he thought.

The voices started so suddenly Flea realised he must have dozed off.

He recognised Shim's voice first. '. . . all be dead before they turn twenty and you know it. Listen, Judas, and listen well. These brats are being given a part to play in something that's bigger than them and bigger than all of us. Pay them off if you want, pay them as much as you want, but tomorrow we need them. It's been decided. There's an undercurrent of . . . fear in the City. Of violence. If we're surrounded by children it softens our image and reinforces our core message.'

Jude's voice was exasperated. 'An undercurrent of fear? Yours, you mean. You want to use the kids to –'

'Enough!' Shim said. 'We all agreed. None of us likes it, but it has to be done if the prophecy is to come true. Think of it, man! The world is going to change forever and we – and your precious kids – are going to be at the heart of it. The very heart. You know what the Master would say. Be strong.'

'Except he wouldn't,' Jude said. 'He stopped talking to me weeks ago.'

Shim's voice was clever and soft. 'If he cuts you out it's because he knows you don't believe in him. It's like a slap in the face when he needs you most. You saw what he did in Bethany. You saw –'

'Bethany! Don't talk to me about that place! Where can it lead?'

'But that's the point! That's the test! You've got to come with us on the journey. You've got to rejoin him. We're doing it, Jude. We're going all the way. He's found the courage. We've found the courage. Question is, old friend, have you found the courage?'

'I'm not that brave,' Jude said.

'Then borrow his courage. Have faith. We're now in a world beyond choice. We're in the place to which every choice has led since the devil corrupted Eve in the Garden of Eden. This is where every road ends. This is the point of everything. And this is the end of everything. This is the Plan.'

'So it can't make any difference what I do, can it?'

'It makes a difference to him. It matters more than I can say.'

A pause. A sigh. 'All right, then,' Jude said. 'So . . . what are we doing tomorrow?'

Shim laughed and wagged a finger. 'Nice try, but I'm afraid I don't quite trust you yet. I'll tell you this: we're having our feast a day early.'

'Tomorrow night? You'll never get a room.'

'Friends in high places.' A pause. 'Perhaps we should be getting back?'

'Give me a minute. I'll be in shortly. Feel a bit . . . you know.'

'Think over what I've said, yes? Good man.'

As Shim's footsteps *slap-slapped* their way back across the court, Flea sat very still, aware of the sound of his breathing.

Then Jude said, 'It's all right. You can come out now, Flea. And don't pretend you're not there. I can see your dirty little foot.'

# 20

Flea stood up shakily. His heart was thumping, but the edge of the fountain no longer moved and the flagstones stayed more or less level under his feet.

'So, what did you make of that?' Jude asked.

Flea swayed slightly.

'This isn't what I meant by keeping alert.' Jude sounded bleak, as if the night had drained the colour from his voice.

'Who caresh? Jus' wanna . . .'

Jude grabbed Flea by the shoulders, shook him, then shoved his head under the water.

Lifted him out and shoved him down again.

Lifted him up and dropped him on the flagstones.

Watched him splutter and said, 'Make sense of that?'

'What's the matter?' Flea spluttered, outraged. 'What have I done?'

'I wanted you to concentrate. I told you not to drink.'

'I can concentrate! And I'm only a little bit . . .'

Jude picked him up and held him at arm's length while Flea tried to kick any part he could reach. When he stopped thrashing, Jude said, 'Finished?'

Flea tried one last kick, thought about biting, thought better of it and nodded.

'What did you hear?'

'Nothing. Everything. Nothing made sense.'

'Tell me what you remember.'

'Something about the Garden of Eden and the end of everything.'

Jude sighed. 'Things are worse than my worst fears. If I'd known, I would never have involved you. I want you to get away from us as quickly as possible. I want you out of the City and far away.'

'Why? Where?'

'Because there's going to be trouble, big trouble, and anyone linked to us is up to their necks in it.'

'We're always in trouble,' protested Flea.

'Not like this. They're using you. The idiots! No wonder that smiling spy was after me. Tell you what, though, you horrible little infant: I'm grateful you found out about him. Thanks to you, I might just have time to salvage something out of this mess.'

'So it's all to do with the plan you were talking about?'

'The less you know the better. Go back inside, pretend everything's fine and tell Shim that you saw me stagger off to be sick somewhere. They won't be surprised about that. Then tomorrow, get everyone you know or care about away from the City. The riot in the Temple yesterday was nothing compared to what's coming. They're looking for trouble. That's the part of the plan. Now go. Go!'

'What are you going to do?'

'None of your business.'

'Whatever it is, why don't I do it? They suspect you.'

'Didn't you listen to a word I said?'

'You hired me for another day's work. I don't want you weaselling out of it.'

'After what I've just said, you're thinking about money?' Jude threw his hands into the air in frustration and howled silently at the night sky. Do you really think –?'

'Do I really think what?' Flea interrupted furiously. 'You tell me to listen, but you don't listen to me! Every day is dangerous for me. If I'm not being kicked around by Big and the rest of the gang, I'm being chased by muggers who'd slit my throat for a copper mite and no one would give a damn. Get it? Nothing you say frightens me because nothing that can happen because of you can be worse than what happens to me EVERY SINGLE DAY!'

A pause, and the moonlight got a bit brighter. Jude

looked at Flea levelly. 'Well, you got that off your chest all right. Are you sure you won't be too hung-over?'

'I'm fine. I'll be fine tomorrow.' Flea felt sullen and shaky. Jude's assault followed by his yelling had almost sobered him up.

'All right. I'll let you help on one condition: that you promise to get out tomorrow evening. There are powerful forces at work here. It must be Yusuf who's been arranging things inside the City for Yesh. A feast like this takes weeks to arrange . . .'

'Oh,' Flea said. 'The man carrying the pitcher of water from the bridge. I saw him hanging around in the kitchens.'

'Making sure everything was going to plan, for sure,' Jude said. 'So, as well as looking out for Romans and the Temple Police, we have to keep on the right side of one of the most powerful men in the City. Most likely he'll have someone keeping an eye on me, but you'll be able sneak around.'

'Thanks.'

Jude ignored the sarcasm. 'This supper Yesh has planned for tomorrow – I need to find out where it is. If I know Shim, he'll go there early to make sure everything's as it should be. So in the morning, when Yesh and the others come to pick you up, stick to Shim. If he leaves the group, follow him. Make a note of where he goes and then come back to me. Remember, all I need to know is where this meal is going to be. As soon as you know, find me. I'll be at your gang's shelter or nearby.'

'All right.'

'Now go back inside and act normally. And if anyone asks after me, tell them I've probably passed out.'

Flea made his way back into the hall. He didn't want to eat anything. He certainly didn't want to drink anything. He wanted things to be back the way they had been, but most of all he wanted to sleep.

In the hall, Shim was sitting with Yusuf up on the dais, talking earnestly. On the floor of the hall Yesh was walking between couches, talking to people, making them laugh, Tauma following.

*They all know what to do*, Flea thought. *This is what being an adult is all about. You plan. Things work. You move on.*

Slaves moved between the couches, pouring more wine and bringing wet towels for people to mop their faces. Food was still arriving, though no one was paying much attention to it. Flea had never seen so much food in his life. The glut and the waste made him feel sick.

He sat and he watched and he waited. All around him, adult faces grew redder and redder and voices grew louder and louder. A chant started in the back of the hall. 'Live forever, live forever, we'll live forever.'

People started banging tables, clapping hands,

stamping feet. 'Live forever. Live forever. Live forever.'

And in the middle of the room, Yesh; very much the centre of attention, but somehow very alone.

one day to go

# 21

Rats were everywhere – chattering under his feet, rushing through the houses on either side of the road, leaping across the alleyway over his head – stopping him reaching the little courtyard he knew was home.

And now they could talk and knew his name: *Flea*, they chattered and squeaked. *Fleafleafleafleaflea*.

His eyes were stuck shut. *Better in the dark*, they said. *Better, Fleafleafleaflea*.

The dark was the crack in the pavement and Flea could see down it. There was another alleyway underneath, and streets under the streets and houses under the houses: an entire underground city, a dark copy, peopled by rats: soldier rats, priest rats, beggar rats.

'Flea, Flea, Flea.'

*It's not them calling*, he thought, *it's someone real*. But when he managed to force his eyes open there was silence, except for a tired echo in his mind of someone calling him home.

He was outside the gang's shelter, wrapped in a cloth he'd nicked from Yusuf's house. The gang had been too drunk to get back here after they'd been invited to leave Yusuf's palace and had collapsed in the nearest alleyway. At dawn they'd woken and struggled back to the shelter and Flea had followed. He'd filled the water skin and sucked up to the others by offering drinks. If he was going to hang out with them again, he might as well try and get them to be civil.

One by one they crawled out of the shelter to sit in the alleyway, oblivious to the scandalised mutterings from their neighbour and her daughter. The worse for wear, they still managed to swap stories about the night before.

'Did you see me jump on the table?'

'And fall off!'

'And when you threw that beaker of wine over that man . . .'

'It was an accident.'

'Not what he thought.'

'But he thought it was funny in the end.'

'Do you think we'll go back?'

'I'm up for it.'

'I know,' Flea said, in an unnatural voice. 'Why don't we all . . .'

He stopped. Do what? What was it Jude had told him to do? Save the gang and follow Shim? He couldn't do both. Why couldn't Jude have been clearer?

Little Big noticed him. 'Oh look, it's the wimp.'

'Yeah, where were you just when things started getting really good?'

Flea thought quickly. 'Oh, I passed out. You know.'

'When?' Big asked.

'Don't know. Too pissed to remember. Hah.'

'Was that before or after you followed your boyfriend out of the hall?' Big sneered. '*Oh, Jude, Jude, where are you, Jude?*' His snigger was echoed around the gang.

'What do you mean?' Flea tried to sound outraged, but there was not enough force in his voice.

'*I don't like it here with all these big, rough men,*' Big whined. 'Listen, what are you even doing back here? We kicked you out of the gang, remember?'

'But Yesh . . . I just thought –'

'He just thought. Well, I *just thought* I might have to punish you. What did I say I'd do if you carried on hanging around?'

'I don't know.'

'I said I'd shove you down the rat hole!'

'You can't. You wouldn't . . .'

The twins grabbed Flea's arms and Little Big and Red each grabbed a leg and hung him over the rat hole at the end of the alleyway. They started chanting, 'Sacrifice the Flea! Sacrifice the Flea! Sacrifice the Flea!'

Flipped upside down, Flea was helpless. He closed his eyes, clamped his mouth tight shut and held his breath. This time, he wasn't going to scream.

'Come on, rats!' Big shouted. 'We've got breakfast for you!'

They bumped Flea up and down, jerking the breath from his lungs so he had to suck in the thick, musty, rat-stinking air. He could hear rustling, opened his eyes and thought he could see the dark writhing of bodies and the glimmer of little yellow teeth. Forgetting his promise not to scream, he had just begun to bellow when someone shouted, 'Put that child down!'

Flea turned his head and saw an upside down Yesh floating in the street outside the alleyway. Flea was dropped. Big started to stammer an explanation, but Yesh cut him short.

'If you charming little thugs want to make yourself useful, come with us now. If not, try and treat that poor creature how you'd like to be treated yourselves.'

Shocked, because they had never heard Yesh speak angrily before, the gang trailed out of the alleyway and joined the slow river of men, women and children jostling sluggishly as they tried to avoid makeshift stalls that blocked the street. Everyone seemed to be going in the direction of the Temple today, the last chance before the Feast for people to pay their taxes and make a sacrifice.

Jude dropped back until he fell into step beside Flea.

'Well?' he said. 'Are you all right?'

Flea shook his head.

'Look, I know –'

'No, you don't. You don't know anything. They're having a go at me for . . .'

'What?'

'You're always hanging around me and they're . . .

saying things,' Flea said. 'If you left me alone so I could just try and make things better . . .'

'Even though you're earning good money?'

'Shh! They'll nick it,' Flea whispered urgently.

'Nice friends.'

'You can talk,' Flea snapped back.

'I walked into that one,' Jude said. 'Here. I bought you some dried fruit. Should help keep you going. You've got a busy day today, remember?'

It came to Flea at last. 'I've got to stick to Shim and if he goes to a room, remember where it is and tell you.'

'Good. And as I thought, one of Yusuf's people is trailing us. Think you can slip away without him noticing?'

Flea glanced behind and saw the water carrier he'd seen at the bridge and again the kitchens.

'Easy,' he said. 'What are you going to do?' Suddenly Flea was nervous of going it alone, feeling the weight of responsibility.

'Judas!' Yesh's voice cut across the line of followers, sharp and commanding.

'Later,' Jude murmured. 'The boss is in a real mood this morning. Hung-over most likely, so keep your head down.' He called out, 'Master?'

'*Master. Master.* Yohan calls me Lord,' Yeshua barked back. 'Did you know that? Shim calls me Lord. Even Tauma calls me Lord. Only you call me Master. Any reason for that?'

Yesh stopped and beckoned Jude to join him. The followers parted to make two ranks that Jude had to walk between. Flea hurried to join him.

'You know me, Yesh,' Jude said quietly. He stood in front of Yesh, half a head taller, but looking meek. 'We go back a long way. I find it hard to change.'

'Yes. We noticed. But even if you have stayed the same, do you really think I have?'

Jude flushed. 'That's not for me to say, Master.'

They were standing in the middle of the road, forming a solid plug. Above them, washing hung on lines across the alley. People had put benches outside their houses so they could sit and catch the morning sun. Two small fig trees, neatly clipped, stood in pots on either side of a front door. Yesh pointed to one of them.

'So tell me, Judas: is a plant that doesn't grow any use to man or beast?'

'I don't know, Master.'

Two small red spots appeared on Yesh's cheeks. 'Let me tell you this, then. A follower who doesn't follow and a man who doesn't change are like a fig tree that doesn't grow.'

He grabbed one of the trees and lifted it, pot and all. Then he dropped it so the pot shattered and stamped on it until the trunk splintered. The followers huddled around to make a barrier between Yesh and the crowd. They looked wary.

'Do you understand now, Judas?' Yesh said. He was breathing heavily. 'You're about as much use to me as that tree, unless you change. You want to go back to the old days. We can't. As soon as I was chosen, that was it. I moved on. Everyone moved on. That's why we're called a *movement*. But you, Judas, my oldest friend and my first follower, refuse to budge. Can't you see how that might upset me? Can't you see how at this moment, the last thing I want to do is waste my time splitting hairs with you? Can't you? CAN'T YOU?'

Flea did not dare move, even though Jude was gripping his shoulder so hard it hurt. He watched the clench of Jude's jaw muscle and noticed a tick shiver the skin on his scarred cheek.

Jude took a breath and said, 'Yes, Master. I see.'

Yesh turned away. 'Mat, pay for that tree. The rest of you, pray for it.' A twisted smile. 'Now come on. There's still a lot to do.'

'Is that what you call keeping your head down?' Flea asked. 'It's just that . . .'

'Enough!' Jude snapped. 'Listen, there may be trouble at the Temple, and remember what Shim said last night? They'll be trying to use your gang as a sort of shield. It's one thing to chuck us out of Temple Square; it's quite another to hurt little children, especially if Yesh has the crowd on his side. Believe me, that's one thing he's good at.'

# 22

The wide steps that led up to the Temple's southern doors were normally crowded. Today they were empty, the crowd kept back by a cordon of Roman soldiers, watched by a couple of Temple guards. But the crush of people made room for Yesh as he led his followers and the Temple Boys towards it.

'Lord, they're obviously expecting us,' Mat said. 'We won't be able to get into the Temple today. Should we discuss what to do next?'

Yesh did not pause. 'Should the crowd see us run away at the first sign of trouble? I think we can do better than that.' He put his head down and walked through the crush, curious faces all around. The unspoken question hung in the air: *what's he going to do now?*

Then, as they approached the cordon guarding the steps, something unexpected happened. The Imps moved back to let them through. Nodding thanks to the left and right, as if it were the most natural thing in the world, Yeshua began to lead them up.

'Lord,' Mat said, 'they're not letting anyone in after us. I told you –'

'Have faith, brother,' Yesh said. He climbed very slowly up the steps. Flea turned so his back was to the Temple gates. Below him, behind the cordon of soldiers, upturned faces and hope rising like a vapour.

'Lord, the people – *your* people – want to hear you speak,' Mat said. 'You can't be seen to enter the Temple while they've been shut out.'

Yesh stopped mid step, turned and looked down. His face was like a stone in a stream, all smooth ridges and dips. The murmur from the crowd dropped, rose, then dropped again. Tension grew in the silence like water swelling a skin.

With the Temple walls rearing up behind and the great expanse of marble steps so bare, Flea felt trapped and exposed. He found himself counting and wishing. *One, two, three . . . He's got to say something. Four, five, six . . . Please say something. Seven, eight, nine . . . Don't do anything stupid. Ten, eleven, twelve . . . The Imps will do something . . . Thirteen, fourteen, fifteen . . .* The Imps were turning now. *Nineteen, twen–*

'How wonderful to see you all! Thank you so much! I never expected a crowd like this!'

Yesh's words were a lovely surprise, like a splash of warm water when you were braced for cold.

'And thank you to the soldiers for doing such a splendid job today. I want you all to thank them too!'

Like a magician, he raised his arms and turned to the left and to the right. A huge roar. Everyone liked to laugh at the Romans, but you never got the chance. And here was Yesh actually thanking them . . .

'And a hand for the Temple,' Yesh continued. 'I've

said harsh things about it in the past: it was too big, too expensive, too just about everything. I've said that if I had my way, I'd pull it down brick by brick and not leave a single stone standing, but do you know, I think I've changed my mind. If it wasn't for these fine, impressive steps, how could I see you all? And how could you all see a short-arse like me?'

More laughter and a smatter of applause. *He's got the crowd now*, Flea thought, and when someone called out, 'Give us some magic, mate!' and Yesh called back, 'Sorry, I'm into talking today,' there was a murmur, but it wasn't an angry noise. People were curious. People wanted to know what was going to happen next.

'But thank you for raising the subject, friend, because that's partly what I wanted to say. The time for tricks is over. The time for magic is over. Some of you have said I perform miracles and I'm afraid the time for that is over too. Well, maybe there's time for one more . . . we'll have to see. The thing is, I've got so much to say and I think time may be running out so I'm going to talk and if you stay, my friends, I'll take it as a sign that you want to hear more.'

And then Yesh was off. The followers and the Temple Boys began to sit down around him. Yohan, the youngest member of the movement sat on one side of him and Yak, Yesh's brother, on the other. Flea leant back, his elbow on the step behind, and let the words wash over him.

'You don't have to put up with the way things are. No one should and no one *needs* to. There's a better way – my way – and if you only give me a tiny bit of faith, a scrap of belief, I can change you so that *you* can change anything you want. Want to move a mountain . . .?'

'All right then,' a voice called out. 'How do we do that?'

'Well, maybe not a real mountain – but last night, this gang of young tearaways were the guests of the richest man in the City. If that's possible, anything is!'

The same heckler: 'Can you get me an invitation?'

'Don't push your luck, friend.' Yesh smiled, then his voice changed. 'It would be fantastic if we could just hold this idea in our heads forever and hope it came about. It would be wonderful, but it would be a dream. Time is made of moments and some moments are special. A special moment can move past you like a leaf in the wind and, if you don't grasp it, it's gone forever and the opportunity's lost. And a moment like this is coming, my friends. I know it and feel it. You know it and feel it. And if you want this to happen, if you want better times, if you want change, you have to be prepared. This is all I ask of you. Let me grasp the moment, let me take the hour, but you must be prepared. You know the prophecies. You know the stories. You know the signs!'

The crowd was restless now, pressing up against the guards, and as they shuffled backwards Flea noticed Shim

119

slipping away to one side. Jude had moved down to try and calm people and reason with them because the Imps were scared now and had drawn their weapons. He'd be too busy to talk. Flea knew he had to act and so, making himself small, he set off after Shim.

# 23

Shim walked quickly without looking back and so was easy to follow.

The streets grew less crowded, as if everyone had drained into the lower City. In a broad street that ran straight as an arrow to the City walls, Flea watched as Shim stopped at a simple, square building next to an inn. He climbed up rickety stairs to the upper storey and went in through a wooden door covered in flaking blue paint.

Flea ran to the building and hid under the wooden steps. The door was open a crack. He could hear voices.

'So that's fixed now?' Shim sounded tense and businesslike.

The voice that answered was wheedling but sharp. 'Oh yes, sir. A meal for thirteen, meat to be provided, this evening. Could the master tell me why he is arranging his holy feast a day early?'

'You can mind your own business,' Shim snapped. 'You're being paid, aren't you?'

'Handsomely, yes, by the agent of Yusuf of Ramathain. You are fortunate indeed to have such powerful friends. Of course I had to charge for the whole week because –'

'That's enough from you,' Shim snapped. 'Do you really think I care about your squalid little schemes? The lamb will be delivered from the sheep market later. For that money you can be here to receive it. Is that clear?'

The door was pulled open and there were heavy creaks on the stairs. Flea watched through the open treads of the staircase as Shim's bare, cracked heels descended, then the landlord's. He waited. Shim was walking off towards the City walls, the landlord was disappearing into the inn. Flea thought for a second. Jude had told him to report back when he found out where Shim was going, but suppose he was on his way somewhere else? Surely he should find out where. Surely Jude would want to know that.

Shim was walking with even greater purpose now, so Flea scurried behind as fast as he could. The man was heading for the western gates closest to the Skull, a bare hillock of a stone scoured and hollowed by quarrying, and now used by the Romans for public executions.

Flea had never left the City in this direction. He'd gone scavenging in the Pleasure Gardens on the slopes of Olive Tree Hill – people always left bits of their picnics behind – but that was about it.

Here the landscape was bare and dusty. The road to the Skull was empty and Flea had to keep his distance. The path climbed. There were no crosses on it today – the Romans tried to avoid executions in the run-up to the Feast – and the mid-morning air was clear. In the distance, a pale road snaked between rocky hills. A line of camels showed up on it like carved toys, the red threads of their decorated halters bright as spring flowers.

The sight of them brought Flea up short.

There was a world outside the walls where life still carried on, utterly separate from the struggle on the City streets. It had never struck him before, but now he thought: if the camels were coming from somewhere, then somewhere was different from here. Like a fresh, sharp taste he had never had before, or a dreamy scent carried on a warm breeze, a sense of freedom suddenly gripped him. He didn't have to live his life scurrying through these streets like a rat through a tunnel. He could set out on that road, he could pass the camels heading for the City and nod to the camel driver and in front of him would be . . . would be . . . what?

He shook his head. He couldn't waste time thinking about things like that. He had a job to do. He had the chance of earning money two days in a row. You didn't turn down opportunities like that. Even so, he kept half an eye on the camels as he followed Shim, as if by watching them, part of him could stay with them and be carried far, far away.

Shim followed the road around the Skull. It narrowed to a dusty path then burrowed straight into the lower quarry, whose pitted walls had been dug out for tombs.

Flea slowed. If he followed Shim in there he would be walking into a dead end and he had no desire to confront Shim face to face. Shim might even suspect that he was doing it for Jude. Flea looked around and spotted a path that would take him to the top of the cliff so he could look down.

By the time Flea had reached the top and crawled to the edge, Shim was talking to the tombs' watchman, who was pointing up to the opposite side of the quarry. The tombs were roughly aligned in two levels on the wall, and as Flea watched, Shim started to climb the rough scaffolding to the upper layer.

'I tried to warn him, but he went ahead and bought it anyway. He's been well and truly stitched up.' The watchman had cupped his hands to his mouth to call up and his words bounced back off the quarry walls to Flea. 'More money than sense, that one. Bought the whole row. Useless. Waste of money. Cracks in the ceiling. Cracks in the floor. Whole place has been over-quarried. Look, I'm just the watchman. I keep the grave robbers away. I'm not meant to do quality control, but complaints always seem come back to me.'

Shim called down from the upper level of the scaffolding, 'And the rock that goes across the entrance. How does that work?'

'You just roll it across, but like I said –'

'Can one man do it?'

'Big guy could. Don't see why not.'

*Why is he looking at a tomb?* Flea wondered. *What's this got to do with –?*

But he never finished the thought. He heard the crunch of feet on gravel, smelled old smoke and in the same instant was buried in the heavy folds of a large net.

# 24

'What have we here?'

Flea tried to kick out, but the net held him. The more he struggled, the worse the tangle of arms and legs and knotted rope.

He craned his head round and saw a Roman soldier, who stilled him by placing a hobnailed sandal on his back.

'You see, this is why it's so important to get out and see things for oneself. Such interesting things happen,' a voice said. Flea turned his head the other way and saw the tall, smiling man who had tailed Jude into the covered market. His ankles were on a level with Flea's nose. They were veiny and his shins were dusty. He spoke Flea's language with only a hint of an accent.

Then he gave an order in Latin. The soldier untangled Flea from the net, grasped Flea's waist with two enormous hands covered in short blond hairs and lifted him up. When Flea wriggled the soldier squeezed so hard Flea thought he might break in half.

'What's going on?' Flea managed to get enough breath to say. 'Aren't I allowed to have a lie-down?'

Eyebrows arching comically above his thin, tortoise smile, the man backhanded him across the face. Flea felt the crunch of gristle and a sudden warm trickle of blood.

'Stupid question,' hissed the man. 'Of course you're allowed to rest, and you're allowed to spy, and I am allowed to hit you. At least, I can't see anyone stopping me. Let's carry you down and see what our friend Shimon has to say.'

He rolled the name around his mouth a couple of times as if to get the taste of it, then spat. In spite of the pain and the shock, it struck Flea as odd that he knew who Shim was.

They caught up with Shim as he was leaving the tombs. He looked shattered, Flea thought, as if the skin on his face had loosened and slipped from the bones. When he saw Flea, still held prisoner by the soldier, he gave a cry.

'What?' the thin man asked. 'Does that feeble bleat mean you know this thing?'

'I didn't mean . . . I mean, I was surprised . . . I . . . He's bleeding,' Shim protested.

'Isn't he just? Now, I repeat. Do you know this thing?'

'Yes.' Shim would not meet Flea's eye.

'Any idea why *it* might be following you?'

Flea tried to look innocent, but his face felt as if it had been knocked lopsided by the blow and all he could manage was a sort of leer. His nose was beginning to ache.

'It, I mean, *he's* a charity case,' Shim said. 'Part of a street gang. We fed him and the rest of them last night. Perhaps he thought he could touch me for some money.'

'Ah yes, the meal at the house of Yusuf of Ramathain, if my intelligence is right. Your leader's uncle, I believe?' The man went still, as if a thought had struck him. 'Oddly enough, this horrid little thing looks familiar to me.'

He gave an order in Latin. The soldier held Flea out at arm's length while the thin man frisked him expertly and roughly. His hand pounced on the little ivory-handled spike hidden inside Flea's tunic. His fingers worked it open.

'Ahh.'

It was a sigh of pleasure. The man held it like a precious object, spike pointing at the sky. Flea stopped struggling, wishing heartily that he'd thrown the thing away as Jude had ordered.

'Turn it upside down.'

Blood from Flea's nose threatened to run into his eyes.

'Please, master . . .' Flea wheedled, then started coughing as blood flowed into his throat.

'Shh.' The man turned to Shim. *'The Lord will abhor the bloody and deceitful man*. I'm quoting from your fifth Psalm, I think, and I feel sure – yes, I feel it in my waters – that he abhors bloody and deceitful children too. Like this one. However, as we know, all the gods help those that help themselves and I like to think of myself as a results man. This, by the way, is my little helper.' The thin man waved the spike in general direction of Flea's face. 'I lost it yesterday. I wonder, is it too much of a coincidence that this thing somehow has it?'

Flea opened his mouth and started coughing again. He could not quite untangle what the man was saying, but it did not sound good. The spike was of real concern.

The soldier turned Flea upright and squeezed him till his ribs crackled. Blackness rose in front of his eyes as if he were sinking in dirty water. He felt his spine crack, then kink.

'Don't kill him! I mean . . . I feel responsible.' Shim sounded panicked.

The grip loosened. Air rushed into Flea's lungs with a *whoop*.

'You feel responsible? That's because you are. It was following you and you didn't have the wit to notice. As for me, the fact that it had my little helper suggests I've seen it before, but I'm not sure where. It's just that I'm hearing a very special kind of music.'

'Music?' Shim looked around dimly.

'When I'm on to something I hear distant music. As I get nearer to the truth the music becomes louder and sweeter. Creature, how did my little helper come to be in your possession?'

The soldier gave Flea an encouraging squeeze.

'I found it,' Flea gasped.

'Where?'

'In the street. I don't remember where. I was . . .' Flea fell silent as the Results Man tested the spike's tip against his finger, then put it in Flea's ear. The metal felt cold, oddly wet, sharp and huge.

'A boy gave it to me! He was . . .' Flea screamed as a jag of cold pain lanced through him.

'Beautiful, but not quite there yet,' the man smiled. 'You see, yesterday I was following one of Shim's comrades – that horse-faced old bone-bag who's taken a spear through the side of his face. So, I was following him, lost my helper in the covered market and now this horrid little scrap has been following Shim with my little helper. Coincidence? I don't think so. I think he was following Horse-Face and now he's following Prat-Face, sorry, *Shimon*. While he was following Horse-Face, the man I believe is known as Judas the Ginge, he picked my pocket.'

'I can think of any number of other reasons . . .' Shim began.

'It's true,' Flea gabbled. 'I was with Jude yesterday and he gave me a couple of mites. When I saw Shim go off this morning and I thought maybe I could touch him for a coin or two. Why not? All his lot are idiot do-gooders. They love beggars. I –'

'Shut up,' the Results Man narrowed his eyes. 'You said you were with Judas. That must be a lie because *if* you were *with* Judas, I would have seen you.'

'I was following him, in secret. Like a game.'

'So was I. No, I think you were watching Judas's back, and that makes me worried. You followed me, then picked my pocket in order to do . . . what? Time for more help. Other ear this time, I think.'

'Jude told me to! He thought he might be being followed!' Flea knew he could not stand the pain again.

'Trumpets! Cymbals! Harps! Marvellous!' the Results Man said. 'Did you hear that, soldier? Did you hear that, Shimon? The music of truth! Now, what shall I do with this thing? Deafen it? Blind it?'

'No, no, NO!' Shim said. 'I must protest. I . . . whatever else, we are here to cure, not harm. I cannot allow it. I . . .'

Something dark flashed behind the Results Man's eyes. 'Idea! Might I suggest that I punish it, then you take it away and cure it? Yeshua the Healer is good at that, I hear. My little helper knows a place that will stop it walking forever, but your master could fix that in an instant, couldn't he? But I think there is still more to come.' He narrowed his eyes. 'If this thing was watching Jude's back, the question must be *why*? Why was his back so special it needed watching? Purely technically, I quite admire its skill. So, it's with Jude but not with Jude. Any chance, Shim, that Jude is with your movement but not quite with your movement? Any chance that yesterday he was perhaps not acting in your best interests?'

'Jude might not be quite as . . . committed as the rest of us, but he would never betray us.'

The Results Man snapped his fingers. 'I know. Let's ask our new friend. Shimon – you ask the questions and I'll judge the quality of its answers.'

Shim cleared his throat, faced up to Flea and tried to look imposing. 'Well? Is this how a beggar boy repays kindness? What were you doing? Is Jude trying to go behind our backs?'

Flea tried to swing a foot in his direction. 'It's not Jude who's the traitor! It's you! You're talking to Roman scum! Jude's only trying to find out –'

The words turned to chalk in Flea's mouth. His spit dried out. He tried to swallow.

'Well, Shim! Completely accidentally you seem to have bumbled on to a lead of some sort,' the Results Man said. 'What is Jude trying to find out, pray?'

Flea found his voice. 'Nothing.'

'I would remind you,' the Results Man said, 'that we are surrounded by tombs. One more body here or there won't make much difference, especially one as insignificant as yours.' A scratch of his stubbly chin.

'You wouldn't,' Shim said.

'To get the truth out of him, I would.' The Results Man held Flea's right eyelid up with his thumb. 'You know how much it hurts to get grit in your eye . . .'

Flea felt the spike stroke his cheek, then stop in the dip where his eye socket met his nose.

'I might jab it in and scoop out your eye like an oyster. Do you know what oysters are? They're flesh in a shell and Romans like to eat them raw.' He made a slurping sound.

A tear slid down Flea's cheek.

'So, unspeakable agony followed by blindness followed by more agony followed by death and then nothing. No one will even wonder what happened to you. You don't want to die, do you? Beggars have such developed survival instincts and you've done so well so far. What a shame to throw it all away on, what? Misplaced loyalty to this Judas.'

The tip of the spike ached like ice.

'I'll talk,' Flea said.

'Everything,' The Results Man smiled dreamily.

'Jude knows there's a plan.'

'Yes.'

'He found out that the camel and the donkey on the bridge were rigged for Yeshua,' Flea said.

'The music has started again and it's good. I almost feel like dancing.'

'Then he told me to follow Shim. I found out that Yeshua is planning a feast for tonight – a day early.'

'I'm losing that melody.'

'Jude told me to report back to him, but I didn't. I got caught instead.' Flea had to fight to hold back the tears.

The Results Man started to hum and beat time in the air. 'Carry on.'

'That's all I know. Everything. You have to believe me.'

'And I do!' The Results Man slammed imaginary cymbals together.

Shim's jaw dropped. 'Jude would do that? Jude would spy on us?'

'You're betraying him to the Imps!' Flea shouted. 'You're the traitor. You're a dog. You're a worm. You're the worm in a dog's –'

The Results Man clamped his hand across Flea's mouth. 'You could talk for the Imperium, you could. Shim's not a worm. He's just a man. A man with a plan. But what to do with you? You're close to Jude, aren't you? From now on, you're working for me and you tell me everything he's planning. Do you understand? By the way, where's the rest of your gang?'

The switch in questioning put Flea off balance and he staggered into the trap.

'With his lot, I suppose.' He nodded at Shim with as much contempt as he could express.

'Not any longer,' Shim said. 'We'll be preparing for

our . . . for our meal tonight and they're not invited.'

Flea shrugged. 'Then at the shelter.'

'You don't have a shelter.' The Results Man sounded disbelieving

'Yes we do,' Flea protested. 'Behind the bakery close to the water fountain halfway down the Temple's west wall.' As soon as he had said the words he wished he hadn't, but then again, the spike still ached in his eye.

'Thank you. Shim, you scuttle off. You, helpful thing . . . creature . . . child . . . come with me.'

The soldier dropped Flea on to the ground. Not understanding, but with a sinking heart, Flea picked himself up and followed the Results Man.

# 25

The Results Man walked with long strides and a dipping, questing head, like a heron. Flea had to hurry to keep up. Every few strides the man shot him an unexpected question. How did he join the gang? How did they survive? Who were their rivals? Did he prefer languid summer days or bracing winter weather? Where did they sleep? Had he ever eaten pork? Camel? Would he eat a baby if he was starving? Did he play hide and seek? How far would he go to cling on to his miserable life? This far? That far? *All the way?* Not that far, surely. Just this far. Interesting. In a way.

Flea answered absent-mindedly, trying to work out how he could get away – or at least get a message to Jude. It would no longer be enough to tell him where the feast tonight was taking place; he had to warn him that he'd been found out. Perhaps Jude would be at the shelter when they got there. Perhaps it was a blessing in disguise that he had blabbed its location to the Results Man.

Once they were in the City, Flea said, 'Er, where are we going? The gang's shelter's over in that direction.'

'All in good time. You've been kind enough to tell me where you live. Allow me to introduce you to *my* home.'

'Your home? You mean the Fortress?' He could not keep the quaver out of his voice.

'Come, come. It's not that bad.'

But it was.

The Fortress was the main Roman garrison in the City. All around it, heavy, greasy altar smoke hung in the air to remind you that it backed on to the Temple. Its huge wooden gate was flanked by two towers, with mean windows slashed into the rough grey stone. Behind the gate was a courtyard with a whipping post: stark, stained and plain.

In front of the gate was a square. Even today, with the City as full as it ever could get, the square was deserted. No one liked to get close to the Fortress and the few people who could not avoid it scurried across the cobblestones, heads down. Only a handful of petitioners stood by the gate, begging the guards to find out if a relative had been arrested and taken in for questioning. Sometimes it worked, sometimes it didn't. Sometimes people just disappeared. Sometimes they reappeared outside the gates – dazed, broken, discarded – and all but their mothers thought it might have been better if they had stayed disappeared.

'Now, where can it wait so it won't get into trouble?' the Results Man tapped his teeth. 'Oh, I know.'

They passed through the gate. Flea tried not to look at the whipping post and the bloodstains on the flagstones around it. They entered the main body of the Fortress – a hall with lots of rooms leading off it – and continued down a curving flight of stone steps.

They entered a low underground chamber. In the middle of the floor stood a brazier, its bitter fumes roughening the air. Flea recognised the smell from the Results Man's clothing. The only light came from small windows, set high in walls that were hung with chains and a variety of tools.

'What do you think of my musical instruments?' the Results Man said. 'They make such wonderful sounds.'

Flea's first impression was that he was in the garrison smithy, but then he looked again at the tools on the walls. Knives, pincers, spikes, manacles, whips.

Anything that could hurt.

Flea made a dart for the door, but his way was blocked

by the same soldier who had caught him at the tombs. In this low, dark room he was a dreadful pink giant, expanded by a blanket of flesh that rolled out from under the hard leather of his breastplate. His red face was peeling, but there had been no sun. His eyes were the colour of earth.

'Interested in him, are you?' The Results Man nodded at the soldier. 'He's from a long way away. Germania. All forests and rain and bogs that swallow horses. We had our differences – they killed three whole legions not so long ago – but they let us conquer them in the end. And accepted our gods. Why can't you people? Oh well, never mind. You've seen my instruments. You understand how I can make the truth sing. Remember: *The man that walketh in a perfect way shall serve me; he that worketh deceit shall not dwell in my house*. That's another pithy little saying from your holy book.'

'Are you going to . . . use them on me?'

'What? No. Never. You work for me now, understand? This is part of your . . . education. Now, come with me. Don't dawdle. I've got to get a squad together and there's so much to do and so little time.'

He left with a skip and Flea followed, his heart a dead weight in his chest.

# 26

Flea didn't have to lead the Results Man to the shelter because he had already told him where it was.

There was nowhere for the gang to run. The squad of Imps blocked off the end of the alleyway and moved in. Big tried to fight and was knocked down with a club, but the others were too shocked to resist. The whole time, the Results Man had one hand on Flea's shoulder and the other digging the little spike into his back. Flea could not move and it looked for all the world as if he was just standing there while the others were bullied to their feet and made to stand facing the wall.

Big tried to spit at Flea over his shoulder. 'You sold us out, you bastard!'

Flea was about to protest when he felt the spike's cold pressure increase. He closed his eyes and tried to shut everything out, especially when the Results Man started to speak.

'Boy, boys,' he said. 'I want you to concentrate. I'm arresting you and holding the one you call Flea hostage. Or is it the other way round? It doesn't matter. If Flea behaves, you go free. If he doesn't, none of you will ever see the light of day again. Do you understand? So, if I were you, I'd be nice to him. As you walk past on your way to prison, I want you all to stop in front of him, bow and say, "Please look after us, Flea." All right?'

One by one the Temple Boys passed by Flea, and one by one they looked at him with hatred and said, 'Please look after us.'

Flea shook his head hopelessly. For once he was lost for words. In the end, just he and the Results Man were left alone in the alleyway.

'It's all yours now,' the Results Man said. 'This lovely home . . .' His voice trailed away as he looked at the shelter. 'What are you going to do with it?'

'What am I going to do? What are you talking about? I've got to do what you say,' Flea said.

'Oh no, no, no. You don't understand. We're beyond all that, Flea. Orders, salutes . . . I'm not a soldier, Flea. I'm the Results Man, and if you're going to work for me, you have to start by thinking a bit. Using your loaf. You do have a brain?' He spun Flea round and looked at him. 'I'm letting you go now, and for the rest of the day your job is to work out ways of pleasing me – and what will happen to your friends if you fail. It may be a tiny thing you do to upset me that only takes up the tiniest slice of time, but it will mean that your friends hurt for the rest of their lives. On the other hand, I would not want you to despair. This could be the making of you. You have led a life without purpose, a life without results, and now I have given you both. If you are clever, you will learn from me.'

'But *how* am I meant to please you?' Flea asked.

'I told you: by making sure that I know what Jude is

doing. and anything else you can think of, of course.' The Results Man smiled encouragingly.

'So, by betraying him, I'll make you happy.'

'Of course!'

'And the gang?'

'Their fate is in your hands.' The Results Man's eyebrows shot up into a comical double arc and he pursed his lips. 'There, another thing I've given you. A sense of responsibility. Try and grow into your new role.'


# 27

Flea took refuge on a rooftop a few streets away.

His ribs ached from the squeezing, his ear ached from its spiking and his back felt fragile. He picked black flakes of dried blood from his nose and tried to blame everyone else for his situation.

He failed.

If he hadn't followed Shim to the tombs, if he'd headed straight back to Jude, none of this would have happened. If he hadn't got mixed up with Jude in the first place, none of this would have happened. If he'd been a different sort of person, none of this would have happened.

He thought of the skinny girl and her warning. Remorse tasted foul and bitter, like a rotten nut.

Then he dredged up some reasons to feel less bad. He thought about how the gang had treated him. He thought about how Big had held him upside down over the rat hole and how all the others had jeered and clapped their hands and stamped their feet. Very deliberately he thought about each of their faces as the Imps took them away. Big had cried like a baby. Little Big had grovelled. The twins had tried to run, but been caught. Clump and Gaga had looked betrayed, but what right had they? They were toads like the rest of them and never once tried to stop the bullying.

Bullying? Torture, more like.

They had tortured him and now they were getting a taste of their own medicine. Maybe the Results Man was right. Maybe this was his opportunity. Maybe the Results Man had seen Flea the Magnificent, Flea the Terrible, Flea the Conqueror of All Things. He had given Flea his chance, and when Flea came to him in the Fortress with information about Jude, he would smile and say, 'You have passed the first test, Flea. Now we will begin.'

He would take Flea up to the highest tower of the Fortress. Below, the priests in the Temple would look like ants going about their business and the streets of the City would look like the tracks and tunnels of their broken nest, but all the lands beyond would be ripe with promise: honey-coloured rocks, tawny desert, green fields. The Results Man would say, 'I will show you real power. Join us, join the Imperium, and we will take on the whole world.' And when he was emperor, Flea would bring the Temple Boys before him and make them grovel one by one. Big, Little Big, Clump, Snot, Hole in the Head, the Twins, Halo, Crouch . . .

*Crouch.* Why had his mind snagged on Crouch?

Flea thought back to the arrest. Halo had curled up, Clump had tried to climb the wall, Big had thrown a punch and fallen over . . . Crouch wasn't there. He was sure of it. And yet the Results Man had counted them, one, two, three . . . all the way up to twelve. *Of course!* When Flea had told the Results Man how many Temple Boys there were, he hadn't included himself, so that meant Crouch's absence was not noticed.

He stood up, suddenly excited, and all dark thoughts of betrayal were blasted away by hope. Maybe Crouch would help him by taking a message to Jude and telling him about the Results Man.

Flea jumped as a trapdoor from the roof next to his was flung open and a man climbed out. He headed for a small rooftop shack and carefully opened its door. The explosion of white doves made Flea cower. They clung to the man's hair, clothes and outstretched arms, and when he lifted his hands they flew off with a clapping of wings and circled, bright white against boiling black clouds, then dropped back to their owner. The man plucked them off him one by one and put them in wicker cages.

Sacrifices for the Temple. Everything good ended up there, somehow. A thin, icy rain began to fall and Flea set off for the shelter.

# 28

When Flea got back to the alley, everything had changed.

A family of out-of-towners – parents, three boys and two girls, all dressed in bright holiday clothes – had pitched their tent there and were cooking their evening meal over a fire made from the shelter's struts and supports. A young man, sprouting his first growth of beard, picked up a stone and shouted at Flea, 'Get lost! Beggar! Scum!' A younger boy, about Flea's age, stared at him dumbly.

'This is my home!' Flea yelled back.

'Not any more, loser!'

'I've been here years.'

'Going to cry like the other one?' The stone spat grit off the wall next to Flea, narrowly missing his eye.

'Which other one?'

'That bent-over-double kid. Too old to be sobbing like a baby.'

*Crouch*, Flea thought. 'Which way did he go?'

'Who cares? That way!' He pointed up the hill, but as Flea set off he called, 'No, that way, sucker.' And he pointed in the opposite direction.

Flea felt his hope dashed and stood still, not quite sure what to do next. The young man and his family turned their backs, all apart from the boy of Flea's age. He continued to stare at Flea blankly, then, keeping his hand across his chest so no one could see, he extended his finger downhill.

Flea nodded and left.

He found Crouch huddled against a wall, his hand stuck out for passing trade. As a begging technique it was as effective as sticking your hand into a river and hoping to catch a fish. As soon as he saw Flea he stood and hobbled off.

'Don't hurt me,' he said as Flea caught up with him. 'Don't kill me. Don't arrest me. I'm sorry! I never did anything wrong.'

'What are you on about?'

'They sent me out to get water and when I came back the woman opposite said you'd turned up with a full platoon of Imps and ordered them to kill us all.'

'No, it wasn't like that! She's lying! There wasn't anything I could do. They would have . . . he showed me their torture chambers. He had a spike and stuck it in my eye. He said he was going to hurt me really badly. He took the gang to blackmail me, to keep me quiet.'

'You keep in saying *he*. Who is he?'

'He's like an agent. A fixer. He knows everything.'

Crouch blinked. 'And why is he blackmailing you?'

'He wants to use me, and I know something. Shim's betrayed them all to the Romans,' Flea said.

'Shim? But he's one of Yesh's most trusted followers.'

'That's what I've got to tell Jude so he can tell Yesh and the others. He doesn't know. But I can't tell him – I can't do anything – or else the Romans kill the gang. That's the deal.'

Crouch digested the news, his thin, lined face very still. Then he said, 'Do you really care? We weren't very nice to you.'

'Whatever you did to me, it's not as bad as what the Romans might do to them.'

'That's really . . . that's good of you. If it makes a difference, ever since you were kicked out they've been picking on me. It wasn't personal.'

Flea didn't know if that made a difference or not. And he suspected it wasn't goodness that made him want to save the gang from torture so much as a desire to save *himself* from nightmares.

'I know,' Crouch said. 'Suppose *I* warn Jude about Shim? Then they can't blame it on you.'

'They'll all be at their feast and the room's on the other side of the City. Do you think you can make it?'

'I can try. I should try. I want to.'

Flea's heart gave a little kick. 'Are you sure?'

'To make up for what we did to you. And look.' Crouch opened his hand to show four coins. 'I got lucky. This'll buy us something to eat.'

# 29

At a narrow crossroads they ordered two skewers of meat wrapped in bread. The vendor had greasy grey hair and wore a thick, fat-stained apron. His boy, grey-faced, hollow-eyed and not much bigger than one of his master's legs, was squatting by the wall, staring into space.

'Fan,' the vendor ordered. The boy got up and began to fan the flames with an old palm frond. It took Flea back to the morning the magician rode into the City and how the crowd had thrown palm fronds under the donkey's hooves.

'Need more fuel,' the vendor said. 'Stay there.'

He walked off, and Flea and Crouch stretched their hands over the spitting brazier.

Flea nodded at the vendor's boy, who was staring at them. He had a thin face led by a narrow, prominent jaw.

'You're Flea, aren't you?' he said.

'Might be.'

'I remember you from the Temple steps last autumn. I was there before I got this job.'

'This is a job?'

'It's work and it's food. You used to be with the Temple Boys?'

Flea heard the *used to be* and exchanged a look with Crouch. 'What do you know?'

'There's a mob out looking for you. Some people say it's the Cutters.'

'Cutters? *Cutters?* I thought they were finished.'

A wave of dull sickness swamped Flea. The Cutters were fanatics who murdered anyone they thought was collaborating with the Romans. They did it in public and melted away into the crowds, protected by fear. If anyone pointed out the knifeman to the authorities, they'd be the next to die.

'They say you sold your gang out to the Imps.'

'It's not true!'

'I don't care if it is. Me, I'm here because of Cutters so I hate them. My dad was a leather worker and they killed him because a rival claimed he was mending sandals for the Romans. Stole all his business. Nothing my mother could do to stop them. She died a year later.'

'I'm really sorry,' Flea said. 'But how did you hear about me?'

'People gather round the fire and talk. No one notices me, but I listen. Heard about you about an hour ago. They want to make an example of you tomorrow, when the City's fullest. Another thing: they said the Cutters' leader, Abbas Barabbas, is going to be released. That's why they're getting bolder.'

'Why would the Romans do that? Barabbas is their enemy.'

'Who knows why the Romans do anything? All I know

is what I heard. Something big's going to happen – an uprising. Are you trying to stop it?'

The street seemed to tilt. Flea felt Crouch support him with a steadying hand.

'I'm not trying to do anything,' he stammered. 'I don't know about an uprising. I don't know anything.'

The boy folded soft flat, bread around the skewer and wiped the meat into it. 'If that's what the Cutters think, they'll open you up without asking questions.'

A gust of wind seemed to carry the sound of roaring upon it. It grew and faded, grew again and faded. Four alleyways fed into the crossroads where they were standing. Each one now looked bleak and menacing. Those shuttered windows were surely hiding watchers. Those shadowed doorways could be seething with Cutters.

'What's that noise?' Flea asked.

The street vendor's boy tilted his head to listen. 'Could be the mob. Could be my master spotted you and ran off to tell them.'

'WHAT? Why didn't you say that before? Crouch, we've got to go!'

'Wait!' the boy said urgently. 'Please. You'll be all right for a while. They were heading off to the Lower City and my master will have taken ages to catch up with them. I heard . . . The other thing I heard was that you'd been hanging out with the Chosen One.' For the blink of an eye hope flared his face, lit by the brazier's glow.

'Yes, but . . .'

'What's he like? He must be wonderful.'

'He's just like . . . He's a man. He's . . . I don't know.'

'And the Change? When's that going to happen?'

'I don't know about an uprising and I don't know about a change!'

'You spend too much time stuck up by the Temple. Down here in the slums there are stories. Any day now the fountains will be running with wine and there'll be food for everyone, all the time.' The vendor's boy was really warming to his theme now. 'The Chosen One's fed a whole crowd from scraps. Food just kept on coming and coming and coming and no one was told to stop eating. He's cured cripples, cured leprosy. All you have to do is listen to him talk. I could do that. I could listen to a man talk if he fed me. It'd be better than being beaten all the time. If you have anything to do with him, tell him most of the people are behind him, but he's got to act quick.'

Flea glanced at Crouch, hoping he'd put the boy right. But Crouch's eyes were shining and his face was bright.

'Yes,' Crouch said. 'That's what Yesh said on the steps of the Temple. He said we had to catch the moment for the Change to happen. I know it can happen. Flea, we must do what we can!'

'CUTTERS WANT TO KILL ME!' Flea shouted. 'A MOB IS ON ITS WAY. I DON'T CARE ABOUT

YOUR CHANGE AND I DON'T CARE ABOUT YOUR MOMENT! I JUST WANT TO GET AWAY!'

Was it his imagination or was the awful din getting closer? And wasn't that the flare of torches glowing against the wall?

The boy blinked and shook his head. 'All right. If you tell me which way you're going, I'll say you've run off in the opposite direction. It'll save you a bit of time. I know what that sounds like, but I won't give you up.'

'Trust him,' Crouch said.

And so they ran. It was hard. Crouch could not straighten up or lift his feet high and Flea had to keep hold of him so he didn't pitch forwards on to his face, but somehow they managed.

Behind them they heard the brazier fall and the shouts of angry men, clear and distinct. They zigzagged down the hill as far as the new aqueduct, where Crouch gasped, 'Must rest.'

They leant against one of the pillars. A great arch leapt dizzyingly above their heads then stitched a path across the jumbled rooftops to the Temple.

Flea peered through the gloom, back in the direction they had come from. The boy might have sent the pursuers the wrong way, but nowhere was safe. They were near where the priests left out the remains from the fire altar and Temple kitchens, supposedly for the poor. But in reality it was now a racket controlled by gangs who chased beggars away as a matter of course.

'I don't like the way they're looking at us,' Flea said, nodding at a knot of men under the next arch. A couple of them had stooped to pick up stones. 'We can't stay here.'

'But where can we go?'

'Nowhere is safe for me,' Flea said. 'Not with the Cutters on my tail. You'll be safer on your own.'

Crouch bent his neck up and peered at Flea. 'I don't think I want –'

'Listen,' Flea interrupted, 'somehow Jude and Yesh need to be warned that Shim's been passing information to the Romans. Right?'

Crouch nodded.

'The only way you'll be able to make it – even with me helping – is if we go straight there through the Lower City. The problem is, that's Cutter territory and if they see me, we'll both be dead. So the only route is all the way round the Lower City, but that's too far for you to walk. So that means I'll have to do it on my own and leave your here.'

Crouch shook his head. 'I can't. I'm sorry. I'm too scared and anyway, you need me. Have you forgotten? It's got to be me that warns them. If the Romans find out it's you –'

'I know!' Flea said. 'The gang will be killed. We've been over it.'

'So . . .'

'All right,' Flea came to a decision. 'We'll just have to

do it together, but you be sure to tell me if it all gets too much and you need a rest.'

Crouch smiled. 'It'll be you needing the help especially if you have to carry me.'

Flea laughed. It seemed the only thing to do.

# 30

To avoid the Lower City they had to head deep into the southern slums, where there was barely room to move. Entire families squatted in doorways, water sellers picked their way through the crowd, conmen shouted out the latest deals.

Tomorrow was the Feast of the Angel of Death. Every family had to purify themselves in the Temple, kill a lamb, mark the door with its blood, tie a sprig of hyssop to the frame, then cook the lamb and eat it. Salesmen were busy with last-minute deals. *Genuine charcoal from the Temple stores! Holy lambs blessed by the high priest himself! Herbs from the Temple kitchens! Come on, people: don't risk the Angel of Death coming to pay you a visit. And while you're about it, why not buy a bucket of sand in case of fire?* There were accidents every Feast – some years whole sections of the City caught fire.

But death could come from anywhere, Flea thought. At one crossroads a man was standing on the edge of a water trough so he could scan the crowd. Flea felt a surge behind him and sensed that others were pushing towards them.

Spies were here too!

He hunched down and drew the neck of his tunic over his head. 'This way.' A narrow alleyway off to their left was less crowded.

'What if it's a dead end?' Crouch said.

'It's the only way.'

Damp air clamped their clothes to their bodies. The alleyway was run-down, lined with crumbling houses. Weeds tugged their feet. They became aware of a swelling sense of broken emptiness. A growing quietness that roared a warning.

Stumbling round a corner, Flea and Crouch saw why. A rough barrier blocked the road. It was as high as the houses on either side and built of rubble and old timbers, as if people had piled up anything they could, then left.

This wasn't a recent construction. The wood was blotched with lichen. Weeds struggled out of crannies.

Crouch's weight dragged Flea to a halt. 'Dead Streets,' was all he said.

The Dead Streets were forbidden. Taboo. Utterly unclean. Rumours shadowed the narrow alleyways: the dead from a Roman massacre still lay in the streets, just bones now, mouldy bones, piled so deep they crunched underfoot as you tried to pick your way through them. It was the Romans themselves who first threw up the blockades, to hide their crime from the world. Then the high priest declared the whole area unclean and said that anyone entering had to purify themselves for thirty days if they crossed the barriers. Superstition did the rest. The gang used to dare each other to cross, but no one ever had and, as far as Flea knew, no one had even come this far. And it was almost dark now.

A cold wind nudged them. A banging door somewhere sounded loose and hollow. The power of the dead reached over the barrier. Flea felt it like cold hands on his skin.

Crouch tugged at his arm. 'Come on. We've got to go back.'

'We can't. And we can't hang out here either. We've got to go in.'

'But the ghosts,' Crouch wailed. His face was shrivelled with terror.

'I know, but think of the mob. If it's Cutters they'll gut us. What the worst thing a ghost could do?'

'Gut us too?' Crouch said. 'Drag us down to hell?'

'We've got to risk it. It's certain death or . . . possible death. And you've got to warn Jude.'

There was an abandoned house on their left, its door sagging loose. Flea scraped it open and peered inside.

A small, square room. Empty. A few ashes in the middle of the earth floor. It was dark inside, but there was just enough light to show a rough ladder leading to the next floor.

'No,' Crouch said. 'I just can't. Not here. Not at night.'

Behind them the slap of footsteps faded to silence.

'That's it,' Flea said. 'Someone saw us and has gone to get the mob. I'm not frightened of a few mouldy bones. Think about it. The mob won't follow us into the Dead Streets, so we'll be safe. I'll go first.'

The ladder was old, the wood splintery. When Flea put a foot on the lowest rung he felt it give, but only by a little.

'It's fine,' he called and to his relief Crouch followed. The floor above was lighter and another ladder took them up through a trapdoor on to a flat roof. A small tree was growing in one corner, leaning on to the street. Rags were piled in another, and straight ahead Flea could look over the barrier into the Dead Streets.

The view was an anticlimax and a relief. No old bodies stacked like timber, no strewn bones. No nothing, in fact. The Dead Streets just looked empty and messy and sad.

'We'll be fine,' Flea said. 'We just have to cross one more roof and then we can follow that alley all the way.' He stepped over the parapet.

'Flea.' Crouch's voice was small with fear.

'What?'

'Something's moving behind me, but I'm too scared to look.'

Flea looked, but wished he hadn't. Behind Crouch the pile of rags had shifted and was taking on form: a hunched thing of blackened limbs and tattered cloth.

The hairs on the back of Flea's neck lifted. Terror

strangled him. He tried to speak, but no words came.

Then Crouch was past him, moving faster than Flea had ever seen, stumbling over the parapet to the next house, then the next. Flea followed until they found steps that led down. They half fell down them and finally landed in the Dead Streets.

# 31

Weeds clawed their feet. Tiles crunched and slid. The thing of rags was behind them somewhere, stretching out, trailing shreds. Bent double, Crouch tried to row himself through the air. Flea felt old nightmares gather. Dark doorways spilled horror he had to splash through. He risked a glance behind. Saw nothing. He slowed, panting, while Crouch slid to the ground.

'I'm sorry, I'm sorry,' Crouch gasped. 'I should never have come.'

'It's fine. Look – we've lost it, whatever it was. Come on, we can walk now.'

While they'd been running, they'd been protected by a bubble of panic. Now they were walking, every noise made then jump. Flea tried to remember what had happened here. It was coming back now . . .

There had been a water riot – people complaining that the Romans or the Temple or both were starving the City of water. Whatever the case, the riot had got out of hand

and the Temple Police had driven the protestors into these streets, where the Imps had been waiting.

They had massacred everyone, protestors who had run here and families that lived here, and then left.

A big rat ran in its broken, hobbly way across the road in front of them and Flea lashed out with a foot, connecting with something round and white that had been buried in the weeds. A skull? It crashed into a door. The hollow knock seemed terribly, terribly loud. Unseen things skittered.

'What was that?' Crouch asked.

'Nothing. Just walk.'

'I am walking.'

Flea stared straight ahead, trying to block his peripheral vision. There was a noise to their left now, behind the row of houses.

'That's bigger than a rat,' Crouch said. 'That's –'

He screamed as the pile of rags leapt out of a side street and blocked their way. A ragged man. Ragged hair, ragged beard, ragged skin, ragged clothes. Cracked dirt glazed his skin. Eyes very white. Teeth very absent.

'Bones, bones, bones,' the man said. His mouth stretched into a soft, wet O. 'Bonny bones. Boney bones. Is he coming, bathed in glory?'

Running was useless. They backed against a wall.

'Did you come to see the bones? Did you come searching? Are you looking for the way?' warbled the man.

'Out of here?' Flea asked.

The ragged man winced. His face was blunt; skin stretched like a tight tent across where his nose had once been.

'Out of the bone cage! Out of the skin sack! Into the light!'

He jumped, then pulled his rags apart and beat his chest. His ribs were shocking and white. He smelled like a glue-maker's yard.

'No, master,' Flea said. 'Just . . .'

'I AM NOT THE MASTER. I am from the desert. The Master came to the desert, but now is back among men.' He stretched his arms skywards. 'Oh, why have I been cast away? Why have I been left in this cesspit of sin? In this vat of vileness? In the desert I sought him, but found him not. In the mountains I looked for him and he was not in the rocks, nor in the caves. Where is my saviour? Where is my purity? He has led to me to the filth to find the light. I have followed him to the flesh pits for my salvation.'

Crouch tugged Flea's arm. 'I think he's one of them . . . you know, a Ranting Dunker.'

The man stooped, picked up a bone and began to dance with it, hopping from one foot to another. 'We have seen the light! We have come to the darkness to shine the light. Here! He has come to City, where the truth will become light and bones become flesh. Here the dead will dance and I will see it!'

Ranting Dunkers, Flea knew, lived off insects. They wore animal skins they had cured themselves, which would explain the smell, and meditated in total solitude, which might explain the manner. They also believed that sins could be washed away in river water, not animal blood, which in no way explained the dirt.

But Flea had never heard of a Ranting Dunker hurting anyone.

He whispered to Crouch, 'It's all right. I think he's harmless.'

Then he said out loud, 'Glory be!' It was something he had heard their followers say. 'May I ask a question?'

The Ranting Dunker shot him a sly glance. 'Many are the questions, but only one is the answer.' It sounded like a prepared statement.

'Glory be. When you say *he* has come to the City, who do you mean?'

'He is the answer to all questions. The Chosen One. The Chosen One who is washed clean of sin and is wrapped in glory! That is why I am here among the dead. When he comes, the dead will be reborn. The dead will dance with joy. I have gathered their bones. I have made me a pile of their bones and in the great gathering bones that were parted will gather, flesh that was sundered will join.' He stepped closer. 'Flesh. Will. Gather.'

'I don't think he's harmless,' Crouch whispered. 'He's

just taken out a knife.'

The blade was small, but had been sharpened to a silvered edge.

'And that's why you're in the Dead Streets?' Flea's back was pressing hard into the wall behind him.

'I am here to gather up the dead and save the living! Let me save you!'

The knife point danced between them.

'Er, we're fine,' Flea said. 'I mean, we hung out with the Chosen One and his followers, didn't we?'

He nodded encouragingly to Crouch. They couldn't get past the madman and they had nothing to fight with. All they could do was buy time.

'We ate with them,' Crouch said. 'We saw him cure the sick down at the Healing Pool. We agree with everything he says. Glory be.'

'Can you tell us how you save people?' Flea asked.

'With this.' The knife's tip seemed to be unstitching a seam in the air. 'This. This. This.'

'You kill people?' Crouch's voice rose to a squeak.

'How else can they be reborn?'

'This is what I don't get,' Flea said. 'It's all very well you going around saving people with your . . . er, knife, but who's going to save you? It doesn't seem fair.'

Doubts flickered across the Dunker's face. The knife stopped pecking. 'Who's going to save me?'

'Well, yes. And how are you going to do it?'

'I . . .' He was looking down at his knife now.

'I mean, we could help.'

'Flea?' Crouch warned.

But Flea was on a roll. 'You see, we spent time with the Chosen One and he always banged on about this thing. We should try to save as many people as possible. His orders. So if we saved you, it would be saving us.'

The man peered at him. 'You would do that?'

Flea held out his hand.

The Ranting Dunker held out the knife, then snatched it away. 'Let me save your friend first. My way of saying thank you.'

'No thanks are needed. This is my duty.' Flea tried to look calm and reassuring.

'Your duty.' Tears spilled from the Dunker's eyes and filled the fissures of his face.

Flea hoped Crouch would know what to do. The Dunker handed over the knife, bared his neck and knelt. 'Here?' he asked.

'There!' Flea threw the knife as far as he could over the roof of the house opposite. 'RUN!'

He grabbed Crouch and they surged forwards. Behind them they heard the Ranting Dunker howl. Ahead, the barrier blocking the road loomed, the Upper City rising behind it.

'He's going to catch us,' Crouch said as Flea shook the doors of the houses close by. All locked. 'He's coming!'

'Can you climb?' Flea asked, and almost before he had finished talking Crouch was hauling himself up the barrier, hand over hand. Flea followed and helped him up on to the roof where they collapsed, panting. They climbed half a dozen more parapets before shock caught up with them. Flea could not stop the trembling in his arms and legs. Crouch's skin was grey and pinched from pain. His head kept falling on to his chest as if it were too heavy.

'I'm sorry,' he said. 'I'll be better in a while. I just need to catch my breath.'

'That's all right,' Flea said. 'We'll just . . . Oh no. That sound.'

He crawled to the edge of the roof and peered over. A crowd was marching down the street towards them. Some people were holding flaming torches; others were knocking on doors.

They sounded angry.

'What do we do?' Crouch asked. Flea knew he couldn't walk any further, let alone run from a mob.

'We stay put,' he whispered. 'Don't worry. *Shh*. Listen.'

The banging on the door seemed to come from right below them.

Muffled voices from inside the house. 'What? Who's that?'

'Temple business,' a gruff voice answered. 'We're after two boys. Blasphemers. Trying to disrupt the Feast.'

Crouch crawled across to Flea. 'Blasphemers? Us? That means they want to stone us. All for spending time with Yesh.'

'First the Cutters and now the Temple?' whispered Flea. 'I mean, how can the Temple *and* the Cutters be after me? They hate each other, don't they? Why don't I understand and what am I meant to know?'

'It doesn't matter,' Crouch wailed. 'It's too late. Look!' He was peering over the roof's parapet. 'They're on the rooftops. They'll see us. They're looking everywhere! If we move they'll see us. If we stay still they'll catch us. We stuck. We're . . . Oh no.'

The scrape of wood on wood. A few paces away, a black square appeared as a trapdoor in the roof creaked open.

# 32

Flea looked at Crouch blankly. He had opened his mouth to say sorry when a quavering voice spoke.

'I was right. I was sure I could hear something up here. I knew I was right.'

'We're just beggars. We're lost. We haven't done anything wrong,' Crouch squeaked.

'And I've got a knife.' Flea tried to sound menacing.

'Oh dear,' the voice said. 'Miriam, they're scared. Bring a light so they can see me. That should reassure them.'

A small oil lamp was passed up from below. Its light

showed a very old man with long white hair and a white beard. 'Two little angels fallen on our roof. Our prayers have been answered. Come quick.' The light played in the hollows and wrinkles of his face.

'How do we know we'll be safe?' Flea said.

'Dear child, you don't. But there's no safety up here and the mob's closing in. Even my deaf old ears can hear them. I beg you, come in.'

And before Flea could think of anything else, Crouch was crawling across the roof to the trapdoor and climbing down.

Flea followed him into a small, square room. In one corner a fire burned in a simple clay oven. A roll of bedding was laid out in another. There was a rush mat in the middle of the floor and a few pots and plates stacked along the wall.

'Welcome,' the man said. 'We heard you . . . arrive . . . just as we were saying our prayers. We have no interest in following the mob. The night before the Great Feast is a time for prayer and kindness.'

'We were praying for guests,' the woman said. 'Our prayers have been answered.' She was a tiny concentration of sweetness and wrinkles. On her forehead and chin were tattooed small crosses the colour of the sky at the end of a dusty summer's day. 'Sit, please. They are here.'

'Open up by the authority of the Temple,' a voice called out. The banging on the door made Flea wince.

'We have to run,' he hissed. Panic made him feel sick.

'Have faith. The Temple has no authority here,' the old woman said, with a smile. 'Husband, send them away.'

The old man climbed down the stairs to the lower room. Over the flustered clucking of chickens they heard him calling out to wait and be patient as he unbarred the door.

'We're looking for two children. Law breakers. Blasphemers. Have you –'

'Children?' the old man said. He sounded honestly confused.

'They come from a street gang. Been involved in terrorist activity. Have you seen anyone like that?'

'Nothing like that, but these old eyes . . .'

'Alone, are you?'

'I live with my wife.'

'Well, be careful. These are dangerous times.'

'Oh, I know,' the old man said. 'I know.'

He was smiling when he returned to the room. 'Well, I didn't lie, did I?'

'No, indeed you didn't.' The old woman returned the smile. 'You did very well.'

'When he said, "Have you seen anyone *like* that" . . . the truth is, I have seen the thing itself, so nothing *like* it.'

'You'd split hairs with the barber,' the old woman said. 'What these boys want is a cup of milk and a place to rest, not a lecture on how clever you are.'

'Whatever happens, we don't like the idea of grown men chasing children down the street. We've lived through this kind of madness before. There's always trouble at the Feast, especially when the latest one turns up at the east gate.'

It took a second for the words to sink in. 'The latest one?' Flea said. 'What do you mean?'

'Oh, every other year someone rides into the City on a donkey claiming to be the Chosen One. You know the old prophecy: *Behold your king is coming for you. He is just and will save you. He is humble and mounted on a donkey.*'

Flea shook his head. 'I'd never even heard of the Chosen One before yesterday. We just went to see Yesh because we thought he did tricks, but then it all got complicated. I don't know how it happened.'

'Poor child. Life can be very simple, but people like to make it complicated. They go through the old books looking for prophecies, for example. This "Yesh". Can he heal the sick, do you know?'

'Yes,' Crouch said quickly.

'Of course you know the verse from the Holy Book?' the old man said hopefully.

When Flea and Crouch looked at him blankly, he said, '*The lame will leap like a deer and the dumb will shout for joy.* Did he go into the Temple?'

'Yes,' Flea and Crouch said together.

'*And the Lord, whom you seek, will suddenly go to his Temple*. It's all there, written down in the old books. All you have to do is look. But the problem is, people just don't seem to study the texts the way they used to.'

'Are you saying that if he did all these things, then he *must* be the Chosen One?' Crouch asked.

But Flea's mind had raced ahead. 'No! Don't you see? If they're all written down, he just has to follow them, so that they look like prophecies coming about. The donkey on the bridge: that had been set up in advance. The trouble in the Temple – all done for a reason. The healing and probably everything else he did. That was the plan!'

Crouch stuck out his bottom lip. 'It doesn't matter,' he said. 'If it was prophesied and he did it, then . . .'

'But if he knew about them, then they're not prophecies at all. They're more like . . . instructions. You must see that.'

'It doesn't matter if he really is the Chosen One.'

'It does matter. It has to matter!' Flea's head was like a room full of voices he could not understand. They were getting louder and louder. He thought his head would burst.

'Enough, enough,' the old woman bustled over. 'Time for talk tomorrow. You look exhausted, you poor things. Rest here. Stay with us and tomorrow join us for the Feast.'

The old man put a comforting hand on Crouch's

shoulder. 'Come now. I can tell you've been pinning your hopes on this Yeshua. Well, in spite of what your friend thinks, he has a lot going for him. We heard he's from Gilgad, and that's part of the prophecy you can't fake. He's got quite a following up there, and that counts in his favour. And of course there was that desert prophet who recommended him. Yohan, he was called. So don't lose heart, that's the main thing. And if you . . .'

Flea stood suddenly. The voices had come together to form a single clear question. 'What comes next in the prophecy?' he asked.

Silence. The old man looked away. 'It is best not to meddle, child. Stay with us for the Feast. We shall kill the lamb, cook it and mark our door with its blood so the Angel of Death passes overhead.'

'But I need to meddle! I've messed things up. I don't know how, but if I know the next stage of the prophecy, maybe I can do something!'

'Really, child . . .'

'You know. Why won't you tell me?'

'Because it is a terrible thing.' The old man looked at his wife, who nodded sadly. Then he took a deep breath and chanted, 'He was pierced through for our sins, he was crushed for all the unfairness in the world. He was punished for our comfort and we can only be healed when he is whipped. That's what the writings say. It is not good. You don't want to trouble yourself. Many pretenders claim to be the Chosen One, but all fail when they are faced with the ultimate test.'

Flea swallowed. 'Whipped? Crushed? You mean tortured?' He thought of the whipping post in the Fortress's courtyard and the awful instruments in the Results Man's cellar. He felt sick.

'He will be betrayed, tortured and suffer a miserable death. Is it any wonder that none of these pretenders has ever gone through with it?'

'Betrayed? Did you say betrayed? I've got to go,' Flea said.

'Child, you should not meddle in these matters,' the old man said.

'But he *has* been betrayed. Shim, one of his followers, has betrayed him to the Romans. The Romans are torturers. It's happening like the prophecy says, but we can stop it! We can warn them. I know where they are!'

'Hush, child. What will be, will be. If this is Yeshua's destiny, then trying to stop it will be pointless. A true prophecy is like a river – you can try to block it, but it will always find its way.'

'No,' Flea said. 'It'll be my fault! If I'd just done what I was told in the first place, Jude could have already done something about it. That's what he wanted. But now I know what's going to happen, I can make it right. Crouch, come on. I'm sorry. We really have to go now. They can't be too far from here.'

But when he held his hand out, Crouch would not take it. Instead he turned to the old man. 'If he is the Chosen One, what will happen when all the prophecies come true?'

A little smile lit up the old man's face and his eyes crinkled in delight. 'Ah, now, that is very interesting. If all the prophecies come true, it is said that this world will end and a new world will begin. A world of peace and plenty. A world that will make this one seem like a sad memory. Pain and hunger will be no more – fading shadows on the golden fields of paradise.'

'And the poor will be rich?' Crouch asked.

'All will be rich.'

'And the lame?'

Flea read the twist in Crouch's face and the longing in his eyes and did not like it.

'Snap out of it, Crouch,' he said. 'Yesh might be tortured. Your precious magician might be tortured. And the world will end. Don't you get it? The. World. Will. End.'

Crouch's face was anguished. 'But then there'll be a better one. What will happen to the lame?'

'They'll dance in the streets for joy,' the old man said. 'Glory be!'

'Me too?'

'Of course.'

Flea took him by the shoulders. 'Crouch – you can't mean . . .'

'Child, child, do not blame him,' the old man said. 'It is a prophecy. It has been decided. If he is the One, he will die.'

'No,' Flea said. He stamped on the floor and the little house boomed. 'Don't you see? It can't be a prophecy if it's all just my fault. The whole thing can't . . . hang on that!'

'What about the Temple Boys?' Crouch asked. 'You're risking their lives.'

'If the prophecy goes ahead they're dead anyway,' Flea answered bleakly.

And he went.

# 33

The streets had emptied by the time Flea set off again. He forced himself to jog, trying to run off his tiredness.

Flea had heard the priests chanting in the Temple. You had to be deaf not to. They did a lot of praising, and there was always something to be grateful for: the whiteness of lambs, the juiciness of pomegranates, the plumpness of doves, the yield of the threshing floor and so on.

Flea didn't buy it.

Any good fortune he enjoyed had come about through his own quick wits. Or sheer blind luck, like the day he had found the coin on the Temple steps, or the time he'd fallen through a rotten ceiling when he was being chased by a knife gang and they'd been too scared to follow. Luck was just another link in the chain of disasters that was his life.

But right now, as he climbed the side of the valley heading for the room he had seen Shim visit, he could not see how luck could help him. Shim had already betrayed Yesh to the Results Man and now the prophecy would roll out like a Temple scroll.

Yesh would be tortured,

Yesh would die,

the world would end,

and Flea could not take that responsibility.

The problem was even knottier than that, though. Because if Yesh was the Chosen One and his death led to whole new world that was free of suffering, maybe he should just let that happen. Then everyone would be happy, if (big IF, great big IF, great-big, size-of-a-mountain IF) the prophecies came true.

Too many choices. Flea stopped running and looked up at the sky for guidance.

Big mistake. The stars seemed to be circling around him – HIM – as if he were the pivot of the world. Perhaps the old couple were right. Perhaps he should just accept his fate and let events take their course. Perhaps he should just head back and drink their milk and eat their bread and wait for the world to end.

Once, twice, three times Flea stopped. But something

kept him moving forwards to the upper room where Yesh and Jude and all the rest of them were eating and drinking happily, ignorant of the danger they were in.

An Imp picked him up about a hundred paces from his goal. Flea tried to fight, but he was so tired he could barely struggle. When the Imp put him down Flea just stood still, his head swinging from side to side like a cow on the edge of sleep.

The soldier took him straight to the Results Man, who was sitting on the back of a cart a single street away, swinging his legs, smiling his tortoise smile and picking his teeth with his horrid little spike.

'Wanted to see what happens? Good for you,' he said casually. 'Unless of course you were trying to warn someone?'

Flea opened his eyes wide, tried to look innocent and shook his head.

The Results Man ruffled Flea's hair. 'Because you're cleverer than that. You've worked out that if you said *anything* to Jude, Shim would know and if Shim knows anything, he tells me, and I would take it out on your little friends. Who are fit and healthy, by the way. So far. I showed them my instruments this afternoon and invited them to sing along. None of them took up the offer so I popped them into a little room, gave them a bath, turned out the lights and suggested they have a sleep.'

He pretended to play his spike like a flute.

Flea looked down the street to the house where Yesh and his followers would be sitting down to eat. He could see warm light through the shutters. He wanted to be there. Nothing else. Just to be there. If he hadn't gone snooping after Shim, if he hadn't met the met the Results Man. If, if, if . . .

The Results Man broke into his thoughts. 'You see, what I think is this. I do a job, and my job is to do what's best for the Imperium. Is a soldier who fights for his country bad because he's killed a man or two? Far from it. He's a hero. Well, so am I.'

'But Rome isn't your country, is it?' Flea said.

'Not in your sense. Not in the backwards, old-fashioned sense where you're stuck with a country just because you happen to be born on one particular patch of earth. I mean, who wants this place?' He gestured around him. 'Who wants to be trapped in this hideous, heaped-up dump of a city that runs on blood and smoke? Rome is bigger than that. Rome is an idea. Believe in the idea and you become a Roman.' He paused to smile. 'When all this is over, what are you going to do?'

'I think I'd like go a very long way away from here, from Rome, from everything,' Flea said. He remembered the line of camels, their red halters, and the sense of freedom they had given him.

The Results Man snorted. 'Oh, wake up, idiot. Listen, on the very edge of the world there's an island where the sky is always grey, the land is always green and the people have blue skin. When they kill a man, they eat his heart, cut off his head and jam it on to a spike so they can talk to it. And yet that place is Roman too. You can't travel the world to get away from Rome. Rome *is* the world. Travel to explore, travel to conquer, travel to learn, but do not think for one second you can travel to escape. Anyway, I need you.'

'You need *me*?'

'Perhaps *need* is too big a word, as is *me*. Better to say that I have decided to work a person into my plans, yes, and that person might as well be you. You see, we have a tiny, possible risk of a possible situation. There are Temple patrols out tonight. If I arrest Yeshua too publicly it might lead to trouble, and I don't want trouble I can't control. So, change of plan. When I ask you to, I want you to join the party, find out where they're going next and then come and tell me if it's somewhere nice and quiet.'

It took a second before Flea saw the opportunity this presented. 'All right,' he said.

'Now curl up and go to sleep for a bit. I need to think without being disturbed.'

It was not an invitation. It was an order. Flea curled up in the back of the cart and screwed his eyes tight shut.

Getting to see Jude would not be a problem now, but how could he warn him without Shim noticing?

# 34

Pitch-black. Flea woke up very carefully, the spike sliding coldly up one of his nostrils and the Results Man's breath warming his neck. The spike encouraged him to sit up and was not removed until he did. Still stupid from sleep, Flea slid down from the back of the cart and looked out into the street.

The room that Shim had hired stood out even more starkly now. Warm tints from the lamp-lit windows looked soft and inviting. Distant voices dented the silence.

'Quite a meal they're having.' The Results Man's voice was as soft as a lover's. 'They'll have had a drop or two of wine by now, so they'll be loosened up, and a clever boy like you should be able to find out what we need. Ready?'

Flea stood and nearly fell. His heart was hammering so hard his legs seemed to tremble. He didn't think he could make it.

'What is it?' the Results Man asked. 'Scared? Have I been too harsh? Should I have been nicer? Should I coax you? Go, my sweet little insect. Go!'

A hand in the middle of Flea's back compelled him to take a step. The movement shook down his thoughts and seemed to bring new clarity. If it was a choice between saving the world and saving the Temple Boys, he had to save the world, because if the world went then they would all die anyway. He would warn Jude in any way he could, whether Shim overheard or not. He took one more step and then another, a small boy in an empty street, and then climbed the steps to the upper room.

On the landing, two neat rows of dusty sandals were laid out on the little platform along with a wide bowl of dirty water. It seemed homely and normal. He looked up at the door. No one had marked it with lamb's blood and no sprig of hyssop had been tied to the doorpost. Did that matter? Had the Angel of Death passed over anyway, or was it up there, waiting? If he opened the door, would it slip into the room with him like a deadly shadow?

He pressed his ear to the flaking paint. The magician was talking in a low, pressing voice, occasionally interrupted by laughter or protest. What should he do? Should he just open the door? Make a noise? Shout? He scratched the wood with his fingernails and felt the loose, crumbly grain threaten to give him splinters.

He coughed. No response.

He kicked it gently. No response.

He leant his head against it, the catch gave and he fell into the warm light.

# 35

A meal of lamb, bread, olives and wine was laid out on a cloth in the middle of the room. At the far end, under a shuttered window, Yesh sat on a cushion, cross-legged and upright. The others were sitting or sprawling around him, seemingly frozen by the sight of Flea stumbling into their feast: Yohan with a beaker of wine held in mid-air; Yak reaching for an olive; Shim with his mouth clamping down on a piece of bread. Tauma broke the silence by swallowing noisily. Jude rose to his feet and stepped over the remnants of the supper, reaching Flea in two strides.

'Flea, child, what's happened to you?'

His concern was so sudden and so honest that Flea felt a choking rush of tears. He fought to keep them down and shook his head.

'We'll pop outside and talk,' Jude said, shooing him to the door.

'Wait,' Yesh said.

'But I want a word alone . . .'

'And I said wait! I want to see the child first. He looks terrible. Why's he here anyway?' Yesh's voice was slightly slurred and his eyes were bright. He gestured to Shim, who rose to his feet and closed the door, then ushered Flea forwards.

Jude smoothed the annoyance from his face. 'Master, he must have come to tell me something.'

'And so he can, or this yet another one of your secrets?' Yesh sounded sharp. 'No secrets, Jude. Too late for that. If young Flea has come to do you a favour, the least we can do is feed him for his troubles and let him rest.'

'I'm fine,' Flea said. 'Honestly, I'm fine. I just wanted . . .'

Jude mouthed the word 'Later,' and stepped back.

Yesh smiled. 'Come closer. You're our guest. I've done my best to cheer this lot up, but it's been heavy going. So join us. Please. I beg you. You'd be doing me a favour These sour-faced old busybodies want to stop me having fun. Yohan, bring the boy some food and a little bit of wine, I think, mixed with water. That's it. Now then, you look as if you've been through it today. Life on the street's tough, isn't it?'

'We got into a bit of trouble and had to hide . . . you know,' Flea told him. 'We're sorry. That's why I came. To say I was sorry for not being around to thank you for having us to that dinner.' Like bitter fat, the half-truth slipped greasily between his lips.

'Sorry? Thanks? That's very formal, Flea. What's up?'

*Someone's betrayed you and you're going to die, but I don't know how to tell you,* was what went through Flea's thoughts. 'Just that I heard you'd be off after the holiday. That things have got a bit hot for you in the City,' was what he said.

178

'Hm. Ha. Yes. And of course you're right. But I bet you're hungry too, and thought a bite to eat was worth crossing the City for? Good. I knew you'd come round.' He appealed to his followers. 'Didn't I say it? Didn't I say, *That Flea's the hardest one to catch, but he'll come round*? And now he has and we're all the happier.'

Flea was appalled, not just by Yesh's wrongness, but by the chasm between his wrongness and the truth.

Yesh carried on. 'I was thinking very hard about you boys and wanted to pass something on . . . My magic. All brother Jude's idea – did you know that? When I was just a simple preacher it was his idea to pull the crowds in with a few tricks. It wasn't long before they started saying it was more than that.'

'In your hands, Lord, tricks become something else.' Mat spoke gruffly. He was older than the others and tonight the flesh on his face seemed as though it was sagging. His grey hair grew up like a wiry crown.

'Hmmph.' Yesh cleared his throat and said, 'Yes. That is what we believe, but sometimes I yearn to do a few of the old routines again, just for the fun of it. Life was simple in those days, but we have to accept that it can get a bit more complicated.'

'Life's never been simple for me,' Flea said. 'Just staying alive is hard enough.' He tried to load the words with meaning.

Yesh looked at him sharply, then crinkled his eyes. 'All the more reason for some fun, then!'

He clicked his fingers, leant across to Yohan and pulled a coin from his mouth, then pressed it into his left ear and pulled it out of his right. Yohan continued to smile dreamily.

'You could show him your best trick,' Jude said. 'As a reward for coming to see us.'

That was almost too much for Flea. He shook his head. 'I don't deserve it,' he said. 'I didn't do –'

'Show him, Master,' Jude said. 'Show him how to hunt the king.' He locked eyes with Yesh, who was the first to look away and snap out another smile.

'Yes. Jude's right. You should know how to hunt the king. It should be passed on.' He looked around the room. 'What? No one wants me to have fun? I tell you, I feel a bit let down tonight. Almost betrayed.'

An intake of breath and shocked murmurs. *Let down? Betrayed? No.*

Flea stared hard at Shim, but he was looking down so his face was hidden.

Yesh smiled. 'Good. Someone empty that bread off the tray and hand it over to me. Finish your wine, Flea. You too, Yohan. And I'll get rid of mine.' He drank it in one gulp, then put the beaker upside down on the tray and gestured for Yohan and Flea to do the same.

'You know this trick, don't you, Flea? You've seen it

done on every street corner. But some people don't get it. Shim, for example, has never understood. Want to play, Shim?'

'My Lord, is this the time?' Mat began. 'Shouldn't we be getting ready to move –'

'YES! THIS IS THE TIME. THIS IS *MY* TIME! OR HAD YOU FORGOTTEN?'

Mat flinched as if he had been struck. 'No, Lord,' he whispered.

'Then this night, this night of all nights, we play Hunt the King,' Yeshua said in a quieter voice. 'I need three cups. So. I put them in a row, so, and I hide the coin under one of them, so. Then I move them around to the left and the right and the right and the left and all Shim has to do is keep his eye on the cup that he thinks is hiding the coin. Do you understand me, Flea?'

'Yes.'

'Good, because it's not just a game, it's a lesson about life. And now we begin. Sit in front of me, Shim.'

Reluctantly, Shim shuffled up and sat in front of Yesh, who slid a coin under a cup and moved them in a complicated pattern, talking all the time in a trickster's patter. 'Hunt the king to the left to the right to the middle to the left to the left or was it right to middle or what? Place your bets now. Loser pays double. We're good for that, aren't we, Jude?'

Jude hefted his money bag and pursed his lips.

'Just don't lose too much,' he said.

Yesh nodded. 'I hear you. Brother Shim, hunt the king.'

Reluctantly Shim opened his purse, put a coin down and tapped a beaker.

'Are you sure?' Yesh asked.

Shim nodded.

Yesh lifted the beaker and there was the coin. 'Pay you double,' he said. 'Again.'

Four times Yesh lost, until there were sixteen coins in front of Shim, paid from Judas's purse.

'That's the treasury cleaned out,' Jude said.

'One last time,' Yesh said. 'Loser pays double and here we go. 'Hunt the king to left to the right to the left to the left to the right or is it left or was it right or was it the middle?'

Maybe the magician was getting tired, perhaps he had had too much to drink, but his movements seemed clumsier and when he stopped, Shim said, 'But it's so clear, Lord.'

He patted the centre cup. But when Yeshua turned it up, there was no coin.

'Sorry, Shim,' he said, with a cruel smile. 'Loser pays double. Now you owe me thirty-two silver coins.'

'Thirty-two? Lord, I . . .'

'What? Not good for your debts? Isn't that one of the sins that cries up to heaven for vengeance? For your own good, Shim, you've got to cough up.' Yesh fixed him with a stare.

'I don't have that sort of money. I don't have a mite. I . . .'

'So how are you going to pay me?'

Shim screwed his eyes up. Then his face relaxed. 'This is a joke, Lord, right? Just a joke?'

'I'm not laughing. Borrow the money,' Yesh said flatly.

Shim turned. The followers reached into purses and pockets, fumbled for change, held out what they had. Shim counted it out and handed the coins to Jude with a sour expression.

'Fourteen there,' he said.

'What's in the purse now?' Yesh asked. 'Thirty pieces of silver?' He closed his eyes and murmured, '*So I took the thirty pieces of silver and threw them into the house of the LORD for the potter.*' Which holy prophet said that?'

'Zechariah, Lord,' Mat said.

'And thirty pieces of silver is a suitable price for a slave,' Yesh said, his face suddenly sour.

'A slave, Lord?' Mat rose to his feet.

'Or anyone else that has no say in his destiny,' Yesh said, then suddenly brightened. He slapped his hands together. 'Still, no use complaining. Now it is time to go.'

When he stood, they all stood too and cleared a path to the door for him. Two or three seemed to be holding back tears. At the door he turned, looked down at Flea.

'Now, Flea, it's your turn to make a decision. Should

Jude give you the money I made, or should I teach you the trick?'

'I don't know,' Flea said. He'd gone beyond tiredness, gone beyond confusion and simply felt empty. What had all that stuff about slaves meant? He knew he should be able to work it out, but the sense of it was beyond the limits of his understanding, dancing in the dark. 'The truth is . . . the thing I'd like to know most of all is what's happening to you. Where are you going?'

The words had leapt into his mouth before his brain had time to stop them. Shim closed his eyes and groaned. Jude's eyes widened.

A coin appeared in Yesh's hand. He kept his eyes on Flea as he rolled it between his knuckles, back and forth, back and forth.

'And you'd trade my trick, my brilliant trick, for knowing this simple thing?'

'I need to ask it,' Flea said. He looked desperately at Jude. 'Something is making me.'

'Flea, Flea. You are the strangest child I ever met. It's no secret. We're going to the Pleasure Gardens, though it is a bit late, and the weather . . .'

'Surely, Lord, it is just what we need after that meal. A gentle walk, time to reflect.' Shim pushed between them. He sounded flustered.

'So that is the plan? I see,' Yeshua said. 'Then this is where we say goodbye, young Flea.'

'I could come too,' Flea said.

'No, you could not. You have done what was needed. You have played your part. Now you must go.'

'But . . .'

'Goodbye.'

The group seemed to make no noise as they filed out, picking up their sandals one by one, and walking softly into the street. Flea waited until they had gone and then left himself.

Flea sat on the bottom step. A lamb bleated. The City rasped like an old man breathing, but the overwhelming sense was that of quiet: a quiet that was big and smooth and pressed the breath from his chest. When he finally looked up, he saw the Results Man walking down the empty street towards him.

'The Pleasure Gardens,' Flea said.

The torturer smiled. 'Thank you. The Gardens are outside the City walls. It should make my job easier.'

'Can I go now?'

'Oh no. Your evening's just started. Remember, the lives of all your friends are still in your hands.'

'I'm so tired,' Flea said, and put his head on his crossed arms.

The Results Man picked him up by the scruff of his neck. 'You're alive. That's what counts. Come on. We're going to follow them.'

'And what's going to happen then?'

'A very big surprise, I can promise you that.' He looked up at the night sky, put out one hand and smiled with delight. 'Would you believe it! Snow. Or blossom? Or ash?'

Flakes darted and swooped like butterflies. One landed on Flea's hand. It felt dry, then melted. It was snow in springtime. This was madness. The world really was about to end.

# 36

By the time they reached the bridge the wind was blowing hard and the moon was dodging between thick, fast moving clouds – light and dark, dark and light. The Results Man strode ahead. Flea trailed behind, kicking palm fronds. They were followed by about twenty soldiers, not stamping the earth as Romans usually did, but walking softly.

On the bridge they met men and women who'd been driven back into the City by the weather. Flea tried to wish every shape into becoming Yesh, or Jude, even Shim – anything to suggest they'd given up and were coming back to the safety of the City. No such luck.

The road divided. Turn right to Bethany; turn left and a smaller track wound up the hillside to the Pleasure Gardens, a grove of old olive trees with a ruined oil mill in the middle of it. In the daytime it was popular with families who picnicked under the ancient, twisted branches; at night it was taken over by lonely men and women looking for love. Laws did not apply outside the City walls.

Flea tried to glue his broken thoughts into a plan. In bad weather the old oil mill offered shelter and it would make sense for Yesh and his followers to be there, but would the Results Man know that? Unlikely. If he could get away, there was still a chance he might find Jude in the darkness and warn him without anyone noticing.

His moment came when the Results Man was approached by a soldier and dismissed Flea with a wave of the hand. Another soldier started to describe something up ahead.

Flea stepped away. No one noticed.

Another step. The Results Man was just a shape in the darkness, and his back was turned.

*If anyone asks*, Flea thought, *I'll tell them I didn't want them to think I was listening and moved so far away I lost them.*

He slipped behind a tree and then ran. He was at the back wall of the mill before he knew it, and could hear the low murmur of voices. He stepped away and crept around the ruin until he could see who was talking.

Dark figures huddled round a small fire, the light flickering over their faces. Those were the followers all right, but no sign of Yesh. And no sign of Jude.

The wind dropped and it began to snow properly, with big, fluffy flakes that lay like blossom on the earth for a heartbeat before dissolving. Somewhere close by a nightingale started to sing, its liquid whistle sounding huge in the dark. Beyond that, up the hill, Flea heard the sound of retching and followed it.

In a glade, in the moonlight, Yesh was being sick. Jude was holding his long hair away from his face and rubbing his back. Flea hid in the shadows, watching, listening.

'I told you to get away,' Yesh said hoarsely. 'I just need to be on my own.'

'No! I need you to listen to me, not as my Lord, not as my Master, but as my old friend. I know what the plan is and I can't let you go through with it. I can't believe the rest of them are letting you. You still have a chance. You can still get away. Yesh, you can live!'

'You still don't see it, do you?' Yesh's voice was bleak.

'No. I just see horror. I don't think you've thought this through.'

'And is that why I was being sick? Because I haven't thought this through? Because I lack imagination?' Yesh's voice rose. 'Believe me, Jude, I've thought this through, right down to my last scream.'

'I'm not going to let it happen.' Jude answered. 'The way you've been going on the Romans will have to arrest you. And then they'll scourge you and then they'll bang nails through your wrists – here – and your ankles – here – and hang you from a cross where you'll –'

'It's what I have to do.'

'No. You can't. I cannot allow it.'

'The others have faith.'

'But no love. How can they say they love you and let this happen?'

'They love me enough to trust me. Have faith. If I die and you still do not believe, that would be the greatest betrayal of all.'

'If you die, it will kill me, Yesh. Don't you see? Listen, the Temple doesn't want trouble. Give yourself up and they'll hold you until the Feast is over. When the City's calmed down they'll let you go and we can go back to doing what we used to do: walking from village to village helping people. But let's stop all this nonsense about being the Chosen One and changing the world. Provided we keep out of trouble, you'll still be able to teach. You'll still be able to heal . . .'

'Jude.'

'We can do magic together . . . Remember how much fun it was? Remember how much laughter? Remember on the lake when you saw a shoal of fishes coming and told the fishermen to chuck their nets over it and they thought you'd magicked up the whole lot? Remember when we smuggled the booze into that boring wedding and they thought we'd turned water into wine because we'd tried to hide it in a water jug? Remember when . . .'

'JUDE! Stop it. Stop it, my friend.' Yesh held up a hand. 'It's not going to happen. The only people who are coming here tonight are the Romans. I'm on the verge of . . . becoming.'

'Becoming what?'

'Just becoming. And a new world is coming too.'

'And how much is your uncle helping? I know Yusuf arranged the donkey so you could ride into the City on it. I know he arranged a room in a city where there hasn't been room for days . . .'

'He didn't *help*. He's part of the pattern. You are too. Even the Romans, even our hated oppressors. They're part of the plan. That is our victory.'

Jude gestured angrily. 'How can letting them get their filthy hands on you help anything?'

'Because I have to suffer. And the more I suffer, the more value there is in my death. My life has been about taking the teachings and getting to the heart of them, making them clear. Think of the great woolly tangle of Temple Law. I take that and I work it and I stretch it and I spin and in the end I have thread that can pass through the eye of a needle, but which is strong enough to hold the whole world. Now –'

'Don't try your stories on me!' Jude interrupted angrily, but Yesh, whose voice had been getting stronger and stronger, overrode him.

'Now I'm taking my life and I'm passing it through this eye of agony, but when I'm through, Jude, when I'm through, you'll see the beauty of this wonderful thing I've woven. And in it you'll find me and you and the Temple and the Romans . . .'

All the time he was listening, Flea had felt like a baby chasing chickens, unable to pin down the sense of what Yesh was saying. When he finally understood, when he saw what Yesh was trying to do and Jude was trying to stop, anger exploded in him like a clap of thunder. Before he knew it, he had burst into the clearing and was shouting.

'You knew? You KNEW! I made it halfway across the City to warn you that Shim had sold you out to the Romans and it was part of your *plan*?'

The two men whirled round.

'Flea, what are you doing here?' Jude snapped.

'What am I doing? What's *he* doing?' Flea tried to stare Yesh down.

'Keep out of this!' Jude took Flea by the arm, as if to protect Yesh from his fury. 'Go back to the City. You have no idea what you're mixed up in.'

'Neither do you! I thought Shim was betraying Yesh to the Romans, but Yesh is betraying himself!' He pulled free and gripped his head. It felt like it was falling to pieces. 'But why? You know they want to kill you!'

Then he understood one more thing. The truth had

been so big and so obvious he'd missed it.

'That's the whole point,' Jude said. He sounded old and tired. 'Flea, I would have told you, but –'

'You said you would. You promised to share everything and now because you hid the truth from me, the Romans are coming. And do you know why? I brought them here! ME!' Flea was almost dancing with anger. 'It's the *opposite* of what you wanted because you . . . because I . . . They took the gang! They said that if I didn't do what they wanted, the gang would be tortured. I should have found a way of telling you, but I didn't. I should have just stuck to what you asked.'

He subsided, his throat hoarse.

'Take comfort, Flea,' Yesh said. 'This was meant to be. You see how everything comes together, how your efforts – and Jude's – to stop this only made it happen. Destiny, my destiny, is impossible to resist.'

That brought Flea back to life. 'Oh, well done. That's made your oldest friend feel better. Anyway, I don't believe you. You could stop this if you wanted. Me and my friends, we spend every minute of every day trying to stay alive. How can anyone work so hard to get himself killed? How can you *want* to die?'

Yesh stood straighter, lifted his chin and fixed his eyes on a point past Flea and Jude. 'I am the Chosen One. I am the prophecy. I am dying for you, Jude and you, Flea, and for all the world.'

'Don't do any favours for me, please!' Flea yelled. 'I don't want it and neither does Jude, and anyone who does want it, well, they're not worth dying for.'

That seemed to hit home. Yesh's face twisted and he took Jude by the arms.

'Jude. You are my oldest friend. Help me. I need your strength.'

Flea looped his hand into Jude's belt and pulled in the other direction. 'Forget him, Jude! You did what you could. He doesn't want your help. You've got to get away now. The Romans are coming. Come with me. We just have time to run.'

Jude looked down. 'Oh, Flea. What have you done?'

But Yeshua, on Jude's other side, drew strength from somewhere and was suddenly stronger and brighter. 'You cannot fight it!' he said. 'What has been foretold, has to be. The end of days is coming. The end of time. Join me, Jude, old friend, before it's too late.'

'NO! Come with me,' Flea said. 'Forget him.'

Jude sighed and looked down at him. 'Dear Flea, how did I get you mixed up in this disaster? You deserve better, but you'll have to get there on your own. I'm not who you think I am. We've only known each other for two days. I've known Yesh almost all my life.'

'But he doesn't care about you! All he cares about is himself and he doesn't care about *that* enough to live. He's not worth saving!' Flea found he was crying.

'I'm sorry, Flea. There's so much about me that you don't understand. I have to see it through.'

'That's it? You're just going to drop me?'

Jude gave a sigh. 'Look, if we both get through this, meet me at the tree outside the City walls by the dump.'

'When?'

'Later. As soon as you can.'

'You really mean it?'

'I surely do.' But he was looking at Yesh as he spoke.

Then, all around, Flea heard the sound of men breaking through undergrowth. Orders were shouted.

Someone shouted 'RUN', but Flea was held. He thought it was Jude, but Jude was sprinting from the clearing, a man in a white robe following him. Flea wriggled free and threw himself at Jude's pursuer, hanging on to his robe, wrapping himself in it until the man had to shrug it off. He crashed through the cordon of soldiers wearing only his loincloth and Flea was left with Yesh in the clearing, holding the torn robe, surrounded by glittering spear points.

Yesh stood still, waiting patiently, and Flea felt something freeze inside him. He was cold. He was hard. He would not yield.

'Well, well, well,' the Results Man said, brushing aside a low olive branch and stepping into the ring of soldiers. 'What have we got here? All the others have run away and only two are left. Who is going to betray you now, Yeshua?'

Flea jerked himself free so he could point at Yesh. 'This is the man you want,' he said. 'And he deserves all you're going to give him.'

'Thank you, Flea,' Yesh said. 'You're the only person here with the guts to do this incredibly simple thing. You were the only one prepared to help me.'

the day

# 37

Flea was carried back from the Pleasure Gardens slung over a soldier's back, a shoulder beating time in his gut. Yesh, glimpsed behind him, was a jogged blur surrounded by Imps.

They stopped on the bridge. Flea could hear the chatter of the Black River below. Yesh's face was puffy and swollen – hitting prisoners around the face was a standard Roman greeting. The followers were nowhere to be seen and Flea hoped they were rotting in hell. The Imps breathed and stamped like horses.

The Results Man was giving orders. 'I want a vanguard clearing the streets. Any trouble, kill it. Wake up the governor. It's been arranged.'

'What about this one?' The soldier slipped Flea off his shoulder and held him efficiently by the hair.

'Keep him close. I want him to see the results of his actions. It's important for his moral development.' The Results Man turned his attention to Yesh, whose head was down, chest heaving. 'So, shall we talk before we enter the City?'

Yesh did not look up.

'Am I being too polite?'

'He won't say anything,' Flea said. 'It's no use. You might as well –'

'Shut up. This is where you entered the City in triumph, is it not? This is where the plan started, so to speak. But do you have the courage to see it through?'

Yesh lifted his head and seemed to be trying to read the Results Man's smiling face.

'Oh yes. I know you have a secret. I know you have something up your sleeve like every half-decent trickster and I intend to find it out. My guess is that by the end of tonight you'll be singing like a little bird. You people. You arrogant little people. It's not enough to think you can defy Rome. You think you can use us. But here's the thing: you're in my power now. You don't use me. I use you.'

They marched on through the choked streets. Someone shouted that the Imps had the magician and the crowd swelled. The soldiers pushed down into the Lower City, then up the narrow, zigzagging streets on the other side. Flea had a sense that they were all on display and tried to imagine himself anywhere else. They would stop. The soldier would put him down. He'd worm his way down back alleys, get out of the City and find Jude waiting by the tree. They'd escape to that place the Results Man had told him about – the green place where blue people lived – and if the Romans really were there, he'd go further and further and further and further because there must be a place where they could be free.

He blinked and shook his head. Through a blur of pain he saw the skinny girl flitting in and out of the crowd as she kept pace with them. Hadn't she warned him? Hadn't she told him to be careful? Why hadn't he listened to her?

In the Upper City the marble buildings glowed like bones. They were outside the high priest's palace and the Imps were beating on the door with their sword hilts. When it opened a crack, they bullied their way into the courtyard and turned to stop the crowd following them.

A shutter banged open above them and a man stuck his head out of a window. 'What is it? What's going on?'

'Delivering a blasphemer to the high priest,' the Results Man called back. 'We could have taken him to the Temple, but it's late and we thought we'd save him the trouble of getting there. Who am I talking to?'

'One of the high priest's secretaries. You say you have a blasphemer? Have you any idea of the time, or what sort of schedule the high priest has tomorrow? It's the Passover Feast – the busiest day of the year.'

'Like I said, we're here to save him trouble, which he's brought down on his own head. This man offered a direct challenge to your rule and you did nothing. He threatened to rouse the people, turn the social order upside down, and tear down your Temple. That's sedition, revolution and sorcery. You may not care about small matters like that, but we do.'

'But the high priest can't decide on it alone. He needs the council, and the council –'

'You're stalling,' the Results Man interrupted. 'Get him now.'

'You're taking the law into your own hands.'

'Just do it.'

The secretary blinked, withdrew his head and closed the shutters. Flea looked across to Yesh and shook his head desperately. Yesh looked back at him through bruised eyes. His teeth were bloody and his lips were swollen, but he smiled.

Then a door opened and they were let into a long, vaulted room.

The high priest was small and clever-looking. There were creases on his cheek from his pillow, but his eyes looked sharp under heavy eyebrows. He waved away a fussing priest who trying to straighten his heavy robe.

'The governor will hear of this,' was the first thing he snapped. 'You may be head of his secret police, but even you have exceeded your remit tonight. Where are the lights? Get me light and then throw them out.'

'The governor has been informed,' the Results Man said evenly. 'He is fully aware of the situation, but I just thought I would stop off here first.'

Now the secretary arrived, holding a candle. He stooped to whisper in the high priest's ear. The older man looked down, then asked the Results Man suddenly, 'Why should I do anything?' Flame twisted in his eyes.

'If you spent less time purifying yourself and burning

animals you'd know the streets are buzzing with talk of an uprising that you have done nothing to prevent. This man wants a revolution.'

The high priest's eyes slid away from the Results Man and rested on Yesh.

'What have you got to say for yourself?' he snapped.

Just as he had done in the Temple when confronted by the priest, and just had he had done on the bridge when challenged by the Results Man, Yesh looked down and said nothing.

*He does that when he's planning*, Flea thought. He closed his eyes and wondered what he had started.

One by one, more sleepy priests wearing rich, hastily thrown-on robes had joined them. They now stood in a huddle at one end of the room. The soldiers had been sent out when two of the new arrivals made a fuss about them being impure. Flea began to shiver.

Eventually the priests finished their conference and formed a rough semicircle. One stepped forward to address Yesh. The young priest towered over him and Yesh's body seemed to fold itself around his narrow chest. He kept his eyes lowered.

'You are Yeshua Ben Yusuf and you have been accused by this agent of the Imperium of blasphemy.'

When Yesh remained silent, the priest shrugged and turned to the Results Man. 'We know things he's claimed, and to be honest, it's no worse than the sort of nonsense spouted by any of these northern prophets. They all offer change, a better life, wine with every meal and an end to poverty and disease. But they're like fireflies. They flit about and then they're gone. This one's no different.'

'Even though he has claimed to be able to throw down the Temple . . .'

'And build it up again. I know. Does it look like he can? I ask you.'

'He claims to be the Chosen One: a king in exile come to claim his throne in the holy City.'

'Again, look at him. A half-starved tramp with bloody toes. I'm sorry, but if you want us to take him and you seriously, then you'll have to do a lot better than this. We had a perfectly viable containment plan in place, which you have ruined. I suggest you let us take things from here, and the next time you wake up the high priest in the middle of the night, please have a better reason.' He gave a patronising smile as he turned. 'Oh, and I'm sure you know this, but traditionally Temple and Imperium work together to avoid trouble in the run-up to the Feast. It's quite a good system.'

He turned to leave and the Results Man said, 'Wait,' in a voice as a flat and cold as a skinning knife. 'You'll just leave things like this? You'll do nothing?'

Flea felt himself tense. The young priest said, 'That is the view of the council.'

'Then you will have no problems handing this minor troublemaker over to us for a quick little trial?' the Results Man said. 'After all, if such an eminent council can find no guilt, what could anyone else find? No risk of trouble if we find him innocent. Just a tiny embarrassment for Rome.'

The young priest started to bluster. 'I don't think I quite meant . . .'

'You meant you thought you could get out of bed, outwit the Imperium then hop back into it so you'd be fresh to stuff your face at tomorrow's Feast. Not so, I'm afraid. You see, we value order, and this man has said he wants the lowest in society to be elevated to the highest. It may be my suspicious mind, but I think that also means the highest are suddenly in the position of the lowest. Now, let's paint a picture. You out on the street and the lowest slave in the City is running the Temple. More importantly for us, it means this little brat –' he pointed at Flea – 'will be sitting in the governor's palace while the governor works in the tanneries. No. This will not do. If the Temple does not see the threat or is too scared to act, the Imperium must. We're off to the governor's palace and if you want to have any say in proceedings I suggest that you come too.'

'You don't think that will happen . . .'

'Rebellion starts in the heart. We must stop the uprising or stop a lot of hearts.'

'But, for better or worse, this man has a considerable

following,' the priest said. 'Put him in front of the governor and the mob will go mad. It's a disaster waiting to happen.'

'At last we get to the truth,' the Results Man said. 'Now you admit he has a following, but have grown so fat and lazy up on your rock that you think this little problem will go away if you do nothing.'

'We had a plan in place . . .' the young priest repeated. 'We were handling it.'

'You were not.' Again, Flea was pushed forwards and held in full view of the priests. 'Your plan, as you call it, was undone by this . . . beggar thing and has been a disaster from day one. I repeat: Yeshua is calling for revolution. Yet again the Imperium must stand as the bulwark between order and chaos. Idiots.'

The Results Man spat out the final word and stalked away.

# 38

The governor's palace was only a hundred paces from the high priest's.

They were expected. Flaring torches painted fire and darkness on marble walls. A mob had been gathered. It seethed behind a hedge of soldiers, being angry. In front of it a clear space had been left, then there were wide, even steps and the balcony of the palace.

Flea was released – there was nowhere for him to run and he pushed through into the soldiers so he could see Yesh waiting at the foot of the steps. Yeshua's eyes were closed and he rocked slowly from foot to foot. Flea felt exposed. He didn't want Yesh to see him. He couldn't face his steady smile again. He pushed back though the soldiers and suddenly was face to face with the skinny girl.

'How did you get in here?' he hissed. She didn't answer immediately, but beckoned to him and they pushed through the crowd to a mounting block by the wall. They stood on it, out of the crush and out of the way.

'I squeezed behind the guards when the crowds outside started pushing. No one ever sees me,' the girl whispered.

Flea sized her up. She was stick thin and her face had shadows where there shouldn't be, but she didn't look starved. What's more, she must have crossed the City today and starving people couldn't do that. Her eyes were big and under them her face narrowed to a small chin. Her hair was close-cropped where his was long and matted. That was partly why she looked so vulnerable.

'Have a good look, won't you,' she said when she noticed him staring.

'Why are you following me?' Flea asked.

'Following you? I'm following the action. I warned you to stay away.'

'You thought *this* would happen?'

She looked around. 'I was just trying to save you from a beating from the Temple Police.'

'But why?'

'I hate cruelty to dumb animals.'

Flea couldn't even think of a retort. 'Dumb animal is just about right,' he said. 'Everything's my fault. I messed everything up.'

'I tried to warn you.' The girl's mouth closed primly.

'You never told me the world was about to end!' Flea snapped back. 'You didn't tell me the Romans were involved.'

The girl stared him down. 'You just ran away. From me. Whenever I tried to help you.'

Flea flushed hot. He looked into the black sky. It had started to snow again, flakes swirled in the torchlight then melted with a hiss. He shivered. Instead of the hard brilliance of stars, there was shifting chaos. A singed moth patted his feet and spiralled off.

The girl exhaled. 'Look, don't go all floppy,' she said. 'Truth is, no one knew. I hang out the other side of the Temple, near the kitchens? Sometimes they let me sweep the floors and move the rubbish in the dining hall. You hear all sorts of stuff, if you listen. Anyway, the other day, the Temple Police were going on about this magician who was coming to town and how they wanted to stop something happening. I never heard what. But that's why I warned you.'

'But the Temple was trying to do the right thing and I stopped them,' Flea said. 'The priests thought that if people ignored Yesh, then no one would listen to him. When the Imps arrested him, that's when it would all kick off. But get this: Yesh wanted to be arrested.'

'So he wanted it. So then it wasn't your fault,' the girl said.

'What's it to you? Flea asked. 'I mean . . .'

But he couldn't finish because at that moment the governor of the City, the Roman in charge of them all, appeared on the balcony of his palace. He was wearing a purple cloak. His thinning hair was pushed forwards on his forehead and you could see the grey stubble on his fat cheeks.

With barely a look at the crowd, the governor nodded and the trial began. A succession of men Flea had never seen told the governor that Yeshua wanted a revolution, to change the world, change everything. He would pull down the Temple and throw out the Romans and rule as king.

After the evidence had been heard, the governor turned to Yeshua. 'Well,' he asked. 'What have you got to say in your defence?'

As before, Yeshua said nothing.

More witnesses stepped up, their words tumbling from their mouths like the harsh clink of coins dropping. If Yeshua was innocent, why didn't he defend himself? This was more than surliness, this was more than arrogance; this was rebellion. By refusing to answer, Yeshua was defying the Imperium itself.

The governor himself stayed still, his eyes hooded, but darting to left and right. Outside the palace, shouting rose and fell like a weak wind. Inside, the crowd followed instructions on when to cheer or scream abuse.

Then at last even the governor had had enough.

He stood to cheers from the crowd. When he spoke, he had to shout and Flea only heard fragments of what he said.

'Should . . . him go? . . . Punish him? Temple wants . . . blasphemy . . . Choose . . . Yeshua or Barabbas?'

The governor clapped his hands and another man was brought out. He was stooped and filthy with matted hair, and a shocked gasp went up from the crowd. *Abbas Barabbas, the King of Thieves! He stole from the rich! He gave to the poor! He fed the starving! He disappeared a year ago and everyone said the Romans had murdered him. Now here he is, like he has risen from the dead!*

Abbas clasped his hands above his head and shook them. He looked drugged. More cheers. The governor pointed to Yesh. The crowd started to hiss. He pointed to Abbas. Cheers.

Flea could not bear to look. The Romans had planned this. Yesh had planned this. The crowd knew what to do. Everything was a link in a chain and the chain was dragging Yesh to his death. How could anyone fight this?

The governor shrugged and the crowd began to surge. The skinny girl caught hold of Flea.

'Now's your chance to get away!' she said. 'No one can stop you.'

'But what about Yesh?'

The girl grabbed him by the arm. 'He's finished. Come away with me now. Please. Save yourself. You can do it.'

Flea didn't budge. 'It's no use. You don't understand. I told the Romans where Yesh was tonight. Then I helped them arrest him. If he dies, it's my fault.'

'Then he got what he wanted! Come on.'

Now from their vantage point Flea could see the Results Man pushing through the crowd towards him.

He pulled the girl close so she could hear what he said without the Results Man seeing. 'I can't. I really can't. I'm meant to be meeting one of Yesh's followers by that old tree by the dump tonight. Can you go there instead of me? Can you tell him I'm really sorry that . . . Can you just tell him I'm sorry. Can you do that? Please?'

'But why don't you?'

'Like I said, I just can't,' he said, seeing the hurt and disappointment in her eyes as she realised that he was pushing her away again.

# 39

Yesh was dragged into the street. Scuffles broke out – the crowd outside was less compliant than the hand-picked stooges inside and some were outraged that Abbas had been released. At an order, the Romans started smashing their spear shafts into the ground to clear the street before them. Any feet caught under them would be broken. Any person who fell would get crushed.

The Results Man looked as unconcerned as if he were going for a stroll through the market. He peered from side to side, his head pecking the air, his mouth curled up in his idiot smile. Every now and again he looked down at Flea and opened his eyes wide, as if he were saying, *Look at this, and look at this. Isn't it* exciting. *Isn't it* interesting.

Flea couldn't take it any longer. 'Why?' he said. 'Why do you want Yeshua to die? Why go to all this trouble?'

'You mean, if we wanted him dead why didn't we just strangle him quietly up there in the Pleasure Gardens? Him and all his followers?'

'I suppose.'

The Results Man smiled a humourless smile. 'Big question. Let's just say that Rome wants to make sure justice is seen to be done.'

'But if it's going to make trouble . . . I mean, it's not too late. You could just sort of lose him. I could find somewhere to hide him. People would forget soon enough. And anyway, you're just doing what he wants; surely you don't want that.'

'Oh, Flea. How much you have to learn,' sighed the Results Man. 'Do you think I have a heart of stone? Justice should be hard, but never cruel. Yeshua wants to die. He wants a great send-off. Who am I deny him that?'

'Let me talk to him,' Flea said. 'Please. He thought I was special. He said so. If I could get him to change his mind, then you wouldn't be doing what he wants and –'

'I could hug you,' the Results Man said, stopping suddenly in his tracks. 'You people could start an argument with a wall. I tell you what, Flea – if you can persuade Yeshua to beg me for his life, then yes, I will let him go free.'

'What?' Flea could hardly believe his ears.

'If Yeshua asks nicely, I will spare him his life. Go on. Ask.'

The Results Man shooed Flea along the procession and ordered the soldiers around Yeshua to let him talk to Flea, who was clearly a superior young man and one they could all learn from. The Imps had put a halter round Yesh's neck and were leading him like a donkey. His feet were dragging and his head was bowed.

But Flea could whisper in his ear. He was almost choked with hope.

'Yeshua, listen. I've done it. I've got the Results Man to agree. If you ask him for your life, he'll go along with it. He promised. He'll let you go free. I should never have betrayed you in the Gardens. I know it's all my fault. Please,' he wheedled cleverly. 'Don't make me feel so bad. I'm so sorry.'

For an instant there was life in Yesh's eyes: a gleam of warmth, a glimmer of knowing. He licked his lips, swallowed. 'You helped me, Flea. You did what you thought was right.'

'But it was wrong. I see that now. Please. It's your last chance.'

Another gleam, and this time the bruised lips pulled back in a sort of smile.

'Did you know that Solomon wrote about you? *For the king has come to seek a flea, as one who hunts a partridge in the mountains*. I looked for you, Flea. I found you. You have played your part in the prophecy. Now you must accept it.'

Flea realised he was getting nowhere. 'I don't want to be part of a prophecy. Please. PLEASE.'

But Yesh's face had shut down and Flea knew he would get no more out of him.

*Prophecy*, Flea thought. *What do I know about the prophecy?* But his exhausted brain would not give him the answer, and the Results Man did not help.

He beckoned Flea to him and asked what Yesh had

said. When Flea told him he was part of a prophecy, the Results Man barked out a laugh.

'Do you really think Yeshua can challenge us? Do you really think a threat could come from the gods of this pitiful dung heap in a forgotten corner of our Empire? Flea, little Flea, we make our own gods. We know Yeshua thinks that if we will kill him, his magic will be all the stronger. We know that and we laugh, because that is the very thing that interests us. His power. We have heard he can do a certain thing that interests the Imperium very much, and we intend to find out how this thing works.'

'What?' Flea said. 'A trick?'

'We think it is more than a trick. We think this is the big thing that explains how a mouthy conjuror with twelve tramps for followers thinks he can change the world.'

'What is it?'

'I'll give you a clue. It's not about him being the Chosen One. It's all about *how* he becomes Chosen One.'

Flea looked away and tried to think.

*A prophecy. A change. A secret. What's the secret?* Flea beat his brains trying to work it out as the procession moved from the governor's palace to the Fortress.

# 40

In the courtyard of the Fortress the soldiers wrapped the branches of a thorn bush, spikes as long as a dog's tooth, around Yesh's head and asked him who was the governor now.

Flea was still thinking about secrets and prophecies. He was thinking as they tied Yesh by the wrists to the post in the middle of the yard and the Results Man knelt by his head and whispered in his ear.

He was thinking as the whip sang flesh and blood from Yesh's back so that it pattered on to the flagstones like rain.

He was thinking while the Results Man lost patience, took a handful of Yesh's hair, yanked his head back and hissed in his ear, 'Well? Now will you tell me? Now you must tell me!'

He was thinking as the guards exchanged looks, shrugged and winced.

And Flea also waited. He waited for Yeshua to talk. And when he didn't, Flea waited for heavens to open, for the people to rise and for the Temple to fall. But nothing happened like that. The music of hissing whip and splitting flesh hurt his head and clogged his ears, and Yesh's silence grew huge and squeezed out all other thoughts, all ideas, and just left the knowledge of his pain.

Then Flea saw Shim.

He was standing in the shadows at the back of the courtyard, but the sudden flare of a nearby torch lit up his weak, handsome face. It had lines that had not been there the day before and he was looking around as if nothing quite made sense.

Flea made his way towards him. 'Satisfied now?' he sneered. His voice felt harsh. 'Come to check the job's been done?'

'I . . .' Shim's mouth opened and he tried to lick his lips. 'That's not . . . why I . . . came here.' A particularly brutal snap of the whip made him wince. 'Is it quite necessary . . .?'

'No!' Flea said. 'It's not necessary. It's not necessary at all. That's what Jude was trying to show you.'

Shim pursed his lips. 'Jude didn't understand what was at stake. Jude didn't understand what . . . was needed.'

'Jude loved Yesh and wanted this not to happen. Tell me what you want to happen. Tell me what the secret is.'

'Secret?'

'That's what's happening here. The Romans think Yesh has a power and they're trying to whip it out of him. Jude knew that. Jude wanted to stop it.'

'Jude did not understand greatness. Where is Jude now? At least I've come to bear witness. To accept what we have done. Yesh will die outside the City. He will be sacrificed by strangers out in the world. Now the whole world is his Temple. To show how proud –'

That was too much for Flea. 'Proud! You're proud of this? Hey!' he called out. 'This is one of Yeshua's followers! He loved Yesh so much he wanted this to happen! Here! This one here!'

Shim paled as people turned to look at him. He shook his head and backed away, hands out. 'Don't listen to that brat! What would I be doing here if I was one of his followers?'

'He feels guilty,' Flea shouted. 'That's why he's here!'

'I don't know anything.'

The damage done, Flea ran to Yesh. Guards tried to stop him, but the Results Man waved him through. His face was spattered with blood and he looked tense. 'Will he talk to you? He won't . . . He won't talk to me! He just won't TALK!' The word exploded from his mouth.

Yesh had collapsed now, held up only by his wrists, which were tied to the whipping post. Strips of his back were hanging down like saddle straps. His face was a colour beyond white, beyond anything. He smelled like a butcher's block.

Flea knelt.

'Tell him your secret,' he said. 'Please! You can't have meant this to happen. Not like this! Tell him and he'll let you go. Your back will get better. You could heal it yourself, or tell someone else how to.'

When Yeshua opened his eyes, he looked scared.

'Don't . . .' He licked his cracked lips.

'Don't what?'

'Tempt me.' He tried to swallow. 'Don't leave me.'

The Results Man was there immediately. 'What did he say? I saw his lips move.' He worried at one of his nails. They were bitten down to the quick.

'He asked me not to tempt him. Then he asked me to stay.' Flea looked into the Results Man's eyes. They looked strained and his mouth was pulled into an odd shape. 'You thought he'd crack by now,' he said.

'I don't understand it. Why hasn't he done something? He's meant to have powers. That's meant to be the point. I push him and I push and . . . he tells me.'

A soldier, crested, cloaked, clean-shaven, muscled his way through the crowd. 'Governor wants his report.'

'Not yet. We're not ready.'

'Governor was led to understand that you'd have something by now.'

'Well I don't. Yet.'

'*Yet* isn't good enough. He's to be executed – that's the sentence and it's got to be done now if he's going to die in time.'

'In time for what?' The Results Man looked panicked.

'This Feast means he has to be dead by midday and in the ground before sunset, so local customs can be properly respected. That means commencing the execution now and you reporting your findings to the governor.'

'Rome can't be worried about local customs. Do you know what's at stake?'

'Tell it to the governor. You're coming with me.' The soldier's hand strayed towards his sword hilt.

The Results Man turned to Flea. 'Stay with him. If you want your friends to live, you'd better tell me what happens. What he says as he dies. You're my witness. Make this mess mean something.'

Flea looked up.

Dawn.

The sky was lemon-juice grey streaked with pomegranate red.

It matched Yesh's skin.

The whole sky was Yesh's skin.

His body was a temple as high as the sky and as broad as the world.

# 41

On the top of the Skull, a row of square holes had been chiselled into the rock in front of a rickety guardhouse. A stack of timbers stood nearby. Nailings usually took place at sunup and the soldiers who did it were always drunk.

Crosses didn't kill people. They let people kill themselves with the most pain and the least supervision. They were economical. The upright of a cross was just tall enough to hold the victim's feet off the ground, the crosspiece just wide enough to spread his arms, the wood just thick enough to take three huge nails, one for the feet and two for the wrists.

Try to reduce the pressure on your wrists by pushing upwards and your feet pressed down on the nail that went through them. Relax the knees and the nails in your wrists tore flesh and tendons and ground on the bones. As your knees weakened, you slumped further and further down so your arms rose in a V-shape and squeezed the air from your lungs.

In the end, at the end, it wasn't the cross that killed you. It was your weight as the earth called your body home.

Two other men were due to die that day. They dropped their beams at the top of hill, fetched the uprights from a stack behind the shed, then dropped the beam into a notch and watched the soldiers lash it into the place. The first of them was wrestled to the ground and his right wrist was nailed to the crosspiece, then his left wrist; then his legs were held crossed at the ankles and a single nail was hammered through them. He resisted sluggishly – relatives had bribed the Imps to drug his last meal with poppy – but he began to wail as the soldiers lifted the cross and screamed when its foot slammed into the square hole cut into the ground and held him vertical. The second man begged the soldiers to knock him out then screamed all the way through the process.

Flea closed his eyes when it was Yesh's turn and blessed him for his silence.

He found a boulder and huddled behind it, holding his knees and rocking from side to side. He was hollow and numb, as if he had no feelings left. The world was swirling round him. He wanted to join it, get whisked away like a snowflake, but he was too tired and too weak. Behind him he could hear the dying men groan, but it meant nothing to him. Nothing at all.

He was woken by women's voices. They came from below. He screwed his eyes tight shut and waited for them to reach the top of the hill. They fell silent, then one of them sobbed, another moaned and a third began shouting at the guards.

Flea continued to feel detached from it all until hands grabbed him and shook him.

'The child's in shock, Mari. Leave him be.'

'But the guard said he came here with Yeshua. He must have seen. He must know what happened.'

'He's an idiot. Look, he's drooling.'

Flea opened his eyes. Every colour but grey had fled. The sky was grey, the western hills were grey, the City was grey, the stony hill was grey.

He looked at the person who had lifted him. A woman, tall and beautiful, with tawny hair, full lips and big grey eyes. He wiped the dribble from his chin and giggled. The woman dropped him as if he were toxic.

He got to his feet, swayed and said, 'I apologise.' For some reason he felt drunk, but that was better than feeling nothing. With the tall woman was another with the weather-beaten face of a villager, a frizzy fringe escaping from her headscarf. Behind her was an older woman with a wrinkled face, who was gazing at Flea with deep-set eyes that seemed familiar. They were the same as Yesh's, he realised. The old woman must be Yesh's mother. That woke him up.

Flea tried to stand up straight and met the eyes of the beautiful woman who apparently didn't like him.

'Go on, say it,' she snapped. 'If he's a magician, why can't he magic himself off the cross?' She looked around. 'And where are the others? Where are his friends? His followers? Where's his brother?'

'Only Jude was there when Imps got him. The others must've run away when they heard the soldiers.' Flea told her.

She gave him a sharp look. 'You were there?'

'I'm a friend of Jude. We were trying to stop this.'

'And where is Jude? He said we were all going to meet up! He promised us. We thought we'd be eating with Yesh tonight. It's the Great Feast. Families should be together.'

'You're his family?'

'This is his mother. Matta and I . . . we're friends.' She

nodded to the woman with the weather-beaten face.

The crosses were so low and Mari was so tall that her head was on the same level as Yesh's. His head was down on his chest and the circlet of thorns had slipped down across one eye, but the other was open. Flea could not imagine anybody suffering that damage and living. He couldn't imagine anybody suffering that much damage at all.

Matta reached out a hand to stroke his cheek, but jerked it back as the guard shouted a warning.

The guard marched over, grabbed Yesh's cheeks to force his mouth open and peered inside. 'I said, no touching. You'd be surprised what people do – try and slip 'em all kinds of poison. Mind you, this one won't last long and, between you and me, we've been told to finish 'em off early today so the . . . er, correct procedures can be undertaken before your holy day.'

'Correct procedures?' Mari asked.

'Burial and such like before your rest day. It's a respect thing.'

'You call this respect?' Mari's voice would have frozen Temple oil.

The guard pursed his lips. 'Look, lady, I don't know what it's called. I just follow orders and I know that we have to tiptoe around your people's rules at the present time to avoid so much as a whiff of trouble. I thought it was doing you a favour, but if you don't appreciate it, well, that's as much as I've come to expect.'

He sniffed and stumped off. Mari clasped her head and it looked to Flea like she was screaming silently until she managed to force out the words, 'How could they? How could they? We don't even know where to bury him. How did it end like this? He was going to shine for all of us. He was our hope.'

Flea looked at her ravaged face and suddenly, two thoughts fitted together like two hands meeting.

'He thinks his death is your hope.' The simple words seemed to burn away the puzzlement and confusion of the night before so that more of a new truth was revealed. No, not new. It had always been there, it was just that Flea had not been able to see it. 'It wasn't just that he wanted to die. He thought –'

'What? He *wanted* to die?' Mari looked at Flea as if he had slapped her.

'He set it all up. I even know where his tomb is. It was all arranged. Every detail.'

And now the fog of confusion had been burned away the truth had shape. It was all so clear that Flea could walk around it, see it, feel its shape and horror.

'Arranged?' Mari said again.

Flea spoke slowly. 'Yesh wants to change the world. He thinks he needs to die to make that happen, but we've got to stop it. The Romans know what's going on. They think they can borrow his power . . . I don't know how, but I just know they want a bit of it. He can't die. He mustn't die!'

'Are you insane?' Mari said. 'Of course he mustn't die.'

'No, no! He wants to die and the Romans want him to die and his followers want him to die, but he mustn't, because if he does he thinks something's going to happen.'

'What?'

'There's going to be a change. The world is going to end. It's the prophecy the old man told me. It's –'

'QUIET!' The cry came from Matta. 'He's trying to talk! The Master is talking!'

They crowded round the cross, hands behind their backs so the guard could not object. Yesh had managed to lift his head. His eyes, black and soft as plums, moved from side to side until they came to rest on Flea. His lips moved. 'Find Jude. Tell him I'm . . . sorry. Tell the others they must forgive him. He was . . . part of the story.'

Memories from the night before, sharp and dark and bitter, suddenly rushed into Flea's mind and he was overcome with rage. 'He was right!' he shouted. 'Don't you understand? He was right and you were wrong! I wish I hadn't met you. I wish you'd left us alone because things weren't great then, BUT THEY WEREN'T AS BAD AS THIS!'

Yeshua's back arched as if he were trying to tear himself off the cross, but all he did was open the wounds in his wrists and ankles. Blood began to drip and his head collapsed back on to this chest.

Then Flea felt his anger leave as suddenly as it had arrived. 'I'm sorry,' he said. 'I didn't mean . . . Please don't die. Please, don't use your power to change anything. Use it to live. Cure yourself. I'm begging you. Please.'

He got his fingers round the square head of the nail that pierced Yesh's ankles and tried to pull it free.

'Oi. Get away from that prisoner!' The guard grabbed a short stabbing spear and waddled towards them. 'It's time, anyway.'

'Please. Please,' Flea begged Yeshua. 'You don't understand. You don't see.' He felt tearful and hated it, because now more than ever he needed to explain, but his throat felt blocked and his eyes felt blind. Hands took him and held him.

'Oh child,' Mari said. Flea struggled, but was held against the softness of her breasts. She smelled of musk and cinnamon. 'Hush,' she said. 'Hush. Hush. Don't look. Don't listen. He's killing the others. We'll get through it.'

He heard the sob start inside her and was happy to give up and count down the seconds in the drumming of her heart. If the end of the world was coming, perhaps it was better if the others did not know. Yes, that was it. No one would know up here, at the centre of all things, what was going to happen, and that was right and proper. He would die with the truth.

Flea heard the guard say, ''Scuse us, ladies. It's a

kindness, really. Oh, as you were, this one's gone. Yup. He's dead. Nice timing.'

Flea closed his eyes and waited for the world to end.

And waited.

And waited.

And waited.

Until the truth dawned.

He pushed himself away and looked around.

'We're still here!' he shouted. 'The wind's still blowing. The ground . . .' He jumped and down. 'It's still here.' He pinched his cheek, he slapped his leg, he wheeled his arms until his hands got pins and needles and he jumped up and down a few times.

'Child. CHILD!'

If Matta hadn't grabbed him he would have floated away. Flea felt more alive than he had ever felt before and life was weightless. Life was like the wind. Life was like wings. 'The old man was wrong. He said if Yesh died the world would end, but he was wrong. The world hasn't ended! He's dead! Yesh is dead, but we're still alive!'

Matta slapped him. 'Stop it, child. Stop it!'

'But . . .'

She shook him and he saw where he was.

'Child, child. Come back to us.'

Flea saw the dead people. He saw the living. Something tore inside him. The world was grey again.

'I thought . . .' he began.

'Don't think. You think too much. Don't talk. You talk too much. Don't move, either. I don't know what you saw last night, but it's turned your mind. There is blood on your face and I don't think it's yours.'

Flea felt his skin. The flecks of blood and dried flesh were rough. *When Yesh was being whipped* . . . He rubbed them away and shook his head. He thought the tears in Matta's eyes might even be for him. These were nice people. If you cried, they got sad.

'I'm sorry,' he said. 'I think I must be a bit mad.'

'Child, you have to stop running. What were you talking about? What was all this about the world ending?'

'It was the prophecy,' Flea said. 'Yesh thought he was the Chosen One and the Chosen One had to die. Then when he died, the world would end. But it didn't, did it? The Results Man was wrong. They were all wrong. Everything's back as it should be.'

'Except a good man is dead,' Mari said. 'My friend is dead. What good can come of that?'

# 42

Feast Day Rules or not, the women were bargaining with a man who might willing be carry Yesh's body off the hill. Flea felt there was no need to find Jude just now; now the world was not ending, he felt he had all the time in it. He was also sure the skinny girl would have passed the message on to Jude so he could wait too, couldn't he?

And he couldn't bring himself to go into the City even though he knew the Results Man was waiting for his report on Yesh's death. Now he was outside the City and looking in, the place seemed terrifying. The houses were piled high behind the walls like a heap of skulls, their black windows empty eyes. He remembered the mob that had chased him and Crouch. He thought of the Temple Police. He thought of the other gangs, his own gang . . . what was there for him?

To delay his return, and rather hoping the women might decide to adopt him, he showed them the tomb that Shim had visited. He sat on the cliffs above it close to the place the Results Man had netted him, while they argued with the caretaker, who seemed reluctant to let them open it. The sky grew even darker. The City glowed from countless fires as families gathered for the evening's Feast. Flea could smell the smoke. Last year he had gorged himself on Passover leftovers until he thought his guts would burst. He'd even found wine and that had been good too. This year couldn't have been more different. Matta had brought food – hard bread, soft cheese, onions – but, neither she nor Mari wanted any and gave it to Flea.

Flea did not know how he felt. It was as if watching Yesh being broken had pulled his own body apart. His hands were not quite connected to his arms and his arms not quite connected to his shoulders. The bread and cheese sat in his stomach like shopping in a bag.

Then the women started mourning in earnest and for some reason that was more than Flea could bear. He followed a track that led round the City walls to the north, passing the Black Valley Bridge on his left. His feet pushed through the dry palm branches that had waved so happily when Yesh rode into the City on his donkey and the dry rustling followed him like a ghost. He whipped round. Had a shadow flitted into the deeper shade where the crossing places opened out?

'Who's there?'

No one and no thing. The only movement was the clouds and the only sound was the river.

An echo, then. Just an echo. No wonder he was jumpy.

Up against the City walls Flea began to feel better. The wind was doing something useful by tearing the clouds to shreds so that he could see by the light of the moon.

Low in the sky as it filled with light, it was a couple of days off full. When Flea looked up and saw how it seemed that the walls were toppling he just smiled to himself because he knew they weren't. They were safe, solid and real; he could rub his hand across the stone and feel its comforting roughness. And wait a minute, if he followed them round to the left, in no time at all he would be at the tree by the City dump where Jude was waiting for him.

He laughed when he stubbed his toe and he laughed when he scratched himself on a thorn bush and again when he saw the dark figure under the tree. Jude was there, as he had promised!

Flea's heart lifted and he punched the air in triumph. He'd made it!

The tree leant over the valley, roots wedged under the walls, branches fingering the air. Jude standing under the tree, very still and upright.

Flea only just managed to stop himself calling out. His heart began to thump nervously. First thing, grovel. Second thing, explain. Third thing, do whatever Jude said and stick to it this time.

Almost there now. Close enough to hiss, 'Jude?'

Jude didn't answer. He just turned towards Flea slowly then turned away again, his head tilted to one side rather quizzically.

Flea raised his voice a little. 'Jude? JUDE?'

Still no answer. But when had an adult ever given him an answer to anything? When had anyone?

An owl called, another answered it, the wind panted hard and Flea watched Jude turn again. Towards him and away. Towards him and away. A horrid, easy, smooth motion.

The tree hung over a void. Could Jude be floating? Was this another of his brilliant tricks?

Flea forced himself to move close, then closer still, and

as he did so horror bunched in his throat. He saw the rope, and then he saw the kink in Jude's neck.

Jude was hanging, not floating.

And not waiting for him.

Dead.

# 43

The world rushed away from Flea without getting smaller, then knocked him over as it rushed back. His face hit the earth. It crinkled between his teeth. He was dismantled by this final, ghastly blow.

For a while he lay still. He felt he was floating in a world of nothingness. Nothingness that reached into his body and mind, curled nothing tendrils around every bit of him until there was nothing inside him, nothing outside him. He was not dust. He was the nothing between the dust.

After a while he pushed himself up and forced himself to look properly. Jude continued his patient revolutions, turning his face towards him and away. Flea came back to the world. Shock gave way to sickness, sickness to rasping grief, grief to a sudden, surprising swoop of anger.

Who had done this? Who could have done it *now*, when it was all meant to be over?

Flea became aware of voices and the crunch of feet on gravel. He stood and looked for a place to hide, because the last thing he wanted was to be found by anyone here.

He knew what it would mean. First the questions. *So what's a brat like you doing next to a dead body? Outside the walls after lockdown – what are you playing at? Want us to turn you in? Do you? Do you?* Then the roughing up . . .

His feet loosened a rock that went crashing down the valley side. A voice called out and then Flea was running – because that's what he always did – and not thinking – ditto.

He jumped a bush, nearly fell where the path kinked round a boulder, and saw the steaming mound of the City dump blocking his way, too steep and too soft to climb. If he couldn't go up . . .

He skidded downwards, bounced on to a goat track and doubled back towards the bridge. More shouts from above. He chucked a rock far down into the valley, hoping to misdirect them. When the big, dark silhouette of the Temple sewer pipe jutted out in front of him, he stopped. The mouth was protected by iron bars, but he thought he could wriggle through.

What stopped him was the thought of rats.

Behind him he heard the pursuit catching up. They'd kill him like they killed Jude and anything was better than that. Even rats. The black mouth of the pipe gaped and dribbled blood, run-off from the Temple's killing floor. He threw another rock down the side of the valley, gripped the bars and wriggled in.

Wriggling was an art. If you could get one arm and your head through a gap, the rest generally followed. Flea found the bars widened at the bottom, which meant sliding through the foul smelling liquid, but he managed to scrape himself into the pipe. The harder it was for him, the harder it would be for anyone following.

Further back, in the blackness, he heard a dry scrabbling. Rats. RATS?

He closed his eyes and crawled forwards, his back just touching the top of the pipe and one arm waving in front of his face. After crawling only a couple of arms' lengths in, he reached the end.

Not far enough! And now he could hear the pursuit – they'd found the goat track and were questing along it, calling out as they walked.

Wait. Suppose there was a bend in the pipe? Flea rolled on to his back and felt above him. Space! Was there enough to stand? Above his head was utter blackness. His eyes opened so wide that the lids strained against their sockets.

Men were at the pipe mouth now, rattling the bars. 'Pass me that spear,' he heard one of them say.

Flea stood. The sides of the pipe were vertical and slippery. He felt higher and higher. He just needed something to hold on to: a gap in the stonework, anything. And there was a ledge! He hauled himself up on trembling arms, managed to hook his elbows over it and swung his legs up out of the way. The spear tip knocked sparks off the stone below him.

'Anything?' The voice echoed up the pipe again.

More jabs. Then, 'Nah. Little sod must've gone down the valley.'

'Told you I heard a noise.'

'Leave it . . .'

Grumbling, the men moved off.

Flea held his breath so he could hear the men walk away, then exhaled very, very gently. The sweat cooled on his skin. Just as he was about to move, he heard a man suppress a cough. They'd left one behind to trick him. He hung on. His shoulders and neck started to cramp. His arms began to shake. He gritted his teeth. A little longer, a little longer . . .

'Oi! Wait up!' The call came from outside the pipe. He heard the last man move off and at last he could relax.

He almost lost it as small, cold fingers wrapped themselves in his hair.

# 44

Flea's cry was smothered by another hand clamping down across his mouth. He heard a hissing in his ear and froze.

'Quiet. It's me.'

He recognised the skinny girl's voice.

'I'll help you up.'

The hands moved from his mouth and hair to under his arms. With their assistance he struggled up on to another ledge. In his ear: 'Don't talk.'

Flea curled up and shivered. He couldn't talk anyway. He clamped his jaw to stop his teeth chattering, but the shudders moved down his body. He wasn't cold, at least not in any normal way. It was the memories. Jude hanging. Yesh dying. The spike in his ear, his eye. The memories danced in his head like the mad, murderous Ranting Dunker in the Dead Streets. Flea wasn't scared of the future. He was scared by what had come and gone.

'We have to leave.'

'N-n-n-n-no.'

'If you stay, you'll drown. They sluice out the Temple sewers first thing. This is where it all comes out in a huge gush. You don't want to be here. Trust me.'

Flea tried to uncurl, but couldn't. As an option, drowning was fine.

'I'm going. I'll leave you.'

Flea stayed still.

'Of course, there are rats. Big ones that live off all the blood and guts that get washed off the Temple's killing floor.'

Flea found he could straighten up.

'That's better. Follow me out.'

Out in the open, the girl led him away from the pipe and the tree and headed for bridge.

'I'm sorry about your friend,' she said.

'What happened?'

'Well, I found him and passed on your message. He seemed worried, but he said he'd wait. Then I went away to scrounge some food and when I came back . . . he was like that. There were men hanging around. Sorry, there were men close by.'

'What did they look like?'

'Men. Just men. I didn't want to be seen and hid up the pipe. Like you.'

Flea opened his mouth to say something about being lucky to have found her, but started shuddering again, as if a very large dog had got him in its jaws and was shaking him.

'I think . . . I just n-need to rest,' Flea said.

'Not yet. We need to get away from here.'

He followed the girl along another goat track that cut into the valley side, happy to be led. They dropped down to the Black River and scurried under the great looping arch of the bridge, then climbed a zigzag path. Flea was finding it hard to keep up. The squat towers of the Fortress loomed black above the City walls. A grey dawn just touched the spears and helmets of the guards on the ramparts.

'Don't worry, I know a way in where you don't have to walk past Imps. It's a bit stinky, but I've done it loads of times. And if you *do* see an Imp, just try to ignore him. They're bored, most of them, and a bit scared. They know we hate them so if we're caught, don't do what you normally do.' She put her fists up and bounced around, mimicking Flea's sudden bouts of fury.

Flea found he still had a little fire in him. 'Don't tell me they're all right. I saw their torture chamber. I saw Yesh being flogged in the courtyard. Romans did that.'

She shrugged. 'Try to forget it. Look pathetic. It works for me. By the way, my name's Tesha.'

'Isn't that a number?'

'It's a long story. But your name?' She patted him on the head. 'That's probably a rather short story. Now come.'

# 45

The Fortress had its own dump, but the girl showed Flea how you could climb up the side of it and then squeeze through the waste gate for the rubbish. Then they were in an alleyway and Flea could smell cooking.

'The Fortress kitchens,' the girl said. 'Hardly anyone comes here, but Roman food's the same as anyone else's. Better a lot of the time.' She began to rummage through a row of leather buckets that were lined up against the wall, full of scraps to be chucked out in the morning.

'Posh bread!' she whispered and held some out to Flea.

He took a bite. Roman bread was soft and delicious. More rummaging produced a couple of dried figs. The food revived Flea. A little bit of strength returned to his legs.

'Now we just need somewhere to sleep,' the girl said.

'I know a place,' he said. 'It's a bit of a walk, but I think we'll be safe there for a while.'

And so he led the girl across the sleeping City. At the fountain where he used to fetch the water for the gang he washed the worst of the sewer slime from his hair, legs and arms. The scouring cold revived him. While he was at it the girl slipped away and came back carrying a bundle, but she wouldn't tell Flea what it was.

They skirted the lower slums and turned towards the south until Flea found the right street. He looked up and down it. No one moved. They crossed it quickly, creeping by the walls and keeping their eyes on the shuttered windows overlooking them. Flea climbed the steps, gesturing for the girl to stay behind. As before, the door opened to his push and, as before, the room smelled of wine and old cooking.

He beckoned to Tesha. 'We'll be safe here,' he said.

'Are you sure? How come?'

'It was hired for a week for Yeshua and his followers, but I don't think they'll come back,' Flea said. 'Too scared. Too many bad memories. They won't forget their last supper together.'

'Look, there's more food.'

'And wine. Eat. Drink. I just need to . . .'

He could barely stand. He fell on to cushions, managed to swallow some water, and then was engulfed by sleep.

one day after

# 46

Flea woke suddenly. Shutters sliced sunlight and striped the wall. He felt a sudden spurt of panic. Where was he? What was going on? Where was everyone?

He heard breathing. The girl was lying by his side, curled up on a big floor cushion like a cat. Tesha. She was called Tesha. Flea's mind began to spool backwards. Jude hanging. Yesh dying. The arrest of the Temple Boys. The Results Man. The riot in the Temple. How had he got through it all? He sat up and rubbed his face, waking the girl.

'How can you be awake already? This is the best bed ever.' Tesha stretched and sat up. Unlike Flea, she woke up bright and lively. 'Food! I forgot about the food. And look!' She grabbed a metal goblet and held it up to the light. Beams scattered around the room. 'I want this,' she said. She took a sip of the wine that was left in it and spat it out. 'Yuck.'

'I've got to go,' Flea said.

'Where?'

The words were in his mouth before he knew what he was going to say. 'Back to Jude. I can't leave him there.'

'Look, you're in a bad way,' the girl said. 'All cut up. You need rest and we've got our own place here.'

'You don't understand,' Flea said. 'I let him down. I was supposed to be there yesterday, but I wasn't and someone killed him.'

'Oh, so I understand about rescuing people, but because I'm a girl I'm too stupid to understand anything else. Is that what you're saying? I'm so stupid that I'm the one that stays alive and you're the one that's so clever he gets himself half killed.'

'All right,' Flea said. 'So why are you always trying to rescue me? Why did you hang around the gang's shelter? Why did you follow me halfway across the City? And why did you talk to Jude for me?'

The girl stared at him, breathing hard, her nostrils flaring. 'You really want to know?'

'Yes.'

'It was a bet,' she said.

More humiliation loomed. 'What? With who? Your friends?'

'Me. I haven't got any friends.'

'So what was the bet?'

She opened her mouth. Closed it. Shook her head. 'All right. When I start something I have to finish it. It's how I stay alive. Otherwise you give up. Get that?'

'Yes.'

'So it's got nothing to do with you, this bet. But it was a bet.'

'Nothing to do with me,' Flea said. He noticed Tesha's

expression had changed from sullen to sly and from sly to . . . amused.

'That's right. I saw the smallest, stupidest beggar in the smallest, stupidest gang and I bet that I could do a better job all by myself than you lot could . . .'

'At what?'

'At being in a gang. And I was right. They're all in prison, I'm still alive and I saved your worthless skin. And you know what?' Tesha said. 'It was better than hanging around street corners looking pathetic. I won.'

Flea couldn't work out whether he was hurt or relieved. 'So you won a bet with yourself,' he said. 'Big deal.'

'All right, big deal. What's your excuse?'

'I got sucked in. Then I suppose . . .' Flea shrugged. 'I wanted to stop it, I wanted to put things right. It all just seems so stupid. I mean, Yesh wanted to change the world and he's dead and Jude wanted to save him and he's dead and there's no power, no secret, no nothing, except everything's worse than it was.'

Tesha was silent. A fly droned across the room to batter heavily against the shutters. She tore a piece of cold meat off the ribs, wrapped it in bread and began to chew. The noise seemed intolerable to Flea.

She swallowed. Even worse. 'Except it doesn't make sense,' she said.

'I know. I just said that.'

'No. I don't mean the way grown-ups behave. That

never makes sense. I ran away from the quarry out on the Bethany road – you know it? That's where I got my name. The gangmaster used to wake us up by calling, *Sheva, Shmone, Tesha, Eser . . .* They weren't our names. They were just numbers and if one of us died, the new girl would get her number like it was just borrowed.'

Her voice grew shaky and she dashed away a tear, angrily, before carrying on. 'We had to carry rocks in baskets to make roads. If the gangmaster fed us, we could work. If he starved us, we couldn't. He starved us so we could hardly move and then he beat us and that made it worse so in the end no one could do anything. I ran away because it was all so stupid.'

She looked at Flea, who nodded, then she continued. 'Anyway, the thing your magician wanted doesn't make sense, because how could he be the Chosen One and make everything change if he knew he was going to die? One or the other, surely? Dead guy, Chosen One. Chosen One, Dead guy. How can you be both?'

'Right!' Flea said. 'You can see that and I can see that. How come no one else can see that? Grown-ups. They're so stupid. It was all for nothing. Every bit of it.'

And Flea was on his feet, suddenly angry, his fury bigger than the room. Bigger than the City. Bigger than the world.

'That's why I've got to find out who killed Jude. It can't be left like that. He can't have died for no reason and then nothing happens about it!'

Tesha considered him. 'That's good,' she said. 'I'll buy it. But you can't go anywhere like that.'

'Like what?'

'People are looking out for you, it was all over the City. Cutters. The Temple. Romans. Anybody who wants to suck up to the Cutters or the Temple or the Romans. That's about half the City, by the way. Popular boy.'

She had a point. 'So what do I do?'

'You need a disguise. I thought about it last night while you were staggering along and I raided a tent while you were washing. Remember that family who knocked down your gang's shelter? I nicked it from them.' She pulled a bundle from under a cushion and shook it out. 'It's so nice I almost kept it for myself. Anyway, those rags you're wearing really, really stink.'

She threw it over to Flea. The fabric was soft, unlike the tunic he wore, which was roughly woven out of something like sacking. It flowed. It was dyed dark blue. It was . . .

'This is for a girl!' Flea dropped the dress as if it might poison him.

'I said I fancied it for myself, but your need is greater than mine. No one knows who I am. No one wants to kill me.'

'I do! Why couldn't you have stolen a boy's tunic?'

'Well, it was dark. I had to crawl into the tent. Do

everything by touch. If they'd caught me, I'd be beaten or stoned. I just took the first thing I found.'

'Then you wear it. I'll wear your tunic.'

'It looks like your old one. You'd still look like Flea.'

Flea made a noise like *waaaah*.

'Come on. I'll pretend to be your slave. You can boss me about.'

Flea held the dress up. It was long and had sleeves, which were a novelty for him. Shoved down one of the sleeves was a matching headscarf. 'If you ever tell anyone . . .'

'My lips are sealed, oh mistress.'

'Don't look.'

When he had finished Tesha examined him. Flea screwed his eyes tight shut as she wrapped the scarf more tightly around his head, pushing his hair out of sight. The busy, light fussing of her fingers took him back to a time when . . . he couldn't quite think. He risked a peek. Tesha's face was close to his. The tip of her tongue was clamped between her lips as she concentrated. Gold flecked the grey of her eyes.

'There,' she said. 'And, may I say, you look very beautiful now we can't see your filthy hair.'

He threw a cushion at her. She shrieked and threw one back and knocked over the jug of wine so it spilled on the cushions and rugs. Their eyes met, shocked, then they laughed and ran out into the day.

# 47

As they walked, Flea kept his eyes lowered, concentrating hard. He did not see how anyone could walk in a long robe and his hair itched badly under the scarf. When they got to the east gate they realised something was wrong. An angry crowd was packed into the streets around it and the mood was ugly.

Tesha asked a woman what was going on.

'All day lockdown,' the woman answered, as if it were obvious. 'They're looking for terrorists or something.'

'We'll go out by the way we came in,' Tesha said.

'But that's by the Fortress,' Flea protested.

'Trust me. It'll be fine.'

'I don't know if I can walk past a soldier. I'm serious. I'm scared,' Flea said.

He felt Tesha's hand seek out his and give it a squeeze. 'You're not you,' she said. 'You're a fine lady. Get used to it and remember, that's all the guards are seeing.'

She was right. The soldiers at the back of the Fortress saw two girls – a rich one and her slave – and barely spared them a glance. When they were looking the other way, Flea and Tesha climbed through the stinking rubbish chute and began to retrace their steps along the valley side.

As they got closer to the tree, Flea began to feel sicker and sicker until he had to stop.

'I don't know if I can do this,' he said. 'If he's still . . . hanging, do we have to get him down?'

'Wait here,' Tesha said. I'll scout it out.'

She was back minutes later. 'It's all right,' she said. 'There's a bit of a crowd: Wild People, Samaritans, a few City people locked out. And the body – I mean your friend – has gone. I don't know if that's good or bad.'

Neither did Flea.

The tree looked smaller in daylight, its bare branches poking up above the heads of a small crowd. He saw the black of the Wild People's robes, the striped turban of a Samaritan. He pushed forwards, preparing himself for the horror of what might be lying on the ground.

But there was nothing. The wind played with the frayed rope hanging from the branch. That was all there was to see; that was all these gawpers hoping for a quick thrill were going to get.

'Where are they burying him?' the Samaritan asked someone.

'Down there. At the bottom of the valley. In the blood fields,' a peasant answered.

'The what?'

The peasant drew himself up. 'See that pipe? It takes all the blood from the Temple's sacrifices and pours it all into the Black River. The river's diverted into those flat terraces downstream, see? The blood soaks into the soil, they dig it out and spread it on their fields. Makes the best fertiliser in the world. All the City's vegetables are grown with its blood.'

'Is that clean? Is that pure?' a worried voice asked.

A man with a sharp face and a shock of dark hair answered. 'Don't know if it's pure. They've been doing it for centuries. And that's where they bury all the criminals and beggars. Temple Police cut him down this morning and carted him off. Something odd about it, if you want my opinion. I reckon it's a cover-up.'

'A Temple cover-up?' Another voice.

'Quiet! There'll be spies about.' Yet another.

'I don't care about spies.' The Samaritan again. 'They'll have more on their hands than they can deal with soon enough. You want my opinion? He was one of those troublemakers who want a revolution. The Temple finished him off like they finished off that magician.'

'That was never the Temple. That was the Romans!'

An argument started and Flea wheeled away, horrified. No one was thinking of Jude. They'd turned him into an idea to be batted around like a scrap of rubbish.

And Flea should never have come here. He knew that now. What could he do, a stupid little beggar boy? And more than that, what did it matter? It was like being at the bottom of the City's rubbish tip as it fell in a stinking, steaming mound from the walls into the valley. You could stand at the bottom and try to stop it slipping further down, but more and more rubbish would just come tumbling on top of you and in the end, for all your efforts, you would end up buried in other's people's –

'You all right?'

In turning to get away, Flea had cannoned into a farmer. He felt rough, protective hands on his shoulders.

'You're trembling. Not surprised. This is no place for a girl. Where are your people?'

Flea made the mistake of looking up. The farmer's face was blunt and weather-beaten, his teeth worn down to little brown stumps from eating too much grit in his bread. His expression changed from concern to something else.

'Here.'

Flea knew his face would be dirty, the dirt made more obvious by the tear marks and snot trails.

'You don't . . .'

Also his hair had begun to escape from underneath his scarf.

Tesha saw the danger and shrieked, 'Mistress, mistress. What's happening?'

That attracted even more attention. Heads turned.

The farmer said, 'That's not a mistress. That's a bloody boy!'

He tore off Flea's headscarf and waved it above his head, then grabbed Flea and held him up. The crowd bustled round, keen to have something else to think about.

'That's not any boy either,' a voice in the crowd said.

'That's the boy everyone's looking for, I bet.'

'What? The one with the power?'

'You mean the blasphemer.'

'You mean the little traitor.'

'What does it matter? Hang him!'

'There's some rope here!'

'Come on.'

Flea struggled, but was held fast by several pairs of hands. He felt himself boosted high above the heads of the crowd and passed along like a parcel towards the tree.

'No!' He shouted. 'You don't understand. Jude was my friend. He wasn't a bad man! He just wanted –'

Flea's hands were tied behind his back and he was lifted higher. Someone had climbed the tree and shinned along the branch. Now he was tying the dangling rope into a rough noose. Flea struggled and fought. A scream built inside him. Through wide eyes he saw the valley and the hills beyond. He saw a white sky with the sun trying to break through and play on the lion-coloured blocks of the City walls. He saw the roof of the Temple and then, above his head, he saw the noose.

He felt the roughness of the rope on his forehead, then it was over him and the scream was everywhere, inside him and outside him so the white of the sky shifted and shivered and Flea waited for the drop.

# 48

It didn't happen.

Thumping footsteps, a panicked stampede and the crowd scattered in the only direction it could, down the valley side. Arms windmilled. People tripped and tumbled towards the river. Flea looked down and saw a sea of black. Wild People! He'd been rescued by Wild People. One was holding him. He felt the rope around his wrists being cut, and then scampering along the branch towards him was a little girl with painted eyes and a gold chain hooked from her nose to her ear.

She stuck out her tongue at Flea before lifting the rope from his neck. He was lowered to the ground.

'Are you all right?'

Flea looked up into a fierce face with a hooked nose, black eyes and hollow cheeks. He remembered this man, and the girl, from the early-morning sheep market. Jude had bought a lamb from him. He nodded, his chest heaving.

'Lucky for you my daughter saw through your disguise. She was on watch, just in case you turned up. We were waiting to the south, ready to leave. You'd better come with us.'

'Why did you rescue me?' Flea said. 'Why was she looking out for me?'

'Jude,' the man said simply. 'Come.'

'He's dead.'

'We know. He should have paid us to protect him. He would have lived.'

Flea looked around. There were about a dozen black-robed figures, standing around him in a rough circle, knives drawn. 'I don't understand.'

'We can talk as we walk. We need to get away from here. The further from the City you are, the better for all of us: you and your friend,' he said with a nod to Tesha, who was standing a short distance away ready to run. 'Jude came to us yesterday. He said he was hoping to meet you here, but if anything happened, I was to make sure you were all right.'

'Did he say anything about me?'

'He said a lot of things and some of them were about you. Walk more quickly. That mob will be at the main gate soon and whether the gates are locked or not, if they shout out to the guards that they've spotted a fugitive they'll open soon enough.'

'Won't you be in trouble?'

'The Temple Police may come to the camp and ask us questions, but we'll shake our heads and say it was different Wild People who helped you. Bad Wild People. They don't see our faces – to them we are all the same – so no one will know who was here. But that's not your worry.'

'Can you tell me about Jude?'

'Yesterday evening? He was sad. He said he'd lost his Master and now he was worried that he'd led you astray, but at least he could leave you something. He talked about some prophecy. Said perhaps it was true after all and, if it was true, then he'd got you mixed up in his troubles for nothing. That's what he kept on saying. For nothing.'

Flea's face fell. 'He thought the prophecy about Yeshua being the Chosen One was true?'

A shrug. 'Maybe. Nothing you City people do makes sense.'

'But Jude wasn't from the City.'

'You're all from the City. You're all called back here. This is where the madness lies. He came to the tree. He died. When I heard, I told my girl to watch and wait and the rest, well, it happened to you so you know.'

'Do you think he killed himself?'

'Among my people it is not a sin.'

'But he said he would meet me.'

'Saying you would do one thing and then not doing it, that is a sin. Do you think Jude was a bad man?'

'No.'

'Then . . .'

They walked on. The walls followed a slight rise to the part of the City called David's Hill, then the ground fell to a small plain where the Wild People's main campsite was stationed. You could hear the bleat of the unsold lambs. The tents were being taken down and loaded on to donkeys and camels.

Flea's mind caught up the Wild Man's words. 'You said that Jude left me something. What was that?'

The Wild Man smiled. 'Good boy.' He reached into his robes and handed Flea Jude's purse. 'It's all there. I didn't even open it.'

The purse was warm and plump in his hand. Flea remembered the last supper and the game of Hunt the King. Jude had given the money to him. Jude had wanted him to have it. Jude had wanted him to be safe. He felt the quick rush of tears.

'You're a rich boy now and that means you have to be even more careful,' the Wild Man said. 'If anyone finds out that you have that, you'll be in even greater danger than now. As well as the Temple Police, the Romans and the Cutters, every thief in the City is going to be after you and the people you turn to for help will just be waiting to cut your throat. That is the way of the City. Trust no one, even that girl who's hanging around.'

'I think she's all right.'

The Wild Man accepted that with a tilt of the head. 'Of course, you could always leave. It is my thought that if you stay, you will become part of this prophecy. Your destiny will be twisted to serve its will, as Jude's was in the end. Remember your name. Fleas are meant to jump. Do not stay here. You will be crushed. Leap away while you have the choice. We are heading for the desert and you could come with us for a while, or you could go to Bethany and on from there.'

*Bethany.* Tesha had mentioned Bethany too that morning. Now, like then, it produced an echo in his mind – an echo that had a slightly broken ring. Flea shook his head.

'I can't,' he said. 'I have to stay here.'

'You'll not live another day, even with your disguise.'

'It's not just me. My gang's in prison because of what I did.'

'Because of the Romans. Do not blame yourself for every bad thing in the world.'

'Because of me. Because of the Romans. It doesn't matter. I've got to try and help them. I'm not being good. I just know that if I leave them, I won't stop thinking of them and then I won't be happy.'

'A word of advice: you will stop thinking of them. In a couple of years you can marry a girl and with that money you can buy enough land to keep a family.'

Flea looked at him with such disgust that the Wild Man laughed.

'You'll see,' he went on. 'At least come to the camp. There will be girls there who will be only too happy to wear your dress and you can exchange it for something more . . . Flea-like. One last thing: the magician's followers. Jude said that they would be hiding for three days in the

Dead Streets. He seemed to think that was funny.'

'Then what?'

Another shrug. 'Me and my people will be away from here, safe in the desert where the air is clean and this madness does not reach. I cannot say what you will do, because I am not a prophet. I will not bind you with words. I will feed you, you and that girl who does not behave as a girl should, and then tomorrow, when you are properly rested, you can find your destiny yourself.'

two days after

# 49

Side by side, Flea and Tesha peered through the branches of a small bush and looked out into the Dead Streets. Two nights of proper sleep and a day of proper food and Flea felt well again, though different. At the Wild People's camp the women had taken Tesha off and wailed when they saw she had no gold, but painted patterns on her hands with henna and lined her eyes with dark pencil. Flea had to admit the eyes suited her.

They were hiding by a dry pool that lay at the junction of three roads. Steps cut into the side of the pool led down into its shadowed depths, where a mangy dog was stretched out on its side. It raised its head and coughed out a bark before lying back down. On the steps a sleepy lizard was trying to warm up in the weak sunshine and above them a crow flapped slowly across the sky.

The Dead Streets looked peaceful. You could hear the City roaring, but the sound was cut off and distant. You could see the Temple sitting on its hill like a heavy white crown, but you couldn't feel it. The streets had their own air – Flea did not know how else to put it – and they did something to the pit of his stomach that wasn't just fear.

Tesha tugged his arm and pointed. Two streets away a thin column of black smoke was rising into the still air.

Good. She'd been sulking since they left the black

tents of the Wild People's camp. She didn't see why they couldn't go with them. It wasn't the money. She just did not want to risk stoning, disembowelling or hanging for being Flea's accomplice. 'Then let me go alone,' he had suggested, but she had not wanted to do that either.

'It's them,' he said. 'And I have to find out if they killed Jude. I owe him that.'

'He paid you to get away.'

'I know, but I can't leave it.'

'Suppose – suppose he killed himself.'

Flea shook his head. 'I don't believe it. I want to know what he found out. I want to know why he changed his mind about escaping. The Wild Man said the prophecy had crushed Jude. Well, as far as I can see the people who believed in the prophecy most of all were the rest of Yesh's followers. If they killed Jude, they can't get away with it.'

'And you can do something about it? *You?*' Tesha sneered.

But Flea did not rise to the bait. 'I don't know what. Just something. Anyway, as soon as we find them, you're going to hide. If we don't meet up this evening, you'll go to the Temple and tell them where the followers are hiding. I'll make sure they know that. They'll tell me what's going on and won't dare kill me. It'll work. Trust me.'

'Oh, great. And the Temple Police will listen to me, because they're so kind to beggar girls.'

'You won't look like a beggar. You've got the dress now.

You'll look like a normal girl.' Flea had turned down the Wild Man's suggestion of bartering the dress in the camp. He had simply swapped it with Tesha's old tunic.

'Thank you very much,' Tesha said. 'I still think you're an idiot for not getting away.'

'Then what does that make you for coming with me?'

Tesha unexpectedly burst into tears and Flea, just as unexpectedly, felt sorry. But when he tried to tell her, she bit him on the arm. He supposed it was his own fault for teaming up with a girl.

Lizards flickered into nothing as they moved deeper into the Dead Streets. Tiles crunched under their feet. Tiny blue flowers, growing from cracks in the buildings, mirrored the sky. When Flea looked into one of the empty houses he stopped dead.

'What is it?' Tesha whispered. A dusty carpet lay in the middle of the floor, with mats arranged around it as if the room was waiting for people to walk in. But there was more: a jolt of familiarity.

'It's like I know this place, but don't know it. I can't explain.'

'We're all from here,' Tesha said. 'Didn't you know?'

'What?'

'I thought everyone knew. All the beggars our age . . . their parents . . . you know . . . the massacre,' Tesha said. 'Don't you talk to anyone?'

'I . . .'

'Like I said . . . Flea. Don't go all funny on me now. Flea. Flea!'

But Flea could not hear. The house he was looking at seemed to expand, then become so thin and gauzy that he could see through it and into another room just like it with a window on the street and a courtyard to the side.

Shy memories slid up. He remembered pressing his eyes to the gap in the courtyard gate and peering up and down the narrow street to watch men and women, donkeys and even the odd camel pass by. The crack in the wall across the alleyway always scared him. There was a time in the evening when the bats began to swoop like leaves on the wind and someone would come up behind him and put a hand on his shoulder.

He looked up and down, half expecting to see the same animals and families. Of course. These were the Dead Streets. This was where the Imps had massacred every man, woman and child. This was where he had run from. But more importantly, this was where he had come from.

The memories grew bolder. They were insistent. Relentless. They swarmed. An earth yard where chickens scratched in the dirt, a dark room where water stood in cool, earthenware jars. Sleeping on a mat next to his parents; his mother singing; a ball of rags he could throw and catch.

But something else was trying to break through – a

fist behind a sheet. He tried to shut his memory down, but it was too late. He saw the door exploding inwards and then the room was full of men and their metal. Metal helmets, metal breastplates, metal swords. One sword in particular was shining as it fell, but red when it rose, and then he was falling and when he stopped he was on a street and all around was quiet. He saw people and bits of people lying in the street. There was a lump on the side of his head and a hollow ache in his heart, an emptiness that multiplied in empty doorways and dark windows. No faces looking out. They were all looking up at the sky or down at the ground and their eyes were blank.

Flea had had enough. He began running to escape a pain that was more than hollow; it was the pain of missing whatever had the filled void. First in one direction then another, until the running started to hurt, which was better than the other kind of pain. He so he ran more and more – and the only thing that stopped him was when a hand grabbed him by the collar.

# 50

The hand was not a memory. The hand was real and big and meaty. It reached out from between a pair of broken shutters, lifted Flea into the air and pulled him into one of the houses. And Flea was not the little child about to be set to work in the glue factory; this was Flea, who'd survived all that and a whole lot more.

He twisted and tried to bite, but the hand lifted him effortlessly and he hung in the air, jerking and twisting like a fish on the line.

'Gotcha!'

Flea managed to twist round and found himself face-to-face with Tauma. He was as thick as a barrel and held Flea easily. There was no sign of Tesha, which was good.

Tauma said, 'Call me suspicious and nasty if you want, but I've seen rather too much of you lately. What are you doing here?' He pretended to examine him.

Flea, suspended, missed with his kick. 'It doesn't matter what I'm doing. What about you? Skulking here while half the City's after you,' he spat.

Tauma seemed unimpressed. 'Which half?' he said. 'The half that's too scared to come here or the half that doesn't care?'

'The half that wants you kicked out and sent back to Gilgad where you belong!'

Tauma grinned unkindly and Flea lost it. 'Murdering

pig! Liar! Coward! You killed your own precious leader, you killed Jude and now you're going to die, because no one's going to let you get way with any of this! Don't pretend you don't know. You had him killed. He was standing between you and your prophecy. But you can't kill me. If you kill me, everyone will know.'

Tauma's grin died. His eyes went as dead as dust. He tightened his grip and pulled him so close Flea could smell raw onion on his breath.

Shim bustled into the room. 'What's all this shouting?' He caught sight of Flea and his mouth flattened into a red slot. 'You.'

'Hoping for someone else?' Flea spat. 'Someone you haven't seen for a while? Last time I saw you, you were too scared to admit you even knew your own leader! Or is that just part of the prophecy? You betrayed him, not Jude.'

'How much does he know?' Shim asked Tauma.

'Your guess is as good as mine. He says we killed Jude.'

'Jude's dead?'

'Apparently. How –?'

Shim waved his words away. 'We can't let that distract us now. We have to keep on track. He doesn't understand. The secret is still safe. But we do have to work out what to do with him.'

'I know all about your precious secret and I know you were wrong,' yelled Flea triumphantly. 'Yesh is dead. Nothing happened. You're finished. There's nothing left for you to do, unless you want to hand *me* over to the Romans to be crucified!'

Shim slapped him hard across the face. Flea blinked back stars and tasted blood in his mouth.

'How dare you. Tauma, how dare he?'

Flea spat blood. Tauma looked at him and shook his head sadly. 'Oh dear. Oh dear, oh dear, oh dear. See, I'm thick-skinned. I don't care what you say, but Shim's sensitive. You're in trouble now. Come on.'

The other followers were all sitting in the back room that opened up on to a small yard. The air was close with the fug of bodies. In the yard broken pots lay scattered in yellowed weeds.

'The return of the prodigal flea,' Tauma said, pushing Flea into the room. He stood, surrounded by the followers, all sitting with their backs against the walls.

No one spoke at first. Worry had roughened them all. Yohan's dreamy eyes were bloodshot. Mat's face had sunk and his hair was standing up in a spiked halo. 'What's he doing here?' he snapped.

'Jude's dead. He thinks we killed him, so I imagine he's come looking for us to wreak revenge. There was another kid with him, but it got away,' Tauma said.

'And she's going to tell the Temple where you are if anything happens to me,' Flea added.

'Good planning,' Tauma said. 'If they believe a word she says.'

'Of course they will. And now your prophecy's failed, you can admit to what you did,' Flea snarled.

'Those two statements will take a lot of untangling,' Mat said.

Flea was having none of it. 'You arranged to have Yesh killed. Then you arranged to have Jude killed, too, for getting in your way.'

Mat nodded. 'So that's the second half of the statement covered. Now for the first half. You said the prophecy had failed. How do you know this?'

'Because Yesh is dead. I saw him die, unlike you bunch of cowards. If he's dead, he can't be the Chosen One. If he can't be the Chosen One, you can't change the world. It's that simple a child could see it.'

'Or something so simple only a child could be so stupid to think it. But do you really think we're that stupid? The Chosen One is betrayed, dies and then comes back to life. Praise be!'

'He didn't. I was there.'

'Child, he comes back to life *after three days*.'

'What?'

'It takes three days for the power to gather. That is the prophecy.'

Flea looked around the room and saw that the faces of the followers weren't defeated. They were tense, as if they were waiting. His confidence collapsed like an empty anthill.

'How . . .' Flea began, but he didn't know what more to say. *How?* seemed to sum up how he was feeling right then. *How will this happen? How will you know? How can you have the patience?* 'But that's tomorrow.'

'Indeed. Do you know the story of Jonah and the Whale?' Mat asked. 'For three days he lay in its belly before was he released on to the shore alive.'

'That's just a story,' Flea said faintly.

'*Be ready for the third day*. That's from Moshe's Book of The Leaving. And later it says, *Let them be ready for the third day*. In the Book of The Kings, we read, *On the third day, you shall go the house of the Lord*. And in our Holy Book of The Beginning: *On the third day, Joseph said, do this and you will live*. Yeshua our Lord will lie in his grave for three days as a dead man and on the third he will reanimate. He will revive. He will come back to life. He will rise again.'

'Praise be! Praise be! Praise be!'

'It's just words!' Flea said. 'He can't!'

Mat nearly smiled. 'In all the long days we were travelling to the City our Lord tried to convince us with words, but we were weak and blind, like you. We did not have faith. And then, just a day's walk away we saw with it our own eyes. In Bethany.'

'What happened there?' Flea's voice was a whisper. Now he remembered about Bethany. He had heard Shim and Jude mention it on the night of the supper in Yusuf's house. And Jude had been appalled by something that happened there . . .

'We walked from Gilgad,' Mat said. 'We knew we would be in for a hard time when we reached the City so we wanted a place to rest close by, to gather our thoughts and strength. Are you listening? The place we normally stayed was in the house of a friend, Eleazar. Laz, we called him. But when we reached his house, we found it in mourning. Eleazar had died and was three days in his grave.' He paused. 'Our Lord brought him back to life.'

'No.'

'Yes. Yeshua broke his tomb open and walked inside. No one would follow. The stench . . . Anyway, an hour later he walked out, with Eleazar by his side.'

Flea put his fingers in his ears and shouted, 'Wordswordswordwords.'

Tauma grabbed Flea's hands, pulled them away and said, 'Listen!'

'Jude always said you were clever and Yeshua agreed with him. He said that if we could convince Flea, we could convince the world.' Mat made a face. 'Call him forth, Yohan. Bring Eleazar to Flea so he can witness the miracle. The dead can walk. The dead can live!'

Tauma held Flea again. Yohan left the room and walked across the little courtyard to a shed on the far side. He knocked on the door and stood back. Flea's mouth went dry as the door opened. A pause, then very slowly a man emerged. His skin was the colour of sour milk and his eyes had sunk back into his head. He took a step into the sunlight and winced. In the room, the followers winced too. Flea felt the hairs on the back his neck rise and fought the scream rising in his tightening throat. The man stepped back into the shadows.

'Eleazar was dead and is now alive,' Mat chanted. 'He grows stronger every day. It can happen. Yeshua is the Chosen One. Since the world began and the stars began to move around the heavens and Adam first met Eve it has been waiting for this moment. A new world is coming. All will be unmade and then remade and the dawn will be the light of our Lord!'

'No,' Flea said. 'No.'

'Do you understand now, Flea? We did not have to kill Jude. His life and his death were foretold from the moment he was born, and so shall we all die to be reborn in the new world! Nothing can change the prophecy! The day is coming! The time is coming! The end of time and the end of days!'

His words were echoed around the room.

'PRAISE BE! PRAISE BE! PRAISE BE!'

'TELL THE CITY. TELL THE PEOPLE. TELL THE WORLD. SPREAD THE WORD!'

Tauma led Flea out of the room. 'Do you hear that, sonny?' he said. 'It means Mat's decided that we're letting you go. It's what Yesh would have wanted. We'll all be standing in front of him tomorrow, giving a full account of our actions.'

'Do you really believe that?' Flea asked.

For a second Tauma's face went blank, then he smiled. 'I suppose you could call me a seeing-is-believing sort of man, but in the end it doesn't matter what I think, does it? What will be, will be. And no one will be happier than me to see Yesh again. Walking. Talking.'

'Killing Romans?'

'It won't be like that. It'll be different. It'll be a *change*.'

'But what can I do?'

'Between now and then? Try and put right anything you did wrong and tell the world the news.'

'About what? About Jude?'

'Forget about Jude. He was using you. Do something for yourself. Ask yourself, what do you want to do? What's best for you in this short time?'

'I want to –'

'Don't talk. Do. Now, go, before Mat changes his mind.'

Flea left, an idea growing in his mind until it blotted out everything else.

# 51

Tesha alerted him with a long, low whistle. She stepped from behind an abandoned cart.

'Why did you run off? Are you all right? I was beginning to get scared.'

'I'm fine.' Flea found himself suddenly breathless. 'I know all about it now. We were right and we were wrong. Nothing was ever going to happen when Yesh died, and you were right: he couldn't change the world when he was dead. We just missed the obvious. The real prophecy says he's coming back to life first. And then the big change comes.'

Tesha stared at him blankly, then asked: 'When?'

'Tomorrow. They told me to . . . do whatever I had to do before it all happens.'

'And what's that? What's the big change?'

'The end of the world.'

'Oh, just that?' Tesha sounded sarcastic. 'So what's the point of doing anything?'

'I think the point is that there's going to be a new world where everything's turned upside down. The rich will be poor, the poor will be rich, beggars will be kings, lots of food instead of too little. All good stuff.' So why didn't he feel happier, he wondered.

'And it's just going to . . . happen? And we've got no say in it? But how?'

'It's the prophecy. It's all come true so far, no matter what I've done,' Flea said. 'They're looking after someone in there. They called him Laz. He was dead for three days, but Yesh brought him back to life.'

'No.' Tesha's eyes were wide. 'Three days?'

'He looked it as well. I just . . . I don't have a good feeling about this change. That's why I think I've got to do something . . . else.'

'Which is?'

Flea scuffed the ground with his toe. Broken things shifted under the weeds. 'Get my gang out of prison. I thought I could trade my secret – you know, trade my secret for my gang.'

'To the Romans?'

'I don't reckon it will work. I don't think the prophecy works that way. Look – it's like your bet with yourself, when you didn't give up on me. I just don't want to give up on my gang.'

Tesha shook her head. 'But it's not your gang, is it? They treated you like dirt. You might as well say this is your city. It's not. The gang, the City, they just exist. They're not here for you or me, we're here for them, if you let them use you. They're all using you: your gang, that Roman and now Yesh's followers. You're going to sacrifice yourself like Yesh did, but for what? So you can die like he did?'

'I'm not going to die,' Flea said. 'No one is.'

'And how was that for Yesh?'

'But he's coming back to life!'

'And you want that? It's disgusting. We've both seen dead people. We know what that's like. I rescued you and you just want to throw it away.' Tesha was almost in tears.

Flea put his head down. If he looked at her he would change his mind. 'I've got to go,' he said. 'I'm sorry.'

'Don't go. If you do, you'll never see me again! Never ever!'

But he went.

'Never ever. Ever!' Her voice faded.

# 52

Flea trotted across the empty square accompanied only by the soft shuffle of his steps until he stood outside the Fortress. He thought about what he was planning to do and failed to find the slightest hint of good sense in it. He just knew he had to do it.

The City had felt dark and charged, like the air before a thunderstorm. Flea had flitted from street to street, shutters opening as he came, then slamming shut after him. In side alleys, faces turned to see who passed, then turned away. Only the fire altar in the Temple smoked today; charcoal and ash from thousands of home fires gritted the paving.

So why was the Fortress locked? Surely they could feel the mood? Flea banged on the postern gate with his fists and when nothing happened he found a rock and started whacking it with that.

When the gate eventually opened and a bad-tempered, fully armed Imp stormed out, Flea flung himself face downwards on the ground and said, 'Don't hurt me. I've come to see someone.'

A moment's silence. He felt the sharp tip of a sword prod him under the arm.

'Ow,' he said. 'I surrender. I won't fight.'

That prompted a laugh and he looked up. The soldier was dark and wiry and looked like he came from Saba or somewhere to the south.

'I've come to report to the Results Man. I want to give myself up.'

'You do what?' The accent was short and choppy. He was joined by two others, who looked warily into the wide square in front of the Fortress before staring down at Flea.

'I don't know his real name,' Flea said. 'He's tall. He hasn't got much hair. He smiles like a tortoise and walks like a heron.' He got to his feet and did a passable imitation of the Results Man in motion. 'I've found out something important. He needs to know.'

The men talked in their own language, then the one who had opened the door shook his head. 'Get lost. This is bad day for jokes. We let you go, but don't come back.'

'But it's important! You know who I mean?'

'Of course.'

'Then tell him I know about the uprising.'

That worked. They talked among themselves, stood back to let Flea in, then led him down the stairs to the dungeons.

One hour later and Flea was feeling smug. It was a real dungeon, no doubt about it, with black slime on the walls, filthy straw on the floor, a bucket that was the home of all stenches and a stone bench too narrow to lie on. It proved that they were taking him seriously.

Two hours later he still felt pretty clever.

Three hours later, when no one was taking any notice of his shouts, he felt hoarse and thirsty.

Four hours later when the man in the cell next door threatened to tear his head off, he was beginning to feel a bit stupid.

Five hours later he wished he were with the Wild People, Tesha, even Tauma. Anywhere but here.

Six hours later the cell door crashed open.

'Well, you asked for me and now you have me. I'm all ears,' the Results Man said. His voice sounded flat. He looked tired and there was grey stubble on his chin. 'Talk.'

Flea blinked. Behind the Results Man was his usual

guard, this time holding a flaming brand that seared Flea's eyeballs. 'I thought you'd see me sooner.'

'Why?'

'You said you'd keep my friends to make sure I did what you wanted. Well, I did what you wanted: I stayed with Yesh while you beat him and I stayed with him while he died. Nothing happened. But now I know why.'

'And are you going to tell me?'

'If my gang's all right.'

'You're not trying to bargain, are you? You've seen what I will do to find the truth. I'll peel you like an orange, if I have to. So. Tell me what you know.'

'And then you'll let us go?'

'And then I'll let you go. The truth will set you free.' The Results Man seemed to find that amusing.

So Flea told him about Laz, and the three day wait and what would happen afterwards.

'And the uprising? What did you find out about the uprising? Where will it start? Who will be leading it? Yusuf the Merchant? Is the Temple with them or against them?'

'I don't know any of that,' Flea said. Now he'd told the Results Man everything, it didn't seem to add up to much. He was beginning to feel frightened. 'I just know what you told me to do: to find out what Yesh said. Well, he didn't say anything, but I found out more.'

The Results Man smiled, chucked Flea under the chin, pushed him back into the cell and slammed it shut.

Flea hurled himself against the door. 'That's not fair!' he shouted. 'YOU PROMISED!'

The Results Man spoke softly through the rusty iron grille set into the door. 'Poor Flea. You know just enough to make you slightly dangerous, but you haven't got the faintest idea why. I never break a promise. Tomorrow I shall set you free. And if your Yesh is to be believed, we shall all be free. All of us. Forever.'

Flea watched the torchlight recede. The man in the next-door cell chuckled quietly. Then silence and darkness enfolded them.

three days after

# 53

Flea was not sure if he had slept or not. He could just balance on the bench if he lay on his side, but the stone was cold and if he tried to curl up he would fall on to the rotten rushes strewn around the floor. He lay, he shivered, he got up, he lay back down again. The room was pitch-black. He knew when morning came he would see grey light through the bars, but he wasn't sure if he wanted the day to come. In spite of himself, he eventually fell into a deep sleep.

In fact, the Results Man returned before dawn. Suddenly the cell door was open and there he was, holding a small oil lamp that he sheltered with a cupped hand. Flea woke with a gasp, confused. He'd been having a nightmare. In it he had been going calmly about his business in the City, but all the time he was full of the knowledge that he had crucified Yesh. The memory itself was like a monster that dogged his footsteps. He walked, it walked. If he stopped, it stopped. If he ran, it ran. The monster had no shape. It was just there: a big lump of pain that belonged to him and was the ruin of his life.

So he was relieved to be woken, but then he remembered. This was the third day. The day of reckoning.

'Follow.'

For the first time the Results Man had no guard with

him. Flea trotted after him, down one set of winding stairs then a second. Under the Fortress there was another world. He smelled cooking, heard the ringing clang of a smithy. At the end of a corridor he saw a great vaulted hall where soldiers slept on mattresses. Then more passages. More steps down. Always down. Flea began to wake up properly. He thought there might be something furtive in the way the Results Man was moving. He didn't know if this was bad or good.

At last they came to a narrow door of black wood. Half a dozen soldiers, northern-looking, were waiting. The door was guarded by an old man in a leather apron who was sitting at a table. He was very still and was staring hard at a whip that lay curled on the notched wood.

'Have you ever seen a pet dog look at a stick? He's like that. He can't wait to play,' the Results Man said. The old man glanced up, then looked down again.

The Results Man took hold of the bolts on the door and pulled. It opened with a sucking noise, as if the air behind it was solid.

Holding the lantern, he led the way through into a stench that made Flea gag. In the flaring torchlight he saw a short corridor. Off to the right was a storeroom, with broken jars littering the floor and a raised well head at the back. The flickering light made the shadows jump. Flea heard a sullen splash.

The old man followed and kicked out at a fat, grey-furred rat. It waddled away from them and squeezed into an impossibly small hole. Beyond the well room the corridor was lined with alcoves set over crude wooden hatches in the floor.

The Results Man knelt by the first trapdoor and lifted it. He shook his head. Same for the second one. When he opened the third one he grimaced and held his nose.

'Third time lucky,' he said. He flapped the trapdoor so it blew out gusts of stinking air like a bellows, then called down, 'Hello! Got Flea up here. Says he wants to rescue you, but I'm sure I don't know why. Aren't you happy here at my inn?'

Flea heard coughing quickly stifled and a voice call up, 'Please don't throw water on us again.'

'But you were complaining about the dirt! I was only trying to help,' the Results Man said.

Flea pushed past him. 'It's all right!' he shouted. 'It's me. Flea! I've come to get you out.'

There was a pause. 'Flea. Is it really you?'

'Yes.'

'We're sorry. We're so sorry. We didn't mean . . . to be so horrid to you. If you let us out, we'll promise to be nice.'

'I didn't turn you in because you bullied me,' Flea said. 'You can't think that, can you? I was forced to. It was blackmail.'

'If you say so, Flea.'

Leaning against the wall was a rough ladder. Flea

dragged it to the edge of the pit and slid it in.

'Climb the ladder. It's all right. You're free.'

A lot of whispering. 'And if we don't?'

'This isn't a trap! Climb the ladder! You're free. Don't you see?'

He felt the ladder creak. Big was the first of the Temple Boys to stick his head out of the hole. He was filthy, his hair matted, and after four days in the dungeon he had lost weight. He cowered and kept his eyes screwed up tight, as if he were anticipating a blow at any moment.

When he eventually opened them, he looked around carefully. 'I think it's all right,' he said and went down into the pit again. The next time he appeared he had Clump hanging round his neck. Then he climbed up with Crutches and hauled himself on to the floor, panting.

Little Big was next, then Halo, then Snot, Gaga, the twins, Hole-in-the-Head and Red last of all. They stood with their backs to the wall, heads down. There was an awkward silence.

'That's it,' Flea said. 'We're free. Oh, and Crouch is fine by the way.' He beamed at the Results Man. 'A result.'

'You have no idea what you've achieved,' the Results Man said. 'No idea at all. Now, to turn a good day into a great day, let's talk about plans. Good plans. Fun plans.'

'Oh,' Flea said. 'I thought –'

'Didn't I say it doesn't matter what you think? Now, everyone follow me and off we go.'

And suddenly Flea was worried. The worry felt like bad food in his stomach. 'Follow you? Where?'

'I'm taking to you the one place you want to be. It's where you'll find your end, or a new beginning. Now move!' The Results Man's voice snapped.

'Tell us where we're going.'

'To the tomb where Yesh is buried. We need to be there when he comes back to life. I don't think it's going to happen much before dawn, but we should hurry. I've spent the past five – no, six – days working towards it. You boys are the honey on the pastry. The lark's tongue in the jelly. The – you get my drift.'

'What are you asking us to do?' Flea moved over to where the Temple Boys were huddled against the wall, as far from the Results Man as possible.

'Asking? I'm not asking anything. Sometimes people come together against a common enemy. In this case, what could possibly unite the greatest power the world has ever seen – the source of all power and glory on earth – with a tiny cult in a dusty, forgotten corner of its great empire? What could unite Rome with your people? Come on, come on, think!'

Flea's mind was blank, but he knew he was not going to like the answer. He shook his head.

The Results Man sighed. 'All right. I'll tell you. *Death*. We are all going to die – or rather, we *were* all going to die – and what better place to conquer death than in this ridiculous, death-ridden city? How many times has it been destroyed and its people killed? How many times have they come back?' He winked. The effect was vile. 'Now, that's what I call power. Imagine an army that can't be killed. Chop 'em down and up they jump. You've got to admit it's an exciting proposition.'

'So if there's an uprising and the Romans are killed . . .'

'They come back to life! If I can find out what the secret is.' The Results Man winked again.

Flea's mind jerked into motion. 'But if you put down the uprising and kill everyone in the City and *they* come back to life . . .?'

'I don't care, because by then I'll know what the secret is. Immortality. Eternal life. Not just a big secret, but the biggest secret of all. I'll get out of here with my secret, with the power, and I'll conquer every part of this world. I can leave this place be. I can afford to.'

'But it's going to be a whole new world . . .'

The Results Man smiled horribly. 'And I fully intend to rule in that one too. If I can lead an immortal legion into Rome, they'll have no choice. I will be the master. I will be the emperor. I will be the Lord. I will be God. You see, Flea? You should have stuck by me. Me, God. You, God's helper. Super Flea. Flea the All-powerful. Too late now. You've shown me where your loyalties lie and that they'll never change.'

'But what have we got to do with that? We don't have

to go to the tombs, surely?' Flea pleaded.

'If that's where Yesh is coming back to life, that's where the power will be greatest, by my reckoning. I want to see what happens to you and your friends.'

'Happens to us? Happens to us when?'

'When you're dead, dull boy. You die, you come back to life. Could be good.'

'But we're not dead.'

'You will be when I have you all killed.'

Flea gawped at him.

'You've got it. Right there! Right then! You will be the first, and we've got to hustle because I don't want to miss the show.'

'But suppose it's not true? Suppose Yesh doesn't come back to life? Suppose none of the things that are supposed to happen come about?' Flea's voice trembled.

The Results Man shrugged. 'You'd have died anyway. And remember, you were prepared to sacrifice yourself for your friends.'

'But I don't want to die.'

Three things happened then in quick succession. First Flea remembered Yesh being sick in the Pleasure Gardens and understood for the first time what Yesh had been going through as a human being, as a man. Then a feeling of queasy fullness in his belly took him over and he was sick himself. And, last of all, the impossible happened.

The world shifted.

# 54

The earth was eating them. The walls ground like giant teeth and the dungeon floor writhed like a flat stone tongue. They all fell over in the sudden churn. Flea could not see, could not breathe. He opened his mouth to shout and it clogged with dust.

Then everything stopped. No one moved. Movement might set it off again. Men groaned. The dust settled.

And then came a tremor that shook them like dogs shake rats. Rocks crashed. The air thickened.

Then nothing. Flea opened his eyes. They were caked with dust, but he could see dust and he could taste dust and that meant he was still alive.

Outside the dungeon, above the table where the old man in the apron had sat, a torch was still burning. Its flame was a smoky halo in the clogged air.

Flea got on to his hands and knees. The sickness had passed. He saw the others lying where they had fallen, but beginning to move. The Results Man was on his side. The old man seemed to be growing out of the wall. It took Flea a while to work out that a large lump of rock had dropped on top of his head and shoulders and squashed them flat.

'Big! Red!' Flea hissed. 'Are you all right? All of you?'

A quiet chorus of yeses.

'What happened?' the Results Man said. He spat.

'Earthquake,' Flea said. Another tremor shook the ground. A chunk of rock fell from the roof right into the pit where the Temple Boys had been held.

'I've got to get out of here,' the Results Man said. He tried to sit up, then screamed, 'My arm! It's broken! Guards! Help me.'

But the guards stationed at the door had gone.

'Boys. You help me, then.'

The Results Man manoeuvred himself on to his knees, supporting himself with his good arm. Flea reached out with his leg, kicked out and swept it away. The Results Man fell on his face and screamed again as Big and Little Big landed on his back. The others followed. He writhed, then went still.

'Can't breathe,' he gasped. 'Let me go.'

'What do we do with him?' Big asked Flea.

Flea tried to think. In truth, he wanted to kick him again.

'Flea. We need to know.'

'Put him in the pit,' he said, surprising himself by coming to a decision. All you had to do was say it and . . .

The Results Man started to writhe again. 'No. It'll kill me. Let me go and I'll give you free passage out of the Fortress. Out of the City. Anywhere! I'll help you escape. I'll set you all up for life.'

'When you're the emperor.'

'It could happen.'

'No, it couldn't,' Flea said. He was very certain that if

the world ended and a new one was created there would be little room for the Results Man as a god. Equally, if by any chance he did achieve what he wanted, Flea thought there would be little room for himself and the Temple Boys.

'The earthquake is a sign. It's the beginning of the end,' the Results Man moaned.

'Then you'll be all right. Smash, Grab. Pull up the ladder. The rest of you, chuck him in the hole.'

Which they did. The earth grumbled again as he hit the bottom of the pit, so they legged it.

The lower levels of the Fortress had emptied like magic. Blocks of masonry had fallen from arches and ceilings, but they managed to pick their way around them. Hanging dust crunched between their teeth. Pools of oil burned where lamps had fallen.

At ground level, Flea allowed himself to be guided by his nose and led them to the kitchens.

At the door he paused. He could hear something scratching around inside. He peered round the door. It was chaos in there. Tables had been overturned as the kitchen workers had rushed to get out into the open when the earthquake struck. Against the far wall an overturned table was scraping slowly across the floor, apparently moving by itself.

It stopped and a small head appeared above it. Flea's heart leapt.

'Tesha!' he shouted.

Tesha lifted her head, saw him and smiled.

'Just coming to get you,' she said. 'I tried to get in through the front, but this is better. Hurry, the soldiers are getting ready to come back in.'

'How did you know . . .?'

'I knew they'd bang you up. As soon as the earthquake started everyone rushed out, so I came in. It's chaos in the City. It's rather peaceful in here, believe it or not.'

'Everyone, this is Tesha,' Flea said. 'Grab whatever food you can and follow her out. We're heading for the tombs.'

'But that's a girl,' Big said.

'I know,' Flea said. 'She's a girl and she's going to get us out of here. Look – grab that wineskin and that pile of bread. There's dried fruit over there. Do I have to do everything?'

He felt madly active and utterly exhausted at the same time. There was little connection between his head and his feet or his mouth and his mind. He was in a daze, a useful daze of what he supposed was relief, but he wasn't sure. He just knew it was important to keep going, keep going and keep going until he stopped.

And then there would be an end. He would just have to hope that the end carried a new beginning in it, like a gift.

But perhaps it was just the end.

# 55

At the tombs the dawn air was sweet and rich. A silence tingled gently, waiting to fill up with something good. Flea had found space for them all on the cliff above the tombs. He lay back and felt the dew bathe his face. Happiness began to spread through every bit of him, a happiness that warmed, stopped limbs from aching, soothed cuts and bruises, and gently washed away the gallery of horrors in his mind.

Whatever happened, they were here. He had done it – he'd got them out. Whatever happened next was out of his hands.

The sun was rising behind the City to the east and a bead of light, bright and clean as molten metal, was bleeding from around the great rock that blocked the mouth of Yeshua's tomb. Mari and Matta were there with Yesh's mother. They threw their arms in front of their faces and fell forwards.

The scaffold groaned and shuddered. Dust fell and the stone in front of the tomb rumbled sideways. The light, brighter than the sun now, poured from the widening gap and spread. Flea screwed his eyes tight shut and put his hands in front of his face, but it shone through his flesh and it blasted through his bones. He could feel it on his skin, hot as oil, soft as wool. It pierced his skin and his head until the light was inside him and he could see a dark figure in the midst of it, floating.

'Flea,' a voice said. 'Why did you doubt me?'

'Magician?'

Yeshua laughed, a sound that was as deep as gold and as bright as silver. 'Call me what you like. I am what I am. But what are you, Flea?'

'I don't know.'

'But I do. I know you, Flea. I know what you want. I know what you dream of. Open your eyes and look.'

Yeshua's light was a deep draught from a well of glitter and freshness.

Instead of blinding Flea, it allowed him to see more clearly than he had ever seen before. Every detail in the world around him thrummed, from the pebbles at his feet to the distant city walls. Colours brimmed. Smooth shadows quivered. The whole world could barely wait to spill its secrets. Yeshua lifted his hand and a ray like a spear lanced from his palm, so intense that it shone through the City walls and blew them away like silk. The light shone through the huddled houses so they fell like dust. The light blew through the proud palaces so they became thin and fragile as ancient leaves. The light gathered round the Temple and crushed it.

And where the light poured on to the earth, the ground broke and blistered.

In front of the tombs a small white bone appeared, then another. They skittered across the dry earth until they made a finger, a hand, an arm. Still the light shone. Soil gathered, swelled, plumped and became flesh. The earth convulsed and squeezed out bodies. Men and women, girls and boys hauled themselves out of tombs and bathed in the light.

But as soon as they began to move, Flea realised something was wrong. He could see them walk, he could see them nod their heads and when they saw Yeshua floating above them on his cloud of glory they bowed and knelt, but they weren't moving: something was moving them. The way they raised their arms was too smooth. They opened their mouths too wide to show tongues that were as white as salt and as pulpy as berries. When they began to sing it was too loud and too pure and the sound was trying to smother him.

'No! NO!'

'Flea!' He felt a slap on his face and jerked his eyes wide open. Big was leaning down over him. There was no sign of any singing bodies. He was at the tombs and he had fallen asleep, but the sky was grey and the only true thing he had dreamed were the three women who had been at Yeshua's crucifixion. They were waiting outside his tomb and looked finished. The memory of the dream faded to a musty paste in his mind.

'Nightmare?' Tesha asked. She was sitting next to Flea. He leant into her.

'I dreamed people really did come back to life,' he said.

'And?'

'It was bad.' He swallowed. His spit tasted brown. He wanted a drink. 'Last summer I was down at the sheep baths and I pulled a drowned mouse out of the water. It was tiny and weighed nothing, but I just remember its little pink claws and teeth, like grape pips. Anyway, I put it down on a stone to dry – I don't know why – and then after a while I saw it move. I was so pleased because I thought it had revived, but then . . .'

He stopped and met Tesha's gaze. Flea had not noticed before, but with her big grey eyes and heart-shaped face she was very pretty. At some point in the last day she must have washed, and her cropped hair had dried into a sort of dark pelt. He wanted to run his hand through it. He wanted to do that more than he wanted to finish his story.

'Well?' she prompted. Her steady gaze coaxed the words from him.

'Then I saw it was moving wrong. I hadn't brought it back to life. It was ants. They'd got under it and were sort of lifting and pulling it so it looked alive, but it wasn't. That's what the people were like in my dream. Dead but not dead. Alive but not alive. Ant life.'

Tesha shuffled closer. They were both hugging their knees, side by side, hips and shoulders touching. Flea could feel her bones and her warmth. 'It scares me too,' she said. 'If the dead come back, does that mean all the bad people will come back too?'

'I just don't know. Maybe they'll be . . . improved.' He thought of Eleazar and doubted it. 'I'm scared. I'm really scared and there's nothing I can do.'

'Better to do something,' Tesha said. 'Anything. Just waiting here I feel like a lamb in one of the killing pens.' She made a little bleating sound.

'Maybe we should go to the tomb, then.'

'But that's like, I mean if anything happens, that's where . . .'

'Then it will be over quickly,' Flea said. He took a breath. 'And there's something I've got to tell the women. If they're waiting for Yesh to come back to life, I think they're in for a terrible shock. They should be prepared that he might have changed.'

'And you want me to come too?'

Flea was about to say that he would be fine on his own, then realised that he wouldn't. 'Yes, please. Whatever happens, it would be good if you were with me.'

# 56

The rickety scaffolding that clung to the cliff wall creaked as Flea and Tesha climbed it. As they reached the top, Matta and Mari turned. Their dirty faces were streaked with tear tracks. Their hair was stiff with dust. The mother was sitting with her cheek pressed up against the entrance stone.

'I'm back,' Flea said.

'Who are you?' Matta sounded confused.

'It's the child,' Mari said. 'He was with us when Yeshua died. He knew Jude. You must remember.'

'Oh. What does he want?'

Now he was here, Flea found it hard to say the words. Tesha supplied them, brutally.

'You think he's coming back to life.'

Matta burst into tears. Mari closed her eyes and shook her head. 'Who have you been talking to?' she asked.

'He found it out all by himself.' Tesha put her hand on Flea's shoulder and looked at Mari with disdain. 'Is it true?'

'True? Is he here? Is he singing? Is he dancing?' Mari said, defiantly. Then her shoulders slumped. 'Shim came and told us. He said that's why they all stayed away. They didn't want to attract the attention of the Temple or the Romans. I don't know whether to believe them or not.'

'But it's happened before,' Flea said. 'It happened in Bethany, to a man called Eleazar. Yeshua brought him back to life after he'd been dead for three days and now he's going to do it for himself. He's got the power. That's what everyone's betting on: the followers, his uncle Yusuf . . . He's coming back to life and he's going to –'

'End this world, create a new one and rule in glory.' The old woman spoke for the first time. 'He had been dreaming of it since he was fifteen.'

'But the City! The people! What's going to happen to them?' Flea said. 'I don't want to die and come back to life! I don't want to be ruled by him or anyone else!'

'You've got to be ruled by someone,' the old woman said. 'Wouldn't you rather be ruled by the son of God?'

Flea thought of the Temple. The echoing courts, the great empty Sanctuary, the fire altar, the slaughtered lambs, the blood. 'No,' he said.

Mari stamped her feet. 'But it's all nonsense. We knew Laz and his fool of a sister as well as anyone. He never died! He stank because he never washed and he looked half dead because he never ate unless his idiot sister fed him like a baby. She was desperate and asked Yeshua to help. Yeshua's brilliant idea was that they should bury him alive – he was halfway to death anyway – because if he saw what it was really like to die, he might pull himself together. That was all the plan was meant to be until Mat and Shim got hold of the story and started spinning a yarn, claiming that Eleazar had really died and Yeshua had really brought him back to life.'

'There's a Roman spy who wanted to find out what his secret was so he could use its power,' Flea said.

'Yeshua never had power,' Mari said. 'Not that sort, anyway.'

'I saw it,' Flea said. 'One of my gang couldn't talk and Yesh cured him.'

Mari's expression hovered between pity and impatience.

'Kids like you, a moment's attention makes a difference. It's no bad thing – I don't think that for a minute – but it's no big secret either, no great power. Be kind to each other instead of cruel and the world's already a different place. Yesh knew that. He should have stopped there.'

'That's it?' Flea asked. 'Just, "be nice"?'

Mari gave him a level look. 'It's hard enough, believe me. Do you know what I am?'

Flea shook his head, though he had an idea.

'I give myself to men,' she said. 'So I know bodies. I know flesh. I know what can come back to life and what can't. Yeshua – my dear, sweet, kind, stubborn, clever, impossible Yeshua – is beyond bringing back.' She smiled sadly at Tesha, who had been standing very still all the while, trying to make it look like she wasn't staring. 'I was like you once, sweetheart. A pretty little girl. I became a prostitute so I didn't starve to death. But, there was a trade-off. Hunger wasn't killing me, but little by little the work was. You know, I tried to drag Yeshua into bed the first time I met him.'

'I tried to rob him,' Flea said.

Mari gave him a quick smile. 'He just looked at me nicely – your word – and said, "Let's do this the other way." He meant, Let's do love the other way. He meant, You don't have to sell yourself to me. He meant, I love you anyway because you're you. He meant, There could be a world made of people being kind to each other and this could be the start of it.' She paused. 'But why couldn't he have just left it at that? Why do men always have to bring death into it? And power? And destiny? And movements and leaders and followers? Or maybe I'm just tired. Or maybe it's the only way to things get done. I mean, we're angry enough with that fat, pompous uncle of his, but at least he got him buried.'

'What?' Flea said.

'Of course we did the women's work – washing that poor, torn body – but after that we were kept well away. Yusuf owned the tomb, so he took care of it. How could he? How could they?'

Grief replaced anger and her howl seemed to tear away the last shreds of her dignity. She collapsed, crawling over to the mother and curling up so her head was in the older woman's lap.

Tesha tugged at Flea's arm. 'We should go,' she whispered.

Flea shook his head. 'We're missing something.'

'What?'

'I don't know. It's a like a big hole. It's there, but it's not there. What's there but not there? Tesha. Help me.'

'There and not there? Is that a riddle?'

'Not a riddle. But like a riddle!'

'A trick, then? What are you on about?'

Flea's mind blazed. 'A trick. He loved tricks. That's it! Hunt the King! You put down three beakers, move them around and ask the crowd which one of them has got the coin under it. But what's the trick? What is the only way it could work every time?'

'I don't know,' Tesha said, 'because I have no idea what you're talking about.'

Mari lifted her head. 'People called him a king, like David and Solomon. What are you thinking?'

Flea closed his eyes and thought. 'When he pretended to pull coins from people's ears, was there really money in their head?'

'No.'

'Then why on earth did I ever think there was a coin under the beaker? How could I have been so thick? It's misdirection. There's no coin under the beaker and there's no body in the tomb! Hunt the King! That's what we've got to do!'

Now Mari and Matta were on their feet.

'I should have known.' Flea slapped his forehead with his palm. 'I learnt it when I was a grave robber. Kings always had two tombs: one that looked like a real, royal tomb and another secret one. The robbers were meant to go for the big tomb, but the body and the grave goods – the treasure – were in the secret one. Did you see actually see him buried?'

'No, like I said. It was his uncle Yusuf. Are you saying . . .' Mari gestured to the tomb mouth blocked by the big rock, but was interrupted by a piercing whistle from the cliffs above. Big was waving and pointing to the floor of the quarry, where a small procession was approaching: the followers, led by Mat and Shim.

Then Yesh's mother said, 'The earth will eat us,' and the ground started to shake.

The scaffold trembled, knocking Mari against Flea. He threw himself flat as she rolled past him. She threw out a hand and he just managed to grab her as she fell from the platform. For a heartbeat she was hanging on to Flea and he was gripping the splintery wood of the platform, which was rocking and swaying like a tree in the wind. Flea felt her weight begin to drag him over, then a thin, tattooed hand snapped down on to Mari's wrist and held on long enough for her to swing her legs back on to the platform.

Flea found himself looking into the shrewd eyes of Yesh's mother, peering out from under her headscarf. 'Not the first time she tried to get a man in trouble,' she said. 'This time it was your turn to rescue her.'

As Mari hauled herself up, Matta gave a quiet cry and pointed to the tomb.

The earth tremor had shaken the round stone that blocked the entrance. It had rolled away and left a gap big enough for a man to walk through.

'It's a sign!' Matta cried.

Flea stood shakily. The tomb's roof must have cracked, letting in light.

Inside, a shadow moved.

Through the gap left by the round stone, a hand appeared.

It was clean and the wrist, where the grave robe fell back, was hairy.

Mari fell to her knees. Matta screamed. Flea felt as if his entire skin was shrinking. It lifted his hair and stretched his mouth and eyes wide open.

'Is it time?' a voice asked. 'It is time.'

Grey light fell on a figure, dressed in white, taller than Yeshua ever was and better formed.

'What does it mean?' the mother asked in a cracked voice. 'Is it my son? Is it my son?'

It was Yesh and it wasn't Yesh. It was man and it was not man. It was there and then nothing was, because the earth shook again, the scaffold cracked and everything changed as the dust rose and the sun broke through the low cloud and turned the air golden.

many days after

# 57

Although the world did not end, although the City did not rise and throw out the hated Romans, although beggars did not become kings and the dead did not dance in the streets, they all heard about Yeshua in the days and weeks that followed.

He had been seen again at the tombs, bathed in light and robed in glory. His followers had been approached by a stranger out walking and, guess what? It had turned out to be him.

Or Him.

You could touch His wounds – you could even put your hand right inside His body if you dared. His blood could cure anything, if only you could drink it. He floated. He flew. Finally, He was taken up to heaven in a flaming chariot. Then His followers went north and took the stories with them.

The stories made Flea smile. He remembered how he had first imagined the magician when he came to the city, and although he'd lost his appetite for making up stories of massacres and world-saving heroics, he had told a particularly fine tale to the Grinderman.

The old knife-sharpener had been setting up his grinding wheel on the street near the fountain where Flea used to get the water for the gang.

'Hey Grinderman – got anything for me?' Flea called out. 'Any gossip? Any news?' He threw him a copper coin. The Grinderman caught it and pretended to faint.

'Heard one about a flea,' the Grinderman called back. 'Bit a lot of people and when they tried to squish him he just hopped away.'

This made Flea feel very happy. 'Here's one for you. You know that old magician that got himself crucified? They say his blood's magic after all. One drop will cure any disease. Two drops and you live forever. Yusuf the Merchant's hanging on to the body. Going to make himself another fortune.'

The Grinderman winked and tapped his long nose with a dirty finger. Within hours a mob had gathered outside Yusuf's palace, calling for Yeshua's blood. They broke in, wrecked the place, set it on fire, then set off to loot his warehouses. Yusuf escaped with his life, but not much else.

Flea felt it was justice of a sort. He had gone to see Yusuf just as soon as the earth had stopped shaking and they'd stopped running from the tombs, screaming like a bunch of babies. Flea had led them into the City through the Dead Streets and then headed straight for Yusuf's Palace: Flea to get answers, the others to beg for food.

The City was rank.

All the people who should have left after the Feast were still squatting in their makeshift shelters, huddled in doorways, staring out of windows.

They looked angry. Bored. Confused.

Fathers guarded their families with knives and lengths of wood. The streets stank of human waste, rotting food, smoke. On one corner two men screamed at each other, one saying it was the end of the world, the earthquake proved it, they should all go to the Temple and make sacrifices. The other man was shouting that they should band together, attack the Temple, raid its coffers, get back some of the money they'd been pumping into it all these years. Each man seemed to have supporters, who knotted together into sides . . .

Flea led the gang through the slums and into the Upper City. Earthquake damage showed more starkly in the wide, empty streets: jagged cracks in walls, broken tiles in the streets, breaks in the smooth paving where the ground had heaved. At Yusuf's palace one of the doors was off its hinges. The children peered in. Water from the fountain gushed over the marble flagstones and drained through gaps in the slabs. The place seemed deserted.

'Smash and Grab should get to the kitchens and nick as much as they can,' Flea said. 'I'm going up.'

He pointed to the steps that led to the banqueting hall and the main bulk of the palace. Tesha and Big came with him: Tesha because they did most things together now, Big because he was unimaginatively brave.

They found Yusuf up two more flights of stairs, in a small tower room that looked out over the City. He was there with another man whom Flea knew only too well. Swags of flesh drooped from Yusuf's face. His beard was untrimmed and his blue robe with the golden stars was crumpled.

'What are you doing here?' he barked.

'We came from the tombs,' Flea said.

'All the people were meant to be there to bear witness, but the City's on lockdown. They were meant to rise up. It's too late, isn't it?'

Below them the slums looked like a rotten honeycomb. After the earthquake fires had started all over the city and their smoke mixed with the fumes from the Temple's fire altar.

'What was in it for you?' Flea asked. 'Yesh said beggars would become kings, but you're not a beggar.'

Yusuf laughed. 'You thought that he was talking about you? Still, I suppose everyone thought Yeshua was talking about them; that was his particular gift. But no one had the faintest idea what he really meant, and maybe that was his gift as well. You could make it mean anything you wanted.'

'So it was never going to happen? The poor were never going to be rich?'

'Everything's relative, boy. When you live under foreign occupation, you learn to talk in code. The Romans make beggars of us all. We grovel to them for favours, but they're quite capable of snatching everything away. It's intolerable, you understand. Intolerable. No one can live like this, and that's what I wanted to change.'

Yusuf drew himself up, as if he were giving a speech, then collapsed. 'It seemed so straightforward. Poor old Yesh would sacrifice himself like he wanted to and Yak, his brother, would take his place in the tomb. A crowd would gather, the stone would be rolled back and there he'd be! Not that bruised, ruined figure broken by the cross, but a fit man, reborn bigger and better.'

His voice rose and the words tumbled from his lips. 'Have you seen Yak when he sweeps his hair back like Yesh? With a trimmed beard it would have worked. People would have done anything for him. Anything at all. Then it all went wrong. The Romans put the City on lockdown, and then that earthquake . . . I've got Abbas Barabbas out there ready to take on the Roman garrison with ten thousand citizens behind him all calling out the Chosen One's name and no Chosen One to follow.'

'But . . .' Flea tried to think. Just before the final quake he'd seen the followers walking towards the tombs across the quarry floor. Yak had been with them, he was sure of it. Or was he?

Yusuf continued. 'We could have blocked the gates to the Fortress and taken the governor's palace. Held him as a hostage. They'd have negotiated. The City would have been ours.'

'The Romans knew. They would have been waiting for

317

you. But I'm not here to listen to you boast. I'm here to find out about Jude.'

'Jude? Oh, you mean Judas. Why would I care about him?' Yusuf looked honestly puzzled.

'He killed him.' Flea pointed at the man who stood behind Yusuf. His arm shook with fury.

'Really?' Yusuf looked amused. This made Flea even angrier.

'He was everywhere. When Yusuf first crossed the bridge into the City he was there, carrying a water pitcher. He was at the trial, making sure the crowd called for the governor to save Barabbas. I'll bet he was in the Pleasure Gardens when Yesh was arrested so he knew Jude had arranged to meet me under the tree by the City dump. Jude was the only person who was trying to stop the madness. He killed him all right.'

'And what can you do about it?'

'I don't know. But if I matter so little and you're so important, maybe you can tell me why. I just . . .' But his voice was trembling too much. He felt Big step up next to him.

'Come on,' Big said. 'Tell us. Whatever the story is, we can't do anything about it. Or maybe you're not as powerful as you claim to be.'

Now Tesha was on his other side and Flea felt stronger.

The silence stretched, seconds that Flea counted with the thud of his heart. At last Yusuf spoke, an odd twist to his face and tension thinning his voice. 'It's true, Jude could have made things very difficult. He didn't get through to Yeshua because my nephew was a very remarkable man, but he could have influenced the others. In any movement there are leaders and followers, there are doers and there are passengers, people along for the ride. I thought Jude was a passenger. Oddly, he was a doer. He should have been eliminated weeks ago.'

'Eliminated. You mean murdered.'

'You think any of this has been easy for me?' Yusuf's eyes were suddenly hot. 'You know, Yeshua used to love my stories when he was a boy. I used to fill his head with sailors' tales, from the east, from the west. He listened, oh, how he listened. I told him about a land where the teachers go around with a begging bowl because they think happiness only comes from having nothing. I told him about green lands to the north and west where they spill their gods' blood on the ground every spring to make sure they have a good harvest. I told him about lands of ice and fire where the people don't feel the cold. I told him how we could travel there together, but he wanted to die! Do you understand? He wanted to! I just wanted to make sure he didn't die in vain.'

'I watched him die,' Flea said. 'He felt he had to. I don't know if that's the same as wanting. I still want to know about Jude.'

'Are you sure?' Yusuf asked.

'Yes.'

'Then . . .' He nodded to the man, who stepped forwards. He was medium height, medium weight and looked forgettable.

'He was dead when I got there,' the man said. 'There was no one else around. For my money, he killed himself.'

'He would never do that. He would never have left me.'

'You have to face it,' Yusuf said. 'Who mattered most to Judas, you or Yeshua? Come on, child. He killed himself as an act of faith. He couldn't stop Yeshua going through with the prophecy so he decided to join him. If he died, he died with Yeshua; if he came back to life, he would join him forever. At the end, he showed himself to be a coward.'

'No!' Flea screamed. 'You're the coward. You sent Yesh to his death while you sat in your palace getting fatter and richer. I hope it falls down around your ears. I hope it crushes you to death! You just use people. You're as bad as the Romans. No, you're worse. They conquer people and exploit them. But you, you screw over your own countrymen.'

'Get out! Get out now before I –'

'What? Have us whipped? Executed? Like I said, you're just like the Romans, except you're not as strong and I'll get even with you.'

'LEAVE!'

Yusuf's spit was bitter. He took a step towards Flea,

his hand raised to deliver a blow, but before he reached him he staggered. Flea felt himself lurch. Tesha grabbed him. For half a dozen pounding heartbeats, the walls and floors of the palace turned to jelly. Outside the open window he heard wails and the sound of things falling.

'Another earthquake,' Yusuf said. 'God save us all.'

And that was that.

So Flea ruined Yusuf, and felt no better. He watched the City start to repair itself and get back to normal, as if there had been no earthquake, as if Jude hadn't died, as if Yeshua hadn't died. That was a lesson to be learnt, Flea thought, but he did not know if it was a good one or not.

And anyway, things had changed for the Temple Boys, who now had to deal with the thirty pieces of silver Jude had left for Flea and that he had managed to hang on to against all the odds. A miracle, of sorts.

They were, however, proving to be a bit of a headache.

Little Big and Clump didn't see coins, just jugs of wine, large amounts of meat and piles of bread. Big, oddly, got religion and thought they should spend it at the Temple on sacrifices. Flea floated the Wild Man's idea that thirty pieces of silver would buy a flock of sheep and a tent. He saw them all joining the Wild People and becoming another tribe. He'd have to become competent, grizzled and of few words, but he could learn.

In the end they sacrificed a sheep to keep Big happy,

then ate and drank to their hearts' content until fourteen coins were left.

Everyone got one and no one felt much the better for it.

'The thing is,' Tesha said, 'I haven't got a clue what to do with mine.'

She and Flea were sitting on a hillside to the south of the City. It was a warm day. Spring, proper spring, had come at last, with blue skies and fresh warm winds. Tesha flicked her coin into the air so it glinted in the sunlight. She screwed it into her eye. She stuck it on her tongue. Below them lay the blood fields. Farmers were digging out the blood-rich mud and loading it on to carts to spread on their fields. Jude was buried down there, but Flea did not like to think of that.

'Maybe drinking it away would be the sensible thing to do,' Flea said. 'No one can tell you not to.'

He stole a sideways look at Tesha. Her hair was growing and her skin was taking on colour. He would have liked to kiss her, but had no idea how she would react. Getting close to her seemed to heat up his skin in a way that was fantastic, but sometimes awkward.

'But there might be other things to do. Better things,' Tesha said.

'Then you have to think of them.'

'What if I can't?' Tesha protested

'Then go and get drunk for a week,' Flea said.

'You're no good at all.'

'It's the same for all of us,' Flea said. 'I was going to hire a professional mourner to wail over Jude, but I don't know if that's the right thing to do. I have a feeling it's just a big waste of money.'

'Then go and get drunk for a week,' Tesha said with a hint of acid in her voice.

Flea shrugged. The memory of Jude was a cold ache in a very deep place. He should still be alive and he wasn't. He should have wanted to live, but he hadn't. Right now that seemed like the saddest thing in the world.

'I sort of imagined that me and Jude were going to travel,' Flea said, rubbing his newly cut, almost clean hair. 'There was a storyteller I heard once. He talked about a shipwrecked sailor who landed on the back of a giant fish, and there was another about a carpet that flew. The Results Man said there's an island at the end of the world where the land's always green and the people are blue.'

'That'd be good,' Tesha said vaguely. 'How do you get there?'

Flea made a face. 'Dunno. I used to dream about being this magic, powerful person. Flea the Magnificent! Flea the Terrible! I'd tell stories to myself about having fantastic powers, but I don't seem to want to do that any more. I just want to go far away. I want to find blue people and tell them this story and I want it to seem as crazy to them as stories about them seem to us. That's what I want. I just want people to shake their heads and say, *Who'd believe that?* But we'll know it's the truth.'

'I'll pretend to drink to that,' Tesha said. She had stolen a silver cup from the upper room where Yesh and the followers had eaten their last meal together. She held it up, empty, and tipped it to her lips, then handed it to Flea to do the same.

He wondered where they would end up if they went off together. He didn't care at all and he did care very much, both feelings at the same time. Together they made him happy, excited, frightened. And ready.

'Do you think we could do that?' Tesha said. 'I mean, just go?'

Flea looked across the valley to the City on the hill. Smoke drifted gently through the tight pattern of its enfolded streets. To survive in that maze you had to make a plan, find a way, decide you had a destiny and stick to it, or you'd just give up, wouldn't you? But other people had destinies too and where one plan clashed with another, people died.

That was the problem.

The Imperium, Yesh, the Temple . . . they all thought that if only they could follow their own destiny, they'd be free. But it was just a dream. They were all stuck together in the maze, forced to turn left or right by the hard edges of what other people wanted, what other people needed.

Then all of a sudden the empty land behind Flea seemed

like a deep and generous promise that he could fall into. He understood in a way that made his breath quicken and his heart pound that, if he was brave, he could lean into the future, and if he didn't try to think about the crash at the end he could keep moving until he stopped.

And that would be enough. And that would be good. And that would be the best way to remember Jude, and to keep remembering him.

'Flea?' Tesha asked. 'What is it? Suddenly you look all . . . different.'

Flea sniffed and wiped away a tear. Like morning dew, it had come from nowhere. Somewhere in the City, somewhere in the maze, the old Flea was waving him away, telling him to get lost and that he'd be trapped forever if he didn't make tracks. Standing next to him, Tesha was more or less saying the same: there were other, better things to do.

He closed his eyes and waited for Flea the Magnificent, Flea the Traveller, Flea the Hero to make his decision, but he was gone too. The time for thinking up stories really was over. Perhaps it was time to become one.

'Well?'

'Yes,' said Flea. 'Let's go.'

'Just for the record, you did say earlier that you made up names for yourself. Flea the . . . ?'

'Flea the Terrible. And the Magnificent.'

Tesha punched him gently on the arm. 'You'll never

live that down, you know. I'll keep reminding you of it.'

'I know. And I don't care. I am magnificent.'

'You're terrible.'

'Well . . . nobody's perfect.'

## EGMONT PRESS: ETHICAL PUBLISHING

Egmont Press is about turning writers into successful authors and children into passionate readers – producing books that enrich and entertain. As a responsible children's publisher, we go even further, considering the world in which our consumers are growing up.

**Safety First**
Naturally, all of our books meet legal safety requirements. But we go further than this; every book with play value is tested to the highest standards – if it fails, it's back to the drawing-board.

**Made Fairly**
We are working to ensure that the workers involved in our supply chain – the people that make our books – are treated with fairness and respect.

**Responsible Forestry**
We are committed to ensuring all our papers come from environmentally and socially responsible forest sources.

**For more information, please visit our website at www.egmont.co.uk/ethical**

Egmont is passionate about helping to preserve the world's remaining ancient forests. We only use paper from legal and sustainable forest sources, so we know where every single tree comes from that goes into every paper that makes up every book.

This book is made from paper certified by the Forestry Stewardship Council (FSC®), an organisation dedicated to promoting responsible management of forest resources. For more information on the FSC, please visit **www.fsc.org**. To learn more about Egmont's sustainable paper policy, please visit **www.egmont.co.uk/ethical**.